LIONBOY

LIONBOY

THE FIRST BOOK IN A TRILOGY

ZIZOU CORDER

SCHOLASTIC INC.

New York   Toronto   London   Auckland   Sydney
Mexico City   New Delhi   Hong Kong   Buenos Aires

ISBN 0-439-70862-1

12 11 10 9 8 7 6 5 4 3 2 1   4 5 6 7 8 9/0

Printed in the U.S.A.   40

First Scholastic printing, November 2004

Designed by Kimi Weart
Text set in Stempel Garamond

Lionboy is dedicated to Greenside School, especially Year Six, 2003–4: Kehinde Ogunseitan, Taiwo Ogunseitan, Hannah Laidley, Melanie Phillips, Kitty Wordsworth, Rosie Gravante, Alice Broughton, Daniel da Cunha Blaker, Jake Kidston Kerr, Charlie Raven, Charlie Regis, Madeleine Ellis Peterson, Queenie Ingrams, Theo Caldwell, Cieran Lacey, Salma Ahmed, Tamsin Stewart, Arta Avdullahu, Naim Saleh, Tiffany Copeland, Hafsa Wardhere, Alison Woronkowicz, Paris Rhoden, Lauren Castle, Gavin Burchard de Taunton, Liam O'Neill, Karim Cherifi, Harry Guyan.

A nicer bunch of kids there never was.

And to Mr. Morant, Mr. Andrews, Mrs. Hart, Mrs. Lyne, Miss Ellis, Mrs. Joyce, Miss Barakat, Mrs. Shine and everyone. Thank you!

LIONBOY

CHAPTER 1

One Saturday afternoon in September Charlie's mum was on a ladder in the backyard, doing things to plants halfway up the wall. Charlie didn't know what, or care. He liked the yard, the gorgeous honey-lemon smell of the flowers, and the great Christmas tree that hung over the back wall, with its shiny silver and green and purple fruits that he would harvest toward midwinter and sell at the market. He liked climbing around in the tree and in the ruins beyond, running down to the river, and talking to the cats that lived down there. But he didn't care what his mum was doing on the ladder—until he heard a shriek and a clatter and a rude word, and he ran out to see.

His mum was on all fours, on the fallen ladder, on the ground, with festoons of the honey-smelling plant around her, her red hair wild and her face as white as ice.

"Stupid, stupid," she was muttering.

"No you're not," said Charlie. He offered her his hand and she pulled up to her feet, wincing. "You wouldn't be a professor if you were stupid."

"Clever people can do stupid things," she said. "Let me into the house."

She hobbled inside and Charlie followed, worried but not worried, because his mum was the strongest, cleverest, bravest person in the world, apart from his dad, of course, and if anyone could handle falling off a ladder, she could.

"Owwwww," she said. Charlie had already passed her the aloe, a piece of chocolate, and a small bottle of her secret shock remedy, which she made in her laboratory and which smelled of comfort and brandy and sweet winter herbs.

"Best take a look," she said, and slid carefully out of the long leather breeches she always wore for outdoor work.

"Owww," they both said, at the sight of the raw red scratches, the pinky purple swellings, and the nasty gashes that adorned her shin. Charlie handed over a clean paper towel and Mum dabbed at her wound.

"Bring me some Bloodstopper Lotion," she said. "Twenty-seven Red. It's in the rack." She handed Charlie the keys to her lab. Charlie smiled. Mum, Professor Magdalen Start, PhD, MD, PQRST, LPO, TP, kept her laboratory locked on strict instructions of the government, indeed of the Empire, because her work was so important that no one was to be allowed to know anything about it. Except of course for Charlie's dad, Aneba Ashanti, Doctor of Endoterica and Tropical Sciences at the University of Accra in Ghana (currently on sabbatical at London University), Chief of Knowledge of all the Tribes of Akan, and Brother of Lions, who knew all about it because they worked together. Charlie's dad knew everything that had ever been known about the plants of the West African forests, what they were good for, and what was good for them.

"Your mum and I have different ways of knowing about the same thing," Dad would say. "Very good system."

Charlie was honored. Every day these days he was allowed to do new things: new things that showed they realized he was growing up. Last Christmas he'd been allowed to sell the shiny fruit at the market by himself, alone; on his way home from his lessons he was allowed to hang out for a while at the fountain, drinking sherbets and playing football or oware with the other big kids. And now he was allowed to fetch a lotion from his mother's lab. It felt good, being big.

"In the rack by the door," Mum said with a little smile.

He'd been inside the lab before, of course. As a baby, after they'd come here to London from Africa, he'd practically lived in there. While Mum worked, mixing and smelling and flicking between her burners and her computer screen, he would paddle around the place in a sort of pair of shorts hung on a wheeled frame: He could scoot and whiz, and once disappeared completely under a table, so Mum couldn't find him. He'd loved his shorts on wheels.

He loved the lab too. Because it was in a separate shed in the backyard, it had always seemed like a different world. Pushing open the door now, he got a waft of the smell of it: somewhere between a cake baking, old books, sweet strong incense, and underneath it the hard cold smell of science. It looked like it smelled. The walls were old and paneled with well-polished dark wood. The tables to the left were gleaming steel with glass cupboards, VDT screens and instruments of the most precise and modern specifications, while to the left a huge old wooden table stood empty except for a massive globe beneath a rack of hanging dried herbs. Along the back wall were stacked shelf upon shelf upon shelf of books—ancient leather-bound tomes, colorful paperbacks, smart-looking hardbacks, parchments laid out flat, and scrolls, rolled tight and piled carefully, plus CD-roms and DVDs, and old, old thick black vinyl discs, which played on a machine with a huge curling horn. It seemed to Charlie that all the knowledge in the world, past and present, lived in his mother's laboratory, and if it didn't you could find out here where it did live.

By the door was a tall flattish wooden rack, made up of rows of shelves. On each shelf was a row of small, shiny, colored glass bottles, held in place by a little wooden bar along the front. If you looked carefully you could see that the color was not in the glass, but in the contents of the bottle, and they were arranged in order of color like a rainbow: Red Orange Yellow Green Blue Indigo Violet. Charlie craned up to where the reds began in the top left-hand corner, and scanned along the shelves looking for 27 Red. There it was: a deep crimson, blood-colored, only not so thick-looking. He reached up to take it and, giving the lab a last yearning look, took it back to where his mother was waiting in the kitchen.

"Thank you, sweetie," she said, and was just about to lift the lid and drip a drop of the lotion onto her still-bleeding wound, when she hesitated.

"Bring me a pen and paper," she said suddenly.

Charlie fetched one of the strong swirling glass pens that they used for every day, and the green kitchen ink, and a scrap of envelope.

"Proper paper," she said, and he brought a piece of heavy clean parchment from the drawer.

Mum pulled herself up, and as she did so the movement made the blood bubble a little more from her shin. She took no notice. Instead, she lifted her leg and laid it along the kitchen table, as if she were doing her yoga, or ballet. The parchment lay on the kitchen table; the ink was ignored. Mum took the Venetian pen and cautiously dipped it in the beading blood of her wound.

Charlie stared.

"Don't worry," she said to him. "I just thought of something I've been meaning to do for a while."

He still stared.

Mum started to write. By dipping the sharp little nib in her deepest cut she had enough blood to write a full, elegant paragraph, and a signature.

"What is it?" he asked, feeling a little ill.

"You'll know soon enough," she said. She flapped the parchment gently and watched the scarlet turn to a delicate brown. It looked like a magical text, an ancient spell, a decree by some all-powerful and long-dead king or queen.

"I'm putting it up here," she said as she rolled it up, tied it quickly, and popped it behind the photo of her and Aneba on their honeymoon in Venice, on the top shelf of the cabinet. "And Charlie . . ." Here she stopped and looked at him, her blue eyes sure and clear: "If you need to go anywhere, take it with you."

A sudden sharp sense of importance welled up inside him. She didn't mean "take it to the bathroom," or "take it when you go to bed." She meant something bigger, more grown-up, more important. Sometimes Charlie felt that the grown-ups around him existed on that other level—talking of things they didn't mention to him, taking care of things, dealing with things that were not to do with children. Until recently he'd ignored it, and carried on reading his book or taking extra cake while they weren't paying attention. But lately . . . lately there'd been a lot of talking down-stairs after he had gone to bed, a lot of hushed telephone calls, and furrowed brows. This look in his mother's eyes, this sudden mysterious writing in blood, were to do with the same things, he was sure.

Just then the great noise that heralded the Return of Dad started up. There was a Ghanaian song about dinner—delicious mamuna with spicy dawa dawa—that he sang to himself whenever he wasn't doing anything else: *"Tuwe tuwe, mamuna tuwe tuwe, abosom dar ama dawa dawa, tuwe tuwe . . ."* You could hear it from the distance as he strolled up the street. Then the firm, solid tread of his feet crossing the yard, and the jangle of his big bunch of keys because once again he hasn't noticed that the door is unlocked. "Three, two, one . . ." Charlie counted down in his head, and his timing was perfect: On "Blast-off!" came Dad's huge voice calling out, "He-llo! He-llo! Where's my family?"

Charlie's dad, you ought to know, was huge. Not just a big man, but huge. He wasn't technically a giant, but Charlie thought he

might have giant blood, and this worried him sometimes because if his dad had giant blood, then so did he, and that made the whole thing of "you're a big boy now, growing nice and big like your dad" a different ball game. Charlie was proud and happy to be brown—both black like his dad and white like his mum, he said—but he wasn't sure he wanted to be giant as well.

Once, in a museum, Charlie had seen some armor from ancient Greek times, a breastplate made in the shape of a man's body, with all the muscles and even the belly button molded in beaten bronze. That's what Charlie's dad looked like with his shirt off. Like he was still wearing armor. He had huge arms, and the veins on them looked like rivers on a map, only they stood out; he had huge legs, and shoulders as wide as a small shed, and a neck like a tree, and he walked straight and tall and smiling, and everyone got out of his way and turned to look at him after he had passed. When he closed down the smile in his eyes, and let his mouth lie stern, he was the most frightening-looking man. Then when his smile burst through and his white teeth shone and his eyes crinkled up and his cheeks went into little apple shapes, he was like the god of happiness.

"We're in the kitchen," called Mum.

"She's broken," called Charlie.

"No I'm not," said Mum, finally dripping the Bloodstopper Lotion onto her cuts, and the evening descended into a sweet time of Mum lying around telling jokes, Dad cooking dinner, Charlie watching *The Simpsons* and staying up late because there are no lessons on Sunday. He forgot all about the parchment written in blood, and didn't think of it again until six months later, when he came home to find that his parents had disappeared.

CHAPTER 2

He'd been at his lessons with Brother Jerome: Arabic, Latin, mathematics, music, and the history of human flight, and his head was aching from the amount of studying he had done. Mum said he learned more being on his own with a tutor and no doubt it was true, but sometimes he just wanted to fool around a bit during his lessons, like he'd read about in stories, and how could you do that on your own? So after his lessons on that day he headed down to the fountain to play football with the schoolkids. Steve Ubsworth might be there, or Lolo and Jake, or Becks and Joe Lockhart.

None of them were around. But Rafi Sadler was. He was leaning against the tree and calling younger boys to him with a flick of his head, and whispering to them. Rafi certainly wasn't a schoolkid, and he was too old to be called a boy, but he wasn't really an adult either. Everybody knew Rafi. He was tall and handsome with sleek shaved black hair, and he gazed at you from big brown eyes with the thickest lashes—almost girly lashes, but no one would say that. He wore a long leather jacket and had a funny little light beard, shaved into shape. He wasn't really old enough to have a beard and it wasn't a very good one. He always had money and adults sometimes wondered where it came from.

Today Rafi deigned to join in the football for a minute or two. People let him through, and didn't tackle him, and not just because he was strong. Soon he went back to leaning, and talking on his cell phone. Part of Charlie longed for Rafi to call him over, but Rafi had never taken much notice of Charlie.

The football had made them hot, so they all got some cherry sherbet off the guy with his white wooden cart piled high with crimson cherries and jugs of sugar-cane syrup, and drank it frothy and cool from his tall glasses. One of Rafi's boys took him a glass, but he didn't touch it. Instead, he strolled over to where Charlie was.

"Nice haircut," he said. Charlie's mum had shaved his head the day before. This time she'd cut in a design of two crocodiles with one belly—each had a head and a tail and four legs, but they were set like an X, and the center of the X was their shared belly. It was an Adinkra symbol from Ghana: It was about how, though we all eat with different mouths, we have only one belly between us.

"Thanks," said Charlie, surprised. Rafi never talked to him. Charlie's parents used to know his mum, Martha, and Charlie knew that Rafi lived alone with her, and had left school years ago and had been in trouble, and he knew that Rafi was not the kind of guy who would talk to him. That's all he knew.

Charlie couldn't think of anything else more interesting to say. He smiled again, and then kind of nodded. Then Rafi had strolled away again, and Charlie was so embarrassed that he went home.

The sun was heading west, and as he got back toward his street he could smell the evening river smell rising up cool and damp to meet the evening cooking smell of woodsmoke and garlic. The flowers hung heavy on the trees in the front gardens as he turned into his street. He was wondering what was for supper and hoping there would be some cherries left over from breakfast. He'd be sorry when the cherry glut was over—but soon the gardens would be full of strawberries, so there was that to look forward to. And who knows, maybe a ship full of fruit would come up from the south. As he approached his house, he was fantasizing about the old days, when you got all different kinds of fruit at all different times of year, coming in airplanes from far, far away . . . Ah, well. Cherries would do for now.

When he got to his front garden, the door was closed. There were no lights on, and there was no good smell seeping out. He banged on the door: nothing. He peered through the window: He couldn't make out much in the dim light, but he could see there was no movement, no sign of life.

Charlie went around to the back. Back door shut, no lights. He banged on that door. Nothing. Turning to the wall to see if there were any cats around, whom he could ask if they'd seen anyone, he saw something that clutched his heart. The door of his mother's lab was open. Not just unlocked—open.

He stared at it for a moment. Then he went over and peered in. If there is anyone in there who shouldn't be, they would have closed the door to hide themselves, he reasoned, therefore no one is in there who shouldn't be. Therefore maybe someone is in there who should be, i.e., Mum. So he looked in.

Nobody. Everything was just as it should be—except that it was open and empty, which it really, really shouldn't be.

Stepping back into the yard Charlie closed the door carefully and quietly behind him. At least it looked right now. As right as an empty, dark, locked-up house can look when you've come in for your parents and your supper.

He felt a strong twining furry thing around his ankle and looked down. It was one of the skinny, tough, big-eared cats from the ruins. He bent down to talk to her, because you don't pick those cats up. Cuddly they're not.

"Hey, Petra," he said.

"She's gorn," said the cat in her scrowly voice.

"Gone where?" said Charlie immediately.

"Dunno," she said, her yellow eyes large in the dimming light. "Gorn orf downriver. It was some of them half-wits saw it. Least they arksed the river cats to keep an eye out for 'em. Ain't 'eard nuffin yet."

The cats were always having feuds, so Charlie wasn't concerned about the "half-wits."

"Who's 'them'?" he asked.

The cat stared at him unblinking.

"Your mum," she said. "And some humans." And she leaped up onto the wall out of Charlie's reach, a gray arc flying through the dusk. Her tail flicked. "Humans," she hissed again, and disappeared.

Charlie sat down on the back step and felt sick. Why would his mother go off with people the cats didn't recognize?

Marshall your thoughts, he told himself. Marshall. Charlie couldn't even get his thoughts to line up and keep still, let alone stand to attention so he could inspect them. Only two thoughts stood out: One, he didn't like this one little bit, and two, Dad would know.

Charlie reached down into his tutorbag, and as he rummaged his little phone lit up, clear and turquoise like the sea in summer. He pulled it out and dialed his dad's number. A computer voice with an Empire accent answered: "The apparatus is not functioning. Please try later. The apparatus is not functioning. Please try—" Charlie cut it off and huddled down into the step. It wasn't that warm either.

Dad's probably on the train and that's why his phone's not answering. That'll be it. I'll go up to the station and probably meet him on the way. Otherwise I can wait for him, and he'll know what's going on.

Charlie leaped up before the comfort of this version of things deserted him, and raced around to the front of the house, out of the yard and onto the street. There were a lot of people, all coming the opposite way from him: a tide of people returning from work, coming down from the station. He forced his way against the tide up to the marketplace, where the stalls and tents were still up and open, festooned with fairy lights, selling last-minute treats to tired commuters. A handful of sheep were still in the pen beyond the fountain, and their plaintive cries added sadness to the bustle. In this darkness everything familiar was different, and he didn't really like it. He hoped he wouldn't bump into any alcoholguys—the loud lurching ones who made no sense and smelled so bad, and could appear at any time.

Up by the station he parked himself in a pool of yellow light under a lamppost. People flowed around him: all sizes, all colors, but no Dad. Charlie didn't want to try phoning again because someone might see his phone and steal it, like the big schoolkids do off the little schoolkids, even though it's useless because as soon as the little kids' parents find out they cancel the phones anyway so they can't be used. Pathetic, Charlie thought: people trying to prove how cool they are by stealing something useless off a tiny kid.

Come on, Dad.

Perhaps he came by bus. The bus stop is over at the other side of the market.

Perhaps I missed him in the crowd and he's gone home and found neither Mum nor me.

Or maybe he's working late—maybe I could go to his office at the university. But Charlie knew that was dumb because he had no idea where Dad's office was, except that it was by the river, a long way from here. Up there, across the city, the river was twice the size it was here. There were huge ships and warehouses, and great shiny buildings full of people making money, and it smelled of the sea because the sea tide came flooding up, bringing wet fogs and gulls and the heavy salt smell. Here, the riversides had only the ruins and the cats and the fisherguys with their small painted boats, and it smelled of frogs and slimy weeds. Perhaps I should just go to the riverside and walk along until I get to where Dad's office is, he thought. I'd probably recognize it. Probably.

No, that's foolish. Dad wouldn't be there at this hour. Better to go on home.

Charlie dived into the flow of people and let them sweep him back to where the houses were, and peeled off at his street. He didn't look forward to seeing his house still dark and silent and empty . . . but maybe Dad would be there and the lights on and dinner on the stove.

The lights were on, but Dad was not there. Instead, framed in the lit-up doorway, stood Rafi Sadler.

He held the door and invited Charlie in, for all the world as if it were his house and Charlie were the guest.

"Hey, Charlie boy," said Rafi. "Come on in."

Charlie was surprised. "Hi," he said warily. And went in.

He looked swiftly around the kitchen. Mum's lab keys were not hanging in the small tree where they normally lived. Rafi's big gray dog, Troy, was panting at his feet. Troy's tongue always hung out of his mouth, wet and slathery like a flat pink slug.

"Where's my dad?" asked Charlie.

"There's been a change of plan," said Rafi.

"What plan?" said Charlie. "Mum—" But he didn't finish the sentence because he suddenly caught sight of a flash of yellow eyes outside the kitchen window, and a clear warning in them as a dark arc flicked beyond range of the light, and Petra was again invisible in the gloom. Perhaps she'd heard something.

"Yeah, I know, it's a drag," said Rafi. "Mum asked me to come around and tell you. Your mum and dad have had to go on a trip or something. Some new job. They left a note. Here."

Rafi held out a folded piece of paper. Charlie looked at it. Rafi's hand was strong like a man's.

He reached for the letter. Mum *and* Dad? It was in Mum's writing.

"Dear Charlie," he read, "I'm awfully sorry but Mummy and Daddy have had to go away for work business, would have let you know sooner but we couldn't. You're to go and stay with Martha and we'll be in touch as soon as we can. Be a good boy and do as you're told and we should be back soon. Tons of love, Mummy."

Charlie nearly laughed. He hadn't called her Mummy for about five years, and she never called Dad "Daddy" like that. She called him Aneba, because that's his name, or sometimes "your dad." "Work business" was a stupid phrase she would never use—she called work, work, and hated the word *business*: She said it made her think of rich people in horrid suits working hard to get even richer. As for "be a good boy and do as you're told"—she always said she couldn't care less about his being a good boy in the "doing what you're told" sense: She said people often told you to do foolish or harmful things, so it was much better to get in the habit of working out for yourself what you should do. "Imagine if you bought every single thing that advertisements told you to buy," she said. "Or—for example—there were times and places where black people and white people were told they weren't even allowed to be friends, or to work together, let alone to love or marry or have babies . . . so where would that leave us?"

"I'd have to cut myself in half," Charlie had said, unhappily, at about age five. Mum had dropped a kiss on his head and her face had turned a bit sad.

Clever Mum. She had let him know so clearly that this letter was a sham.

Charlie looked up at Rafi.

But if the letter was a sham, then what was going on? And why was Rafi here?

Rafi was smiling at him, in a bored way, as if he had to.

"Come on then," he said, a little impatiently, in the way a big kid would to a younger kid who's been foisted on him.

But Rafi was far too cool to have kids foisted on him by his mum. Rafi never did what his mum said—he'd been ruling himself since he was eight. Charlie had seen Rafi ignore his mum in the street. A long, long time ago Rafi had come over to Charlie's house. He'd said—and Charlie had never forgotten it: "Your house is really nice, isn't it? And your mum. And your dad." He'd said it in a way that made Charlie think he wanted to set fire to all of it.

Charlie didn't believe Rafi. His mum's letter proved that he was right not to.

Or perhaps he was in shock. All he'd done was come home for supper, and . . .

Anyway, all he said was: "Shall I go and get a bag then?"

"Good boy," said Rafi, smiling nicely. Charlie felt a surge of strength knowing that he was being a good boy the right way—clever and brave, not the way Rafi thought—dim and obedient.

He was a little angry that Rafi seemed to think he was so young and dim. He wanted Rafi to know he was more clever than to fall for *this*. But the clever thing now was to play dumb.

He went up to his room thinking quickly. He had no idea where he would go, but he was pretty sure he wasn't going to be staying at Martha's. He had to get himself ready for anything. Picking up his strong leather backpack, he put into it his Swiss army knife, a pair of socks, the little solar panel that would recharge his phone, and—after a moment's hesitation—the big furry toy tiger without which he found it hard to sleep. He hoped Rafi wouldn't notice it.

From the bathroom he got his toothbrush, his asthma medicine, and a small bottle of Mum's Improve Everything Lotion (42 Green), which should have been in the lab, but was inside because she was trying it out on his asthma. It hadn't really helped with that, but it was great for everything else—even your mood, though Mum wouldn't let him use it for that. Then he went into his parents' room and took two hundred dirams that he knew his mother had in the back of her lingerie drawer in case she needed it. "Well, I need it, for her," he said. Her handbag was sitting there on the bed. Normally he wasn't allowed in her bag, but . . . he emptied it out. There was her wallet, with its library cards and pictures of him and Dad, her phone, her lipstick, and some other things. Two little glass pill bottles full of pills. A small, polished sphere of lapis lazuli, deep blue and gold, like a little world from a long way away.

In a quick gesture, almost as if he were pretending he wasn't doing it, Charlie scooped all these things of his mum's into his own bag. Then he hurtled downstairs. Rafi was leaning on the wall by the front door, waiting.

"Be with you in a moment!" Charlie called. In the kitchen he grabbed a couple of apples, and his leather water bottle, then stuck his head out the back door into the yard. The lab door was shut. Checking over his shoulder swiftly to make sure Rafi was not looking, he stepped out into the dark and tried the door. Locked. And the keys missing. So someone had locked it since he had last been here, and so that someone had the keys. Rafi probably. Charlie suddenly and very strongly wanted to punch Rafi. How dare he be locking and unlocking his mum's lab?

The furry twining around his legs that indicated a cat distracted him—which was just as well because punching Rafi would have gotten him nowhere. It was Petra.

"They're gorn down toward the sea," she hissed. "River cats 'ave put the word about round the sea cats. We'll see what we see. Where you off to?"

"Martha and Rafi's, only I'm not going," Charlie whispered into the dark. "I don't know where I'm going, or how. Did anyone see my dad?"

"Dunno," came Petra's voice, light and rough. "We'll see. Off you go. You need anyfink, arx a cat. One of us. Don't worry—there's more to this 'n you know."

"What?" said Charlie. "Petra, what?"

"You ain't alone," she said, but he couldn't see her, and some change in the air told him she was gone.

Well, that's good, I suppose, he thought to himself.

"Hey!" Rafi called from the front of the house.

"Coming," Charlie called back. "Just locking up." One more thing, he thought as he pulled the kitchen door closed. He looked up to the top shelf and sure enough there it was, tucked behind the honeymoon photograph where Mum had put it: the letter, or whatever it was, written in her blood. He leaped nimbly up onto the hutch, smiled briefly at the photograph, slid it and the piece of paper into his pocket, and then, gripping his bag in one hand and his courage in the other, he went out to join Rafi.

CHAPTER 3

There was a long silver car waiting in the street. Charlie looked at it and sneered to himself. When his parents were young everybody had cars. Nobody had ever thought they'd have to be banned, even though they knew they were dirty and that the oil that makes the gasoline that makes them move would run out sooner or later. Sooner, as it turned out.

Ever since the great asthma epidemic of fifteen years before, when so many children fell to wheezing and creaking and coughing all at once that the schools had to close, and the government finally realized it had to act about car pollution, cars had been banned from the housing areas. The Empire, which loved cars, had tried and tried to convince everyone that cars and asthma had nothing to do with each other (they said cats were to blame, and certainly more and more people seemed to be allergic to cats), but for once the government had stood up to them and said, in effect, you can poison your own children, but you can't make us poison ours. So now most people used electros—little scooters and vans that ran on the electricity from the sun or the windfarms. There was very little oil left (planes couldn't fly at all, because there was no fuel for them) and very few people had cars with gasoline engines. Even fewer had permission to use them in the housing areas. Usually it was only government people, or really rich people—Empire people, mainly.

But the car was beautiful—long and low like a shark, and inside it smelled so sleek and leathery (not rough leather like Charlie was used to, but smooth and expensive). It was peculiar—tempting but sickening at the same time. Charlie knew it was these things that made him sometimes unable to breathe, that made his chest so tight and his shoulders high, so that he would cough and cough to try to get some air into his lungs and oxygen into his blood. But sitting inside one as Rafi pulled out and the car sped off down the road, he was amazed and delighted by it: so fast, so smooth, so powerful. It would be fantastic to drive one of these.

Troy, in the back with Charlie, slobbered on him.

"How come you've got a car, Rafi?" Charlie asked.

"Did someone a favor," said Rafi. "He lets me use it."

Up on the main road the low lights cast their orange pools on the dust as the car slid through town. Charlie stared out the window. He felt very separate.

Rafi drove to a housing tower a mile or so from home. The apartment was on the tenth floor and had no curtains.

"Sorry it's not very homey," said Rafi. He looked amused.

It was cold and empty with old tack marks on the walls where there might have been posters once. There were two small bedrooms with two small beds, a sitting room that they didn't go into, and a small kitchen with nothing in the fridge. There was no sign of Martha and it was quite clear that nobody lived here.

"Your supper." Rafi gestured to some damp fish sticks sitting on a plate. They'd obviously been there for hours.

Charlie was only interested in the locks, the doors, the windows.

"My room, your room," said Rafi, waving a hand lazily. "Mum'll be along later."

Charlie knew perfectly well that this was not Martha and Rafi's home. He wondered exactly how stupid Rafi thought he was. He could see that a guy like Rafi wouldn't give him much credit, but really—did he think he was a baby? But then if Rafi didn't think he was clever enough to escape, he might not bother locking up very thoroughly.

"Great," said Charlie with a smile. He tried to look a little confused and very accepting.

In his mind, his plan was already falling into place. He would pretend to go to bed when sent. He would escape when all was quiet. He'd have a head start and not be missed till morning.

"I can't believe I let this happen," Magdalen was muttering. "I can't believe I was so dumb."

Aneba was looking at her irritably. "No," he said. "It's not your fault."

"I should've known," muttered Magdalen.

"No," said Aneba.

"Yes," said Magdalen. "I was stupid."

"No," said Aneba.

They were sitting side by side on a metal bunk in a cramped cabin—more of a storeroom, really. It was very small and smelled of wet metal and salt. The furniture—two skinny bunks, a tiny metal table, a tiny metal sink, and a metal toilet with no seat—was all built in. There were no windows. The door was locked. There was no way out.

One whole wall (that makes it sound big, but it wasn't, because the cabin was so tiny) was made up of a brownish mirror. In the slightly more comfortable cabin next door, on the other side of the mirrored wall, two men—one big and fat, the other skinny and snivelly looking—were staring at it. Or rather, they were staring through it, at Aneba and Magdalen, for from this side the mirror was a dark-looking window.

"I thought they were, like, meant to be like really clever," said the big fat one.

"Yeah," said the skinny snivelly one.

"So how comes she's saying she's stupid?" asked the big fat one.

"Yeah," said the skinny snivelly one.

(The big fat one was called Winner; the skinny snivelly one was called Sid.)

They stared a little longer.

"If I'm not stupid," Magdalen was saying, "then how come I went with that slimy yob Rafi Sadler in his horrible car?"

"Because he said Charlie was hurt," said Aneba. "Anybody would have done that."

"How come I drank his drugged drink?" said Magdalen. "In the old days, the first thing a girl learned was not to get in a car with someone you don't know. The first thing! Stupid. And the second was not to accept drinks from strangers."

"Yes, but we know Rafi," Aneba replied. "What kind of parent wouldn't go in a car with someone they know who says that their child has been knocked down? Who wouldn't accept a drink from him? Stop it. Stop blaming yourself. Also, you may remember I fell for just the same trick with Martha, so you're calling me stupid too."

"Well," said Magdalen, "all right. What I really can't believe is how we were tricked by such stupid people."

Winner and Sid glanced at each other.

"Did she just say Mr. Rafi is stupid?" said Winner.

"Yeah," said Sid.

A curious gurgly noise came out of Winner's throat. It sounded a little as if he was choking, but then when he opened his mouth it became apparent that it was actually a laugh. Sid snickered.

Then Winner stopped laughing, and his jaw fell open a bit to one side.

"Did she just say *we're* stupid?" he said.

Skinny snively Sid stopped snickering to think. It was quite hard work for him, thinking. You could tell by the look on his face, as if he badly needed to go to the bathroom.

"Yeah," he said at last.

Winner screwed up his face and said a rude word. He didn't like being called stupid at all. Sid was used to it—from Winner, usually.

"Yeah, well, we're here now," said Aneba. "And yes, we weren't careful enough. We'll just have to be a bit cleverer from now on."

"Not much chance for cleverness, while we're locked in here, being taken Lord knows where," said Magdalen.

"You know what I mean," said Aneba.

"Yeah," said Magdalen. They were both thinking the same thing, though neither of them said it: Charlie. Where was he? What was he going to do without them? They were going to have to be clever to get back to him in one piece, as soon as possible.

Aneba squeezed Magdalen's hand.

"Sweet," sneered Winner, the other side of the two-way mirror.

"Yeah," said Sid.

"Courage," whispered Aneba.

"Oh, all right," said Magdalen. "Let me just dip into the handy bag of it that I take with me everywhere." She was cranky because she was scared.

"Come on," whispered Aneba.

"Sorry," she whispered. "I'm just . . ."

"Me too," said Aneba.

"Aneba," she said. "Why would Martha and Rafi do this? And who are these guys? What's this about?"

"I'm going through in my head what it's not," he said. "I haven't got to what it is yet. Or why."

"I just don't know . . ." she whispered. She was a scientist. She was used to knowing things, discovering them, recognizing them. She was almost as annoyed about being taken by surprise as she was angry at having been stolen away. "It can only be because of . . . I suppose . . . but why? Why now? And who?"

"I think this is a submarine," said Aneba suddenly.

"What!" cried Magdalen.

They looked at each other. So much for escaping.

Aneba was hitting his fists gently against each other. He looked up. "And . . ." he said, and went and peered closely at the brown glass wall.

He stepped back again, and then, suddenly, he stuck his tongue out.

A muffled expostulation came from the other side.

Magdalen gasped. "Really?" she said, her eyebrows flying up her forehead. She moved behind him and made rude waggly donkey-ear gestures behind his head.

They giggled.

It didn't really help, though. Not in a practical way.

Chapter 4

Around three or four in the morning, in the real dark when even the slugs and the night creatures have gone back to sleep and before the birds have woken, Charlie leaped up with a start.

Rats! How much time had he lost?

The apartment was quiet. His bedroom door was closed.

Charlie tiptoed over to it. Locked—on a latch. Well, that was easy: He got his ID card from his bag and slid it gently into the crack of the door. Jake at the fountain had taught him how to do that years ago. A little twitch of the wrist and—bingo. The latch jumped out of its slot, and the door eased open.

Dark in the grimy hallway.

Breathing sounds from the other bedroom: steady, heavy, male breathing. Heavy dog breathing filling up the gaps.

Stay asleep, you big lugs, Charlie urged, inside his head.

His bag over his shoulder, he crept to the apartment door. Locked: two bolts, easily slid, and a double lock needing a key.

Charlie peered through the dim light, and then almost laughed out loud. Here was the key, on the hall shelf. Rafi obviously thought him totally useless. Well, he'd show him.

He slid silently through to the communal landing of the housing tower and let the door shut behind him. Rather than call the noisy elevator, he opened the glass door to the stairwell and scampered down, down, down, down, flight after flight until he was giddy. He stopped to get his breath and his balance back: His head was spinning. Outside he could see the cold gray that begins to light the sky before dawn, and the morning star hanging like a distant gold coin against the gray.

By the time he got to the bottom and out into the yard, crimson streaks were shooting up the sky, gray was fading to let through a beautiful clear blue, and a few strands of white cloud blew like flags high, high up. First hurdle crossed, and it was going to be a beautiful day. Charlie lifted his nose, caught the river smell, and started to run south, following the sweet damp smell that would take him to the river and to the sea.

He was starving when he got in reach of the Thames. In front of him was one of the pleasurebanks, which during the afternoon and evening would be bouncing with rides and games and stalls selling fluffed sugar and sweet fruit. Now it was silent, the rides wrapped up in canvas against the damp, and the pleasurebank people all still asleep, or beginning to fry up their bacon for the new day. The smell tormented Charlie's nose, which actually began to twitch. "Bacon sandwich," he murmured.

So he skirted the pleasurebanks, feeling rather grown-up (because his normal reaction would be, I want to go on the rides! I want to go!), and moved east toward the rising sun. He started along a towpath lined with pretty houseboats: He could hear the people inside yawning, and see them popping up out of their painted hatches to stretch in the morning air. He kept hurriedly along. He didn't want people to remember that they had seen him. Rafi would be waking up. The "humans" of whom Petra had spoken might have friends or helpers. Charlie pulled his head in and scurried on like a spider along a wall.

It was only another half hour or so before he was back on the riversides near where he lived. Ahead of him were the ruins, left over from the times when thousands more people lived here, before they fled the car fumes and treachery of city life for the New Communities (Private Gated Village Communities, Space Communities, Empire Opportunity Communities—all kinds of promises of a safer, cleaner life). Along the edge, the muddy flats of low tide, he could see the little fishing boats. Better still, he could see a shimmer of heat rising from near the shore end of the jetty and hear the low crackle of a grill, and smell the unmistakable smell of a riverman's breakfast: eel, gasper, and sparrowfish, by the sniff of it. Charlie leaped over the little wall from the towpath to the fisherguys' territory, landed in a shallow splat of salty mud, and ambled over to the jetty.

He recognized the fisherguy at the grill: It was Mr. Ubsworth, Steve's dad. Mr. Ubsworth looked a lot like a fish himself—long and grayish pink and wet-looking. Behind him was a large canvas with a small mountain of slithery silver fish: last night's catch. Mr. Ubsworth had a big old eel up on the table and was cleaning it for grilling, scraping the silver skin and crimson innards off the table into an old sack. A skinny brown cat was picking around it.

27

Mr. Ubsworth looked up and saw him. Too late to be discreet. Oh well.

"Morning, Mr. Ubsworth, sir!" called Charlie cheerfully.

"Hey, Charlieboy!" returned Mr. Ubsworth. Then, "Early!" he commented. Charlie agreed. "Hungry?" Mr. Ubsworth wondered. Charlie agreed again. Two minutes later he was wrapping his mouth around a toasted eel sandwich, buttered up with lemon and pepper, and he'd never tasted anything better. The eels here were huge—eight feet long, some of them. Their meat was more like chicken than fish. Some of the schoolkids said snake tasted like eel, but Charlie had never eaten snake. "Africans don't eat them," his father had said. "Like the English don't eat snails." So Charlie's dad ate snails, and his mum ate snake, and Charlie didn't eat either. When it came to it, he didn't actually want to. Give him a good eel sandwich any day.

Mr. Ubsworth had a cup of tea ready too.

"Where you off to, boy?" asked Mr. Ubsworth.

"Lessons," said Charlie, lying automatically.

"Aye," said Mr. Ubsworth. He carried on with his cleaning, pausing only to take Charlie's diram, until a group of other fisherguys came up from the water's edge.

"Be going along then," said Charlie. "Thank you."

"Aye," said Mr. Ubsworth.

Rafi did wake up. Troy was whining and slathering at him, so he pulled his head out from under his pillow. He listened for Charlie. Hearing nothing, he leaped lightly from his bed and looked into Charlie's room.

First, he was just surprised. It hadn't occurred to him that Charlie would have the guts to run off.

Then he was angry. His lips went thin, and his face grew hard. Turning from the empty bed, he kicked the dog. "Could've bliddy woken, couldn't you?" he snarled. "Barked, or something? Or is that too hard for you?" Troy yelped and skittered across the floor in a way that suggested he'd been kicked often before.

Rafi grabbed his phone and without even thinking started punching in a number so he could shout at someone—when he realized that he couldn't. If he told his people that he had let the boy escape, he would be humiliated. This could not get out—the Chief Executive must not hear about this. Even when you got everything right, it was tough enough being a teenage criminal—getting people to believe you could do stuff, making them have faith in your abilities. But mistakes—mistakes were out of the question. His reputation was at stake here. Nobody—*nobody*—was going to have the chance to call him a stupid kid.

That bliddy Charlie!

He thought fast. Then he called all the contacts he had for friends of Aneba and Magdalen. None of them had heard from Charlie. They all thought he'd gone off on a sudden trip with his parents, to start their new job in a toxic post-flood area where communications were very bad but they'd be in touch in due course and not to worry. The reason they thought this was because Rafi had spent the previous afternoon on Magdalen's computer telling them so, by e-mail.

Rafi had done his job too well.

He couldn't send Sid and Winner after Charlie because they had their hands full on the submarine.

So, what—should he call the police?

He laughed. And then thought: Well, why not?

But he didn't. Rafi knew which side he was on.

"So, Troy," he said. "Shall we go for a run?"

The kid couldn't get far. Troy would track him down, the little rat.

As Charlie shouldered his bag after breakfast, he caught sight of a flick of furry brown tail out of the corner of his eye. He looked around. Again, a brown flick. It was beckoning to him—directing him back onto the towpath. With a gesture of thanks to Mr. Ubsworth, Charlie jumped over the little wall again and saw there in front of him as he landed a very proud-looking cat's bottom, tail waving erect above it as it sauntered away from him. Of course he followed it.

Behind a hedge, out of sight, the cat turned around. Charlie didn't recognize it.

"So 'ow's you gettin' dahn river?" it said briefly. Charlie was used to the quick, brusque way these cats talked, but anyone else might think they were a bit rude.

"Jump a ship, I thought," said Charlie.

"Funny time of day for stowing away," said the cat. "Follow me."

Charlie followed—back along the towpath for a mile or so farther east, then, when they reached the marina, across the larger pool where the pleasureboats lived (again Charlie felt a pang of yearning, to go out on a pleasureboat, with the bunting flapping and the sun shining, and they could eat cherry sherbet and dive off the stern) into the darker, smaller water-yard of the riverpolice. Nearest the entrance was a riverpolice launch; polished wooden deck, extra large engine, riverpolice insignia on the side and a policeguy fast asleep in the cockpit.

"Go in quietly," whispered the cat. "Curl up in the bow on the anchor chain. 'E'll be leaving for Greenwich soon on his patrol. As soon as 'e wakes up. He was drunk last night"—here the cat took on a look of disdain—"and 'e'll be in a rush when he sees 'e's late. At Greenwich he'll tie up and go to the pub. Soon as 'e's gorn, orf you go and catch yourself a seaship. They're 'eaded acrorss the channel. France."

"France!" he exclaimed. France! He didn't know what he thought about that. France!

"Get on," said the cat impatiently. "Ain't got all day."

Charlie would have to climb right over the policeguy to get to the bow. He had to step over him without waking him, then sneak down the companionway into the boat and along to the end. It was all right for cats—they could leap so lightly, it was almost like flying. But a boy makes a thump when he lands.

Charlie edged himself slowly and carefully along the railings that lined the deck, bypassing the policeguy, and was able to sneak past and swiftly down the stairs.

"Whisht!" hissed the cat, and Charlie heard a sort of rumbling snore-y noise, a rumbly, creaking, yawning, groaning sound that could only be the noise of a hungover policeguy slightly disturbed by something and waking up in the open air, on a boat, and feeling stiff and stupid and cold and uncomfortable. Charlie hurtled into the bow, folded himself up in the dark as tiny as he could, and lay still. He could smell engine oil, canvas, turpentine. The anchor chain was cold and hard, coiled beneath him. Never mind. The policeguy, just as the cat had predicted, was already rubbing his head, cursing, and trying to start up the engine. As soon as the noise of the engine was covering any noise *he* might make, Charlie positioned himself so that he could peer out of the anchor's chain-holes, and settled in to think about Rafi.

He hadn't caught up with him! He really hadn't! Yet . . .

He wondered for a moment how much effort Rafi would put into pursuing him.

He couldn't imagine why Rafi would bother with him. But then he couldn't imagine how Rafi could be involved with his parents' disappearance. Rafi was just a kid in the neighborhood—older, and cool, but still just a kid. Kind of. He was still a teenager.

But he could certainly see that someone like Rafi would be annoyed at a younger kid like Charlie getting the better of him.

He didn't like the idea of an angry Rafi.

Then he smiled. "But I'm angry too," he whispered.

Several miles downstream, Aneba was saying: "Who are you and where are you taking us?" It was the seventeenth time he had said it. And for the seventeenth time Winner was sneering and smiling nastily and replying: "You don't want to know, sunshine. You don't want to know." And Aneba's heart constricted—his child, his wife, his wife, his child.

But he wanted to know very much. When they knew, they would be able to work out what to do about it.

He sat back, closed his eyes, and thought. If he thought enough, he might be able to work it out for himself.

CHAPTER 5

There are worse ways to spend a day than chugging down the river, even if you are curled up on an anchor chain, stowing away on a police launch. After his early start and long walk that morning Charlie was tired, so he ate an apple, peered out at the view of the city as it floated past, and dropped off to sleep on a canvas sack. Unfortunately, Charlie was asleep when the riverpoliceguy docked at Greenwich, and asleep when he went for his lunch *and* when he came back, and still asleep when he pulled away and headed his boat down the river to Silvertown.

Charlie was awakened by the shuddering of the boat starting off, and a scrabbly scratchy thing running over his foot.

"Yow!" he yelped, sitting up hurriedly, before remembering that he was in a low locker in the bow and the ceiling was about two feet high. He hit his head sharply.

"Yow!" he yelped again, tears springing to his eyes, and he lay back down, awkwardly. A sneaky-looking black rat, presumably the scratchy scrabbly thing that had just run over his foot, was looking at him with an expression of disdain. The cabin was dim. What light there was, was coming in from the west. The position of the sun and his own growling stomach told him it was certainly past lunchtime.

"Oh, no!" Charlie whispered, remembering now not to yelp, as the policeguy would still be in the boat. "Where are we? What am I going to do, rat?"

The rat gave him a look that said clearly "Waddo I care?" and slipped out through the anchor hole and down into the murky water below.

"Oh!" said Charlie. "I thought you were nice. Well, there you go." He lay on the knobbly anchor chain, being as quiet as he could, wondering if anything good would ever happen to him.

Well, he thought, we're still heading east, i.e., out to sea, and that's where the cats said Mum and Dad were being taken, so that's all right. But now I've missed the chance to meet the Greenwich cats, and hear if they have any more news. He wondered if he should try to slip overboard like the rat and swim ashore . . . Or if he should push the riverpoliceguy overboard and steer the boat back to Greenwich . . . No. Stupid ideas. He had to be sensible.

The problem with having to be sensible is that if you think about it too much, soon nothing seems sensible, and this is what happened to Charlie now. Within a few minutes it seemed to him that he had been foolish to leave Rafi's, half-witted to take the cat's advice, stupid to sleep all day, idiotic to think he could just set off "to sea" and expect to find his parents. The sea is huge. The brown cat had said France. France is huge. How many ports are there on the channel coast? Hundreds. Why on earth had he thought this was a good way to try and find them?

Charlie was a boy who liked to do things, to act. Stuck in that anchor-chain locker, unable to do anything, his misery seemed about to overwhelm him. But then he heard a most peculiar noise.

It was music—loud and raucous music, but not ugly. No, it was wild and exciting, pulsing like drums and wailing like violins, though it wasn't either of those. There was a sound that he half-recognized but couldn't put a name to—a whistling, pumping sound with a swirling melody, like all the things he'd ever wanted to do but couldn't, like adventure and danger and strange, interesting people, like long ago and far away. His heart immediately began to beat faster, and he slid out of the locker into the boat's little cabin without even thinking of the riverpoliceguy.

Calliope Music

As it turned out, it didn't matter whether Charlie thought about him or not because the riverpoliceguy was busy doing his job: He was up against the railings of his little boat with a megaphone, addressing the ship alongside them, saying: "You are breaking the rules. You are causing a nuisance. Under Waterway Bylaw 1783 zx (1), you are not permitted to play music on a public waterway without a license. Unless you produce a valid license within five minutes, I am obliged to board your vessel and prevent further nuisance being caused. You are under a warning. You are breaking the rules . . ." and so on. But Charlie took no notice of all that. He was too busy gazing at the extraordinary ship before him.

For a start, the ship was huge: a great, tall, wide, old-fashioned steamer. And not only was she huge, she was crimson. Not a soppy dolly pink, but crimson like blood, like the sun going down on a burning African night, like blood oranges and garnets and pomegranate seeds. Where she wasn't crimson she was gold: the hair of her gorgeous carved figurehead, for example, with its green eyes and sidelong inviting smile, and the sculpted rims of her many portholes, and the curled leaves and vines carved all over her magnificent stern. She had three masts, a bowsprit, cannons and lifeboats along the decks, and two fine smokestacks amidship. In front of the smokestacks was a low circular canvas awning in crimson and white stripes like seaside rock, and gay flags fluttered in her rigging. She was heading out to sea under power, catching the ebb tide, but her sails were not yet up. Charlie suddenly wanted, more than anything, to see this amazing craft under canvas, bowling along on the high seas.

The wild music was coming from this ship, and it seemed that neither the ship nor her music cared about the pesky riverpoliceguy any more than an elephant cares about a fly on its bottom: He kept on bawling through his megaphone, the ship kept on moving downstream.

And then suddenly a figure appeared on the deck, and seemed to notice the policeguy, for it leaned over the side as if listening to hear what he was saying, and then disappeared for a moment, and then reappeared, casting down a rope ladder from the deck and making beckoning noises. The ship slowed a little to stabilize in the flowing stream of the river, and the policeguy maneuvered his little boat up to the great crimson hull. He made fast to the bottom of the ladder and began to climb up.

Charlie, watching for his opportunity, knew exactly what he was going to do. The moment the coast was clear, he was going to board this ship. It was so beautiful, so exciting. What kind of people could be on board? Who would own such a vessel? He had never seen anything so tempting in his life, and he had to find out about it.

Something was going on up on the deck. He couldn't see clearly because the little riverboat was tied up against the ship's crimson side and the deck was way above him, but he could hear shouting, and scuffling, and suddenly—a great splash.

He looked to where the sound had been.

There was the riverpoliceguy, closer to the river than he would have cared to be: i.e., in it. He was splashing and struggling and trying to catch his breath, which is hard with your boots on when you've been thrown overboard.

"Sorry, fella!" came a hoarse cry from overhead, and then the tempo of the ship picked up, the music suddenly stopped, and the ship began to cruise swiftly, like a fighting swan, on down the river— leaving the riverpoliceguy in its wake, and pulling his little boat along beside her almost as if it had been completely forgotten. Which perhaps it had.

Charlie, sitting alone in the little boat's cabin, being dragged at considerable speed to who knows where, couldn't say a word.

Several miles upstream, Rafi and Troy were standing by Mr. Ubsworth's stall on the riverside. Troy was panting and drooling. He'd run all the way, following Charlie's scent. Rafi had followed him in the long silver car, and was looking cool and pale. He was staring at Troy, his lip twisted.

"You stupid animal," he said, quite calmly to start with. "You *stuuuupid* animal. This is not the kid, it's a fish-stall. Didn't you get a decent sniff of him yesterday in the car? What do you think I feed you for, you plackett! It's not for the charm of your company, it's for your nose! And if your nose can't tell the difference between a boy and a plate of fish, you're not worth your keep! Are you? So pig off! Go on!" He picked up a stick and jerked it in Troy's face.

Troy, whining, his tongue flobbering, went to the edge of the water and ran up and down.

Mr. Ubsworth observed and said nothing.

"You been here all morning?" Rafi said to him.

"Aye," said Mr. Ubsworth, rinsing a sparrowfish in his bucket.

"Did you see a boy? Brown boy, shavehead, about so high, with a bag?"

Mr. Ubsworth looked up. "No," he said mildly. "You the first boy I seen today."

Rafi stared at him. He didn't like being called a boy. "If he comes back this way . . ." he said.

Mr. Ubsworth was back to his fishes' bellies, cleaning out red and blue innards from silvery streaks of eel in the cold water. The heat from his grill shimmered on the air. "Grilled eel sandwich?" he said.

"Of course not," said Rafi. "If he comes back—"

"Ain't been no boy here," said Mr. Ubsworth again.

Rafi stood for a moment, his head down. He was angry.

Suddenly he threw the stick viciously at his dog, then turned on his heel, his jacket flying. He jumped in the car and went home.

Troy lollopped tiredly after the car, his tail down. It was a long way home.

Mr. Ubsworth looked up. He liked lads to have better manners.

CHAPTER 6

Charlie wasn't worried at all about leaving the riverpoliceguy in the middle of the river. Surely riverpoliceguys could swim. He was, however, hungry. He opened each of the two little lockers in the cabin: a half-eaten box of crackers and some tea and sugar cubes and chocolate. He ate three crackers and put the rest in his bag. He pocketed the tea and the chocolate and the box of sugar cubes too—well, the policeguy wouldn't need them now.

Then Charlie settled down in the cabin. He didn't want anyone on the ship to notice him, so he'd stay put until dark, and then make his way up the ladder. He lay back and gazed up at the great crimson hull to which he was tethered, wondering again who would have a ship like that, and where it was going. He could see the ship's name, *Circe*, painted in gold on the curve of her great bow. Circe—he'd heard that name before . . . pronounced Sirky . . . now what was it . . . After a while he recalled that it was the name of the witch who enchanted Odysseus on his way back from the Trojan War. His dad had read it to him. She'd turned all his sailors into pigs and kept Odysseus for a whole year, making him forget his wife and his son at home in Ithaca. Circe. Odd name for a ship, when the Circe in the story had disrupted Odysseus's sea voyage so effectively.

The angle at which the little boat was tethered made it impossible for Charlie to face the direction of the *Circe* for long, as all the blood was going to his head, so he turned himself around and watched the last of the city disappear along the banks. By now they were way beyond the tall, shining buildings of the office district. The wharves and warehouses and stone quays of the big dockyards were giving way to the smaller ship-repair yards, the houses on stilts where the wharf workers lived, and finally the wide, empty mudflats and saltmarshes, where the light hung like gauze, and the silvery grasses rippled, and the tiny voices of hundreds of invisible birds carried over the water, mingling with the rush of the river beneath the little boat's hull. Charlie thought it must be rather nice to live there in one of the stilt houses, with the veranda looking out over the river, and the water slapping underneath. You could fish for your dinner out of your bedroom window, with the great expanse of sky and water all around you, and the sea sliding in beneath your home twice a day. He wondered why they didn't have stilt houses in the west of the city, farther inland, where he lived; why instead people there lived in housing towers or yard houses like his.

He didn't want to think about home. He could feel the presence of his mother's phone in his bag, and suddenly thought—Mum may not have her phone, but what about Dad?

He pulled out his own phone and swiftly dialed in his dad's

number. His heart beat fast and his hands were shaking. His dad might answer. He might.

The phone rang in a dim empty distance. Rang too long. Then— his dad's voice. His recorded message: "Hello, this is Aneba Ashanti, leave me a message and I'll be in touch with you soon."

His dad's voice. Charlie felt it deep in his heart.

He wished he'd thought what to say—what was safe to say. If *they*—whoever they were—were going to listen to the message, he didn't want to give anything away. But he wanted his dad to know—what? And he had to leave the message now, because what if he couldn't get through again? He couldn't waste this opportunity.

Suddenly he knew what to do. He'd leave a message like his mum's note. Clear to them, but not revealing anything.

"Hi, Daddy," he said cheerfully. "Charles here. I'm being a good boy like Mummy said and I'm at Rafi and Martha's, but I'm going out quite a lot and I really hope I will see you soon. I've been sailing on the river today and I hope I'll do some more tomorrow! Ring me soon, I've got my phone on all the time. Lots of love to Mummy. Bye!"

He was really pleased with himself. If Dad got that message he'd understand immediately that Charlie knew what was going on. One: He never called him Daddy, or Mum Mummy—so they'd know he'd picked that up from Mum's message. Plus the "being a good boy" reference and calling himself Charles. "Going out quite a lot" and "sailing on the river" was pretty clear, and the *pièce de résistance*—the best bit, which had come to him even while he'd been talking—was to say that he had his phone on all the time. Of course he had to turn his phone off during lessons—so now they'd know he wasn't going to Brother Jerome's, and they could put that together with the sailing and the "really hope I will see you soon" and know he was coming after them.

Bother. He should have said something about the cats. If Mum and Dad knew the cats were watching out for them, they could maybe send a message . . . Oh, no. Mum and Dad, astonishingly, couldn't understand when cats talked.

When they were living in Africa, when Charlie was little, Aneba Ashanti used to go frequently into the great forests, looking for plants and mosses and funguses for his research. He would go for several days, deep into the dark areas; he would climb the huge trees with the roots tall enough to build houses between, and he would spend days on end in the canopy of the forest where the monkeys and butterflies live, sleeping in his hammock hundreds of feet above the ground while the elephants rooted below looking for big seeds to eat. Sometimes he would take the little toddler Charlie with him, strapped to his back.

One hot, humid day, very early in the morning, Aneba was very carefully scraping samples of bark from a lustrous green creeper way up in the canopy, with Charlie sleeping on his back. Because he was concentrating so hard on getting a good clean sample, and trying not to cut himself with his recently sharpened knife, Aneba did not notice a leopardess down below on the forest floor, making her way delicately toward a waterhole nearby. Nor did he notice the strong, pudgy little cub following her. Nor, of course, did he notice the tiny emerald green snake on which the cub trod in the dimness of the undergrowth.

But he noticed the yowl of pain from the cub as the hot poison sparked into its little body, and the howl of distress from its mother as she realized what had happened. In an instant Aneba swung down from the canopy, his knife in his teeth, and landed not far from the leopards. The snake disappeared: It zipped into the vast green forest and was gone. The leopardess stayed. She stared at Aneba, and for a moment he felt a shot of pure fear. But the animals hereabouts were used to Aneba. They knew he wasn't a hunter, that he just hung around in the woods picking flowers and leaves and digging roots. So she didn't immediately pounce on him and kill him. She just stared. And he stared at her.

The leopard cub's yowling had started Charlie yowling too.

The two cubs yowled. The two parents looked at each other.

Aneba's heart was torn. He desperately wanted to help the baby leopard, and he had in his backpack the antidote to the snake poison—he took it with him everywhere in case he or the child were bitten. But he would have to get it to the cub swiftly—and how to make the mother let him?

Her eyes were expressionless. Aneba's face too was a mask.

There was only one thing he could do.

He was very scared to do it.

Slowly and gently, Aneba unwrapped Charlie from his back and sat him on a flat rock behind him, well away from the leopardess. He didn't take his eyes off her while he rummaged in the bag and found the syringe containing the antidote. Then, holding the syringe up like a totem, so that she could see it clearly, he asked her: "May I help your child?"

She stared.

Charlie, on the rock, yowled a bit more quietly.

The cub was whimpering.

Aneba moved away from Charlie, gently toward the cub.

The leopardess narrowed her eyes. Her ears were perked up, her whiskers twitching. In a swift movement, she dropped her head and moved—away from Aneba, away from her cub, away from Charlie. After ten paces, she stopped, and turned, and sat, staring again at Aneba.

He fell to his knees beside the cub, and swiftly, surely injected the life-saving medicine into the cub's fat back leg. As he did so—

"Baby one!" cried Charlie, who had tottered up to Aneba's side and was now reaching out to pat the cub, who squirmed away from the needle. Aneba gasped, the syringe fell, and a few small drops of blood appeared on the fur. Charlie laughed. The cub, alarmed, put out a claw and scratched, hard. Drops of Charlie-blood were on the cub; drops of cub-blood were on Charlie's bleeding arm.

The leopardess and Aneba looked at each other. The cub and Charlie yowled again: in unison.

Each parent grabbed its child and ran—the cub hanging from the leopardess's tender jaws like a kitten, Charlie tucked firmly under his father's arm.

"Ab ab ab baby one!" cried Charlie happily.

"Mrrrrow!" scrawled the leopard cub.

"Mrrrrow!" called Charlie.

And after that, Charlie talked with cats as much as with people. He was mystified by their constant feuding. Though he understood their language, he didn't exactly understand their feelings and their mysteries, but he loved them and they were his friends. His parents studied him endlessly: They knew what must have caused it, but they couldn't work out why.

"He's modified himself," said Magdalen. "Here's everybody fussing about genetic modification methods, and young Charlie here's done it to himself."

"And can the leopard cub talk English now?" Aneba wondered.

Another thing—he wasn't allergic to cats, when so many other kids were.

"Fascinating," said his parents, over and over again. This was after Magdalen had shouted at Aneba for three days about getting their child into such danger.

Charlie had been really happy to be more clever at something than his parents were. But now—well, it would have been useful if they'd had that particular knack too.

Before the afternoon sun grew too low, Charlie set up his solar panel to recharge his phone. He'd recharge Mum's as well if there was time. There might be messages on it. There might be something to give him a clue.

Clue!

For goodness' sake, thought Charlie. I *have* a clue. His mum had given it to him herself. He reached into his bag and there it was, carefully folded.

Charlie had a bit of a feeling in his chest as he took it out.

This was her blood.

So what had she written?

Oh.

Letters and numbers. Some in brackets, some not. Mostly normal size, some little tiny ones up at the top of the bigger ones.

It looked like very complicated math. It made no sense whatsoever to Charlie.

He looked at it for a moment, wondering if it was a code. He'd played code games with his mum before, and if it was a code, he'd like to think he could work it out.

But nothing they'd ever done had had all these brackets and tiny numbers.

"I know what this is," he said to himself after a while of staring. "This is a formula." He knew what formulas were because scientists use them all the time.

So it wasn't nonsense. But it was nonsense to him, because he hadn't learned nearly enough science yet to work it out.

He folded the paper up and put it away again. He'd learn what it was about. He would find someone who would tell him. He'd be careful whom he asked, though. It didn't seem like something he should show to just anybody.

And in the meantime, it did him no good at all. He still didn't know why his parents had been taken. Apart from him, who would want them?

He thought about it for a bit.

He ran over in his mind the phrases that had come up. *New job . . . Work business.* He knew that the most valuable thing about his parents to other people was their intelligence, and the work they did.

Charlie'd read enough stories.

"Somebody's after their brainpower," he said. "After something they know, or can find out."

He felt happier then. Just having worked that out made him feel he had something to go on.

Plus he had that piece of paper.

The reasons why Aneba had not answered his phone were: 1) because there was no reception under water and 2) because skinny snivelly Sid had swiped it from him while he was asleep to play Snake, and had run the battery down.

Aneba was annoyed about this. Lying back on the lower bunk with Magdalen dozing on his shoulder, he was staring right at the two-way mirror at the spot where he felt Sid and/or Winner would be.

"Berma, mu ye kwasia eni mu ha ma jwi," he muttered. He stared from under his hooded eyelids. His mouth was hard. He hadn't moved for an hour and a half—not a twitch, not a blink, only the tiny movements of his lips, and they were scarcely visible. Basically, he was letting himself look frightening, and he knew perfectly well that he could look very frightening indeed.

"Wo ho ye ahi paa," he murmured. On the other side of the mirror, Sid and Winner didn't like it.

"What's he saying?" said Winner. "What is that?"

"Wo ho ye ahi paa."

"What language is that?" demanded Winner. "What's he saying that for?"

Aneba carried on muttering, and staring, like a block of obsidian possessed by an evil voice.

"I hear he's some kind of wise man, some kind of, like, one of their wizards, isn't he!" said Winner, who couldn't really tell the difference between a wizard and a university professor.

"Yeah," said Sid.

They didn't like it at all.

"He's putting a curse on us," said Winner. "He's putting a hex on us."

Slowly, weirdly, the block of obsidian cracked. Aneba smiled, a long, scary smile. It was working. All he was saying was "you stupid little irritating men, you're beginning to annoy me," but if they wanted to think they were being cursed, that was fine with him. Fat and Skinny, as he called them, were already scared of how huge he was. Skinny had said that he didn't want to go into the cabin anymore.

Suddenly a voice burst over the intercom from the other cabin.

"Stop cursing us!" it cried. "Stop it!"

Aneba lifted his head, flashed his eyes, and gave them a huge grin. The effect, after the hours of motionlessness, was electrifying. Sid and Winner jumped.

"Certainly," said Aneba politely. "When you give me back my telephone, recharged, and tell me where you are taking us, and why, and on whose instructions."

Magdalen rolled her head in her sleep and tried to shift, but there was no room. The ship's cat, a lazy-looking marmalade, fell with a yowl from her lap, where he had been lying, and gave her an irritated look. She half woke.

"Charlie?" she murmured.

Aneba touched her head. He very much wanted to leap up, break the glass, throw the two guys overboard . . . He probably could have too. He was, after all, extremely big and strong. But there was something else he wanted more. He wanted to know why they had been kidnapped, and by whom, and what for. More important than escaping was learning what was going on.

He stroked Magdalen's head, then turned his gaze to the two-way mirror and started muttering again.

> *"Wo hairdresser nye papa,*
> *wo maame ye kwadu,*
> *wo gyime ye sononko,*
> *wo hwene kakraka."*

(Loosely, "You have a very bad hairdresser, your clothes look as if they have been out dancing on their own all night, your mother is a banana, your nose is too big, your stupidity is so famous, they

have statues of it in the city squares . . .") "Your nose is too big"
sounded good, so he said it a few more times, rhythmically, getting
louder and louder:

> *"Wo hwene kakraka,*
> *wo hwene kakraka,*
> *WO HWENE KAKRAKA!"*

"Stop it!" shouted a big fat voice over the intercom.

"I'd be glad to," said Aneba. "You know what you have to do."
And he lowered his lids again, and stared, and muttered, and stared,
and muttered, and stared.

CHAPTER 7

About an hour later Charlie heard noises at the top of the ladder, and realized that someone was climbing down. He had no time to think what to do—even to decide whether or not to hide—before the person was standing in the cockpit, staring at him out of big brown eyes and saying: *"François! Regardez! Il y a un garcon ici—un petit Africain!"*

Charlie's French was pretty good—Brother Jerome was very keen on languages—so he understood that she was saying: "François! Look! There's a boy here—a little African!"

As for what she was, Charlie knew exactly. She was slender but muscular, wearing tights and a tight top with a short skirt, she had her dark hair pulled back in a bun so tight that it made her face look tight too—in fact, everything about her was tight, except her skirt, which flared out like the petals on a daisy. The tight hair even pulled all expression off her face, and she stood with her weight on one leg and her arms crossed. She was quite clearly a ballerina—except that she looked way too tough. And he didn't know why she was going on about him being African. She obviously had African blood too.

François appeared behind her: a black-haired young man in fringed ponyskin chaps, a waistcoat, and a hat. He had a red-tooled holster, fancy Cuban-heeled boots to match, and two shiny little guns, one of which he had pulled out and was aiming at Charlie.

Charlie was not at all sure about being held up by a tough African ballerina talking French and a cowboy in red boots.

"Bonjour," he said bravely.

"Salut," said the ballerina. François nodded. They didn't seem entirely unfriendly.

"Er—could you put the gun down?" asked Charlie politely in French.

The ballerina looked over her shoulder and rolled her eyes to heaven in exasperation. She berated François in a swift and complicated French that Charlie couldn't follow, saying, it was obvious, "Put it away, don't be such a nincompoop, it's only a kid," or words to that effect. Also, as Charlie looked more closely at the little gun, he suspected that it wasn't real. It was so small and shiny, and looked somehow too light. In fact, nothing about the cowboy looked real. He wasn't sunburned, for a start, and his clothes were too colorful. And there was a monkey on his shoulder. And the monkey was wearing fringed ponyskin chaps and a red gunbelt too. No, this was no ordinary cowboy.

François put the gun away and the ballerina said that she supposed they'd better take him up. Charlie, knowing that his only alternative was to try to jump overboard, be pulled out again, and taken up anyway, dripping wet and having annoyed everybody, pult his things into his bag and slung it over his shoulder.

"Come on," said the ballerina, and poked him up the ladder to the ship. Charlie didn't like being poked. She wasn't that much older than he anyway, to be bossing him around.

It was amazing, thought Charlie, how something crimson could look so tough. Because this *was* a tough ship: the great flanks, the thick ropes coiled on the decks, huge fenders dripping salt water and weed over the side, the massive masts and great industrial smokestacks, the brawny sailors with their sunburns and squinty eyes. The ship made a music of her own: a creaking and rumbling, of engines and furnaces, of ropes in the wind, of beams and joists surging through the water. Charlie, nervous as he was, felt a huge thrill at being aboard this great ship as she headed out to sea.

"Go on," said the ballerina. She prodded him along the deck until they came to a cabin door, carved with gold vines, which stood ajar.

"Maestro!" called the ballerina, knocking on the door. *"Y'a quelque chose."* Charlie didn't quite like being introduced as "Here is something," but the ballerina prodded him again and he stumbled into the room, tripping over the little ledge that cabin doors always have at the bottom, to keep shallow floodwater out.

The chamber was small but magnificent, and standing in the middle, leaning on a small desk, was a most magnificent person. He must have been six and a half feet tall, broad-shouldered in white breeches and a green velvet tailcoat, and his fine blond hair, almost as pale as ice, hung down his back in a thick ponytail. His eyes were piercing blue, his skin pale and dry, and he looked as if he stayed up far too late and had done so all his life. In one pale hand he had a glass of what looked like brandy, and before him on the desk was a pile of papers and a large metal box absolutely full of money: masses of it.

Charlie stared. He had never seen a man who looked like this before.

"For Pete's sake," said the man, in French, but with an accent Charlie recognized to be southern Empire. "Now what?"

"I found this boy," said the ballerina, "in the policeguy's boat."

"Throw him overboard then," said the man.

"Okay," she said, and turning around, made to prod Charlie out of the door again. Charlie's heart leaped.

"No, wait a moment," the maestro said. "Bring him back. You speak French?"

"Yes," said Charlie in French. "My name's Charlie and I'm looking for my mum and dad, who have disappeared. I hitched a lift with the polishing machine." (He meant to say "policeguy" but he got the word wrong and said *"polisseur"* instead of *"policier"*—an easy mistake.)

"Really," said the man, unimpressed with this brief history. He looked at Charlie a moment, sizing him up. He took hold of Charlie's arm and squeezed it.

"Boy," he said, "are you strong?"

"Quite, sir," said Charlie. "But I'm more clever than strong."

"How clever?" said the magnificent man.

"I can speak English, French, Twi, Arabic, Latin, Greek, and Italian," he said. (He never told people that he could speak Cat. He had always known, without being told, that it was not something to brag about.) "And I can read and write, I'm quick at calculations, and I can play the piano and drive and I am an experienced sailor." He was thinking quickly of things that might make this strange pale man want to keep him on the ship rather than throw him overboard. "And I can climb, and ride a bicycle."

The man's elegant dark eyebrows rose up his white forehead as Charlie spoke, but he said nothing. So Charlie continued: "And I can cook, omelettes, fufu and soup, and flapjacks, and I can do handstands and cartwheels, and climb ropes, and I can swim, of course, and dive, and tie knots, I can do a sheepshank and clove hitch, and I'm quite used to computers . . ." Charlie faltered to a halt. The man was saying nothing on purpose, just to see how long Charlie would keep on talking.

"Most impressive," said the man, after a little gap just long enough to let Charlie know who was in charge—as if there were any doubt. "But you're not strong."

"Quite strong," said Charlie.

The man took a sip from his glass of brandy, never taking his eyes off Charlie.

"Now tell me," he said. "Of course all boys want to run away and join with us, but what precisely is your excuse?"

He thought Charlie had come to the ship on purpose. Oh, well. That didn't matter. What mattered was—

A very important thought struck Charlie. All these people talking French. Were they going to France now?

"I intend to seek my fortune, sir," said Charlie. "And my parents. Are you headed to France?"

The man put his glass down. He seemed to have made his mind up about something.

"What's your name?" he said.

"Charlie Ashanti," said Charlie. Even as he said it, he thought: Oh. It might have been a good idea to give a fake name. What with Rafi out there, wherever he is . . .

"Charlie. I am Major Maurice Thibaudet." (He pronounced it *Tib-oh-day*.) "I am the Boss, the Leader, the Voice of All Authority around here. I am the ringmaster. You call me Major, Sir, or Maestro. You are Charlie, a little kid we've taken on. You'll do as you're told. Do me a handstand."

Since he was tiny, Charlie had been playing around with the cats in the ruins and he was as agile as a little monkey. A handstand was nothing to him. Now, too taken aback to wonder why the major wanted him to do it, Charlie swiftly upended himself. There wasn't much room, but he managed it without kicking anybody in the face. With his feet in the air and his head down by the floor he couldn't see Major Maurice's reaction, but he felt he shouldn't come down until he was told, so he just stayed there while Major Maurice did his trick of doing nothing to see how long a person would carry on.

"Okay," said Major Maurice eventually. "Come on down now. Could you do that on a lion's back?"

Charlie nearly fell as he brought himself down. What kind of a question was that?

"Yes, sir," he said, with a gulp at his own bravery. He had been doing some thinking, upside down. Ballerina. Cowboy. Music. Striped canvas. Ringmaster. And now lions. "Please, sir—are you a circus? And are you—" He was trying to ask again about France, but the major had started talking already.

"Are we a circus?" said Major Maurice. "Are we a *circus*? We are not *a* circus, boy—we are

THE CIRCUS,
THE FINEST AND BEST,
THE MOST DARING AND THE MOST ASTOUNDING,
THE MOST MAGNIFICENT SHOW ON EARTH!"

He really did talk like that. His voice rose and rose and grew and grew, until the little cabin was full of it and it started to pour out onto the deck, and the blood suddenly came into his face, making him look pink and happy. Charlie could just imagine what he would be like in the ring, filling the big top with his rolling tones, crying out to the audience, shouting about how wonderful the show was, telling them to roll up, roll up for the Most Magnificent Show on Earth.

"We are Thibaudet's Royal Floating Circus and Equestrian Philharmonic Academy," he said, more calmly, "known to those who can't pronounce the illustrious name of Thibaudet as Tib's Gallimaufry, and to those who can't pronounce Gallimaufry as the Show. Play your cards right, young man, and you too will be in the Show. We need a young fella. Work hard, stick around. You can start with the monkeys. Pirouette will take you down. Good day to you."

The ballerina, Pirouette, gave Charlie a smile instead of a prod as she led him down a narrow companionway. It smelled of something Charlie could not identify. Something animal and dusty and musky—not a bad smell, but curious for a ship.

"You really want to be Circus, Charlie?" she said.

"Of course I do," said Charlie. "Of course I do. But listen—are we going to France?"

"Of course," she said, marching on ahead.

Charlie's face broke out in a grin as big as Paris.

The monkeys lived in the depths of the boat, in a smelly little chamber between the zebras and the Hungarian with the troupe of trained bees.

An Indian man—his name was Bikabhai—lived with the monkeys, in a hammock. Charlie could go in with the monkeys too, or he could sling a hammock in the feed hold, even farther down in the depths of the ship, where the smell wasn't quite so monkeyish but the air never changed, so it was still and thick and hard to breathe.

"Can't I sleep on deck?" he asked Bikabhai.

Bikabhai stretched his eyes. "Very cold," he said, slightly shocked. "And if sailorguys tread on you it might be unpleasant."

Charlie's duties were not too hard. He was to bring the monkeys' food, watch Bikabhai as he fed them, clean their quarters, and mend their clothes. Carrying the buckets of water was the worst part, once you got used to the monkey poo smell.

Several of the monkeys were called Dandy Jack.

"Why?" asked Charlie.

"Because they ride the ponies," said Bikabhai, as if that explained it.

"Where do we get dinner?" Charlie asked.

"I do not eat," said Bikabhai. So instead Charlie asked where in France they were headed.

"It matters not, so long as the journey is undertaken with a pure heart," said Bikabhai.

Charlie thought all this less than helpful, and set off to find somebody with a more practical outlook, and an opinion on where the dining room might be.

There were at least three decks that Charlie could make out. In the deep hold was the feed, and who knows what else—it was dark down there, and smelly, and dank, and Charlie found it quite impossible not to think of the deep, cold river water just on the other side of the thick clinkered struts and beams of the hull. The second deck, at the waterline, was where most of the animals lived: The cabins were small, and it seemed almost as if there was something huge in the middle of the ship and everything else had been stuffed in willy-nilly around it, to fit in as best they could. But it was a bit warmer, and through the thick portholes you could see greenish daylight and sky, usually. Tonight, in the reasonably flat waters of the river, the waterline crossed right along the middle of the portholes in the monkeycabin, so you could see sky in the top semicircle, and dark water in the bottom half. The effect was peculiar, and made Charlie feel a bit ill.

The upper deck, where the humans lived, basked in full air and light. Pirouette had said she had a cabin here on the port side, near Major Thibaudet, which she shared with someone she called Madame Barbue. (Charlie thought that was the name. He was having a bit of trouble with the names, and was pretty sure he would be calling it Tib's Show, not Tiboddy's Floating Philharmonic What-have-you.) Charlie decided to go and see Pirouette. She would know about dinner. She had the air of a girl who knew things.

So how to find her cabin? He asked a sailor, got lost, asked another sailor, got lost, and asked another sailor—who directed him to the door in front of his nose.

His knock was answered by what could only be described as a beautiful lady with a large, fine, curling, silky black beard.

He gulped.

"Hallo," she said. She sounded French like Pirouette.

"*Bonjour, madame,*" said Charlie politely, but still gawking. How could a lady have a beard like that? Was it real? If it were fake, why would she be wearing it off-duty? And goodness, what a fine beard it was. He could even smell it—a faint clean tinge of lavender pomade.

"Are you looking for Pirouette?" she asked.

"Yes, madame," said Charlie. He couldn't stop staring. There were no strings that he could see, nor signs of glue.

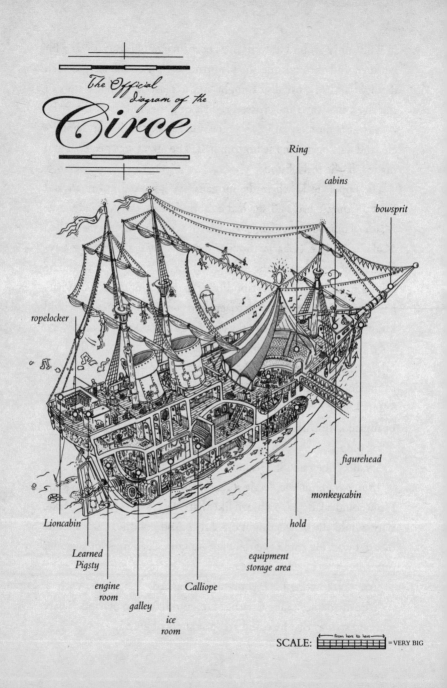

The Official Diagram of the
Circe

Ring

cabins

bowsprit

ropelocker

figurehead

monkeycabin

Lioncabin

hold

Learned
Pigsty

equipment
storage area

engine
room

Calliope

galley

ice
room

SCALE: from here to here = VERY BIG

Then quick as a bird, the lady took Charlie's hand in hers (which was cool and gentle) and put it to her cheek.

"You can stroke," she said, her smile curling up into the corner of her elegant mustache. "You like?"

Charlie couldn't tear his hand away. Her beard was beautifully soft and silky, like a very young goat's ears, or the curls between a calf's horns.

"We are about to eat," said the bearded lady. "You like to come with us?"

Charlie just nodded. Bearded lady. Okay. He could handle that.

Dinner took place in a long narrow chamber along the stern on the upper deck. Everybody took a dish up to the hatch and was given a dollop of food—tonight it was a stew with dumplings and green peas—and a piece of bread. Then they sat around eating and gossiping, and Charlie was able to see for the first time exactly whom he was heading out to sea with. There was a group of about ten tiny Italians, of all ages, with long noses and cheerful expressions, who Charlie guessed were acrobats of some kind. There was a rather fat woman with a squint, wearing overalls—"Snakes," said Madame Barbue mysteriously. A cross-looking gray-haired man sat reading all through the meal. ("Mr. Andrews," said Pirouette with a sniff. "He leads the bears.") An enormous young man came in a bit late, with an enormous dish, and had three helpings ("Hercule. Strong man," said Madame Barbue), and then a gang of energetic boys of about twenty, chatting loudly, playing around and talking about horses, with François the cowboy. ("The trick riders," said Pirouette.) There were various children around the place too, Charlie was pleased to see: a downtrodden-looking boy with mud on his face, a curly-haired boy who sat with two squabbling clowns, ignoring them, and two girls of about nine who had to be twins, wearing matching dresses and imitating each other's every move. They were interesting to watch, but they made Charlie feel seasick.

"What do you do?" Charlie asked Pirouette.

"I am *trapeziorista volante*," she said with a proud little smile.

"Gosh," said Charlie, because he felt he ought to. He could tell by Pirouette's tone of voice that a *trapeziorista volante* was clearly fantastically cool, but he hadn't a clue what it meant. "Gosh," he said again politely. The bearded lady shot him a look and winked at him.

"You will see," she said, "when we do the Show."

"When will that be?" he asked eagerly.

"We go to Paris now," said Pirouette. "We have a date for the big show in just one week. The Imperial Ambassador is having a big party, he invites all the eastern potentates, we are to be the fun for them. They all will come."

Paris! He tried to remember where Paris was. Sort of in the middle, but north. Certainly nowhere near the sea. So, when they got to land he could find a cat and get more information, and move on . . .

Charlie, to tell the truth, was having contradictory feelings. With the circus, he realized, he felt safe. All the activity, and so many people, would give him some protection if Rafi *was* coming after him. So on the one hand, he was looking forward to snooping all over the ship, finding the animals and making friends, and above all seeing the Show, the real magic of the circus. He hoped (and hoped that this wasn't disloyal to his parents) that there'd be chances to see and do loads of things before they got to France. On the other hand, running through this cheerful prospect like an icy current was the constant, repeating knowledge of his parents' danger. And just behind that was the figure of Rafi: cool, unknown, frightening, challenging.

But until they reached France, there was nothing much he could do. Okay. It was frustrating, but he could handle it.

Pirouette was still talking. "We can only make the Show in the big top. We travel to where the people are, then they come on board and we make the Show."

"They come on board!" said Charlie, who had been listening to his fears, not to Pirouette. He wasn't sure if he was understanding right.

"You haven't seen the big top?" said Madame Barbue. She wondered at this boy—so alone, so distracted, yet so accepting. "Oh, Charlie—we have the most beautiful circus ring here on the boat. With the seats and the sawdust and the flying trapeze and the striped tent-roof and everything."

Now, Charlie very much wanted to hear more about how you could fit a circus ring onto a boat, and where it was, and when he would get to see it, but just at that moment another person entered the cabin.

He was not tall like Major Maurice, nor was he huge like Hercule, nor amazing like the bearded lady. He was a brown-haired, brown-skinned man of about forty, or maybe fifty—an African, well-built, quiet, and very calm. What was strange was that he seemed to bring a wake of calm with him. It was as if nothing that was not calm could get anywhere near him, and if it tried to, it *became* calm, no matter what its intention had been in the first place. Silence spread out from him, stillness formed a pool around him. As he walked in, the trick riders stopped laughing and the Italians turned their faces quietly to their plates. Pirouette and Madame Barbue stopped chatting. A forced gentleness descended on the company.

Charlie could not take his eyes off this man, and he could not understand why. Then the man turned to face Charlie, and looked straight at him. His eyes were deep wells of darkness, and then suddenly, from deep within these dark eyes, Charlie saw a flash, a reflection of light like from an animal's eyes, as the man turned his head away again.

"Who is he?" Charlie whispered to Madame Barbue, huddling a little closer to her.

"Ah, he is our dear Maccomo," she said. Charlie was surprised. Was she being sarcastic? "Dear" was not the kind of word he would apply to that man. "He is our lion tamer. Oh—he doesn't like us to say tamer. He is our lion trainer. He is African like you."

He may be African, thought Charlie, but he is not like me. He is like—he is like the feeling you get when your father is angry with you. He is scary, and this calm he carries with him is not a good, relaxed calm; it is the calm of fear. Charlie shivered.

Lion tamer, eh? Well, he certainly seemed to have this group tamed.

Charlie glanced at Pirouette. She was looking at her meal, and seemed not to want to look up.

Maccomo had made Charlie lose his appetite, so he just sat and listened to the gentle conversation that flowed around the cabin as the circus people finished their dinners. One of the Italians was trying to persuade one of the others to get his mandolin and play a song. Mr. Andrews the bear leader had offered part of his newspaper to the Hungarian. Some new people came in, including a large, proud-looking bald man. ("What does he do?" inquired Charlie eagerly, but Madame Barbue just gave him a look, as if to say he should know better than to ask.) There was a small group of wiry Arab boys, and a very tall, elegant, pale man with feathery white hair and exceptionally long hands and feet. Charlie found himself giving

Madame Barbue a pleading look, and she relented enough to say: *"El Superbe Aero: funambuliste,"* which didn't help Charlie much. *Funambuliste, trapeziorista volante* . . . he needed a dictionary.

Gazing around the dining room, Charlie thought they looked like a rather large and odd family. He smiled to himself. He liked it here. At least—he would have. If only . . .

After dinner the twins came over and said—both of them: "Hello, we're the twins. Who are you?"

"I'm Charlie," said Charlie. "I'm helping with the monkeys."

The twins looked at each other meaningfully, then continued: "Major Tib always puts people with the monkeys first. He'll have you doing something else soon. Do you have any chocolate?"

It was amazing the way they talked together. How could they have known to jump from talking about Major Tib to talking about chocolate? If this was a trick for the Show, it was a very good one.

"I do, actually. Would you like some?"

"Yes," they said, and smiled. They were weird.

Charlie said good night to Pirouette (who had undone her tight hairdo and suddenly looked much nicer) and Madame Barbue, who made him promise to come to breakfast with them the next day, and went off with the twins. Part of him wanted Pirouette to ask him to stay with her rather than go off with the younger girls, but she said nothing, so he went. Also, he wanted to find out if the twins really talked in tandem all the time.

Charlie didn't quite know his way back to the monkeycabin where he had left his things, but the twins—"We're Sara and Tara," they said—were able to show him where it was. Well, they could show him where the cabin was, but where the chocolate was, was another thing, and no secret: The monkeys had been in Charlie's bag, and they had devoured the chocolate, the remaining crackers and sugar cubes, and the teabags.

"Yuck!" said the twins. "Raw teabags!"

Maybe they're one person in two bodies, Charlie thought. That would make sense.

Oh, no, it wouldn't, he thought then. How could one person in two bodies make sense?

Sara and Tara then announced that they had some chocolate in their cabin. He followed them back up to the open deck, along toward the bow, right into the bow, as it seemed. And then suddenly the girls turned and disappeared from view.

"Oi!" called Charlie. "Where are you? Where've you gone?"

"We're here!" the girls called, and their heads popped out from a hole in the wall right by the figurehead. "This is where we stay."

Their cabin was right inside the figurehead's chest. It was sort of triangular, and though they had no porthole as such, if you climbed a ladder in the top corner of the curiously shaped chamber, you found yourself inside the figurehead's face, and you could look out of spyholes cut into her beautiful green eyes, and you could peer through a thick glass window behind the great teeth of her beguiling smile. Now of course there was nothing to see but a few swaying stars, misty and far away, but in the daytime what a view that would be! When Charlie had admired the ship from the outside earlier that day, he had had no idea that the figurehead was hollow, with a peculiar little room inside where two girls lived.

"This is absolutely amazing," he said. "This is amazing. I am amazed."

The girls—acting together as always—found the chocolate. Then they unfolded their cot, and there was just room for all three to sit on it (there was no floorspace left) and start to nibble their way into a happy chocolate reverie.

A knock at the door made them jump. "Password!" cried the twins.

"Bucket!" said a voice, and the door opened and in marched the curly boy who had been with the clowns.

"Ah, *you've* got him!" he cried in a cheerful tone. "The twins have got him!" he called over his shoulder, and from behind him Charlie could hear a chattering, scrabbling sound, which turned out to be the muddy-faced boy and four or five of the smallest Italians, who had come to investigate Charlie. They all tried to come into the twins' cabin, the twins told them there wasn't room, and then a great coo-cooing noise started up from behind one of the walls, and the twins said, "Now look! You've woken the doves," and shooed everybody, including Charlie, out.

"Where're you sleeping?" said the curly boy to Charlie.

"Don't know," said Charlie. "I'm supposed to be in with the monkeys, but since they've been through my bag and eaten everything, I don't want to."

"Do you want to come and bunk with us in the rope storeroom?" asked the curly boy. "It's above the galley so we never get cold. It keeps the ropes dry too so they don't rot. It's next to the lions . . ."

The boy was going on about the lions needing the heat too, but Charlie wasn't listening. Next to the lions! There were lions! He'd been told, and he knew it, but only now did it really get through to him. There really were lions on this ship and he was going to be next door to them.

CHAPTER 8

The curly boy was called Julius, and the thin clown was his father. The muddy boy was called Hans, and he looked after the Learned Pig, which was why he was so muddy. (The boy, not the pig. Though the pig was muddy too. But the boy was muddy because of the pig, not vice versa. In fact, the pig would have been a lot muddier were it not for the boy.)

Hans and Julius slept on piles of coiled-up ropes in the rope storeroom. Each had his own shelf, quite big enough for a smallish boy, though without much headroom. Julius had the top shelf and Hans the bottom one, so there was a shelf for Charlie in the middle.

"There's a sleeping bag here already," said Charlie. "Does someone else sleep here?"

Hans started to giggle nervously. Julius shushed him with a furious look.

"What is it?" said Charlie.

Julius snorted. "Oh, well, there was a boy," he said. "He helped with the lions."

"Really?" said Charlie, interested. "And what happened to him?"

"Major Tib had him thrown overboard," hissed Julius.

Charlie stared. "Why?" he whispered, adopting Julius's air of mystery.

Julius shook his head and made a zip-the-mouth gesture. Charlie looked at the shelf and its sleeping bag again, and wrinkled his nose a bit. "Bad luck isn't contagious," he said to himself. "Bad luck doesn't exist. It's all in the mind." This is what his mum always said—though when she did, his dad tended to raise an eyebrow and say, "The mind is a very strong thing, Professor."

Charlie decided that he wasn't going to mind about the sleeping bag: "It's all in the mind and I don't mind," he said to himself.

"You staying then?" said Julius. "Or have we scared you off?"

"No way," said Charlie. "I'm staying."

"Well, if you need any help, I know everything," said Julius in such a friendly way that Charlie decided to try him out then and there. He liked the look of Julius: He liked his curly hair and his freckly nose.

"What's a *funambuliste*, what's a *trapeziorista volante*, and why are monkeys called Dandy Jack when they ride on ponies?" he blurted out.

"Tightrope walker, flying trapeze artist, and after Major Jack Downing, who was a very famous trainer of trick horses," said Julius, without batting an eye. "That's also why naughty people are called Jackanapes—an ape who thinks he's as talented as Major Jack was."

Charlie blinked. "Thanks," he said.

"*De nada,*" said Julius.

"What does that mean?" said Charlie.

"It's nothing, in Spanish," said Julius. "I mean, it means nothing, the word nothing, not that it doesn't mean anything, though of course it doesn't mean anything, it means something: It means nothing. Nothing is what it means. Not it doesn't mean anything."

"No, it means nothing. I know what you mean," said Charlie with a straight face.

They started to giggle.

Although things on this boat were so interesting that it was easy to be distracted, the thought of his parents was only ever a speck away from the surface of Charlie's mind.

He needed to check his phones and see if there were any messages. But privacy is very hard to find on a ship—especially when you're sharing a ropelocker with two other boys—so he went out on deck into the cold night to be alone. The moon was up, like a big pearl button on a navy blue suit. Charlie shivered and pulled his jacket around him, then curled himself up in a corner by one of the smokestacks and tried first his own voicemail, then his mum's.

There was still nothing on Mum's. Why wasn't anyone calling her? Probably they're just leaving messages at home, sending her e-mails . . .

He tried his own line.

The voice leaped out at him.

"Now listen here, you disgusting little rodent. Personally I don't know why your stupid smug stubborn parents didn't just drown you at birth, but as you seem to exist, and as your existence is giving me grief, I just have this to say: I know where you are, I know what you're doing, so you just stay there and I'll be along soon to get you. All right? I'll be along. Soon. To get you."

And the phone banged down.

Charlie stood staring at his cell phone. He was shaking. He'd never heard such anger in anyone's voice. He'd lived his whole life in the city, he'd seen fights and been in fights, he'd yelled and been yelled at, but no one had ever spoken to him with such—such deep nastiness.

Very quickly he pressed the delete button.

Then he cursed himself. He should have kept it for—evidence. To listen to again and learn from . . . But he knew he wouldn't ever listen to that again.

He had heard what it said. He knew whom it was from. He didn't need anything else.

It wasn't that he'd thought Rafi would just let him go. He just . . .

His hand was still shaking from the violence of Rafi's message. He'd had no idea Rafi could be like that. But he still couldn't quite believe Rafi was involved in his parents' disappearance—not directly. How could a kid kidnap adults? Anyway he'd been at the fountain that afternoon, relaxed and playing football—

And talking intently on the phone, and taking notice of Charlie for the first time ever . . .

So there must be other people involved too. Someone had paid Rafi to take him, Charlie, out of the way . . .

When Charlie curled up on his ropes that night, he pulled his tiger out of his bag, secretly so the other boys wouldn't notice. Listening to Hans scratching himself on the shelf below and Julius shouting orders in his sleep on the shelf above, for a moment Charlie wished that his mum were there to say good night to him and check that he had taken his asthma medicine (he had), and that his dad could come up and look at him just as he was dropping off to sleep. He said a prayer quickly and firmly under his breath: "All gods, watch over my mum and dad and help them be safe, please please please." His mum and dad hadn't brought him up to be religious at all, but so many other people believed in so many different gods, and seemed to get help from them, that sometimes Charlie did join in, quietly. "All of you, whatever your name is, please, watch over them," he whispered. Just in case.

Lying there sleepless on his shelf, he felt very unwatched over. He couldn't get comfortable—either his mind or his body.

It occurred to him to check where the call had come from.

The number lit up turquoise in the dark. Charlie smiled grimly, and stored it. What name should he give it? He didn't want to put just Rafi, as if Rafi were a friend of his.

Funny. He used to really want Rafi as a friend.

He stored it as Cocky Slimy Git. It was childish, but insulting Rafi made him feel a tiny bit better.

When he felt a lot better, he might give him a call. See how he'd like that.

No one, though, was watching over his parents—just skinny snivelly Sid. He was in a dilemma. Winner said he would punch him if he gave Aneba back his phone, and tell on him to Mr. Rafi so he would be fired and then Winner could get a partner with more than four brain cells and a vocabulary bigger than one word, because it was bad enough being hired by a sniking teenager without having to put up with a half-wit partner as well. Aneba, however, was still staring at him and muttering.

Which was scarier? A punch on the nose and being fired, or a curse from a giant African wise man?

"I'm going on deck," said Winner. "You keep watch." (Subs do have decks, for when they come to the surface, which is where they were now.)

"Yeah," said Sid.

Winner's heavy footsteps echoed down through the metal of the sub's hull. Aneba, still lying on the bunk (there was nowhere else to go), heard them. He pulled himself to his feet, smiled to himself, and squatted down. Then he started to mutter again, in a deep, low, chanting voice:

> *"Sid, oh Sid,*
> *You poor pathetic little blokey,*
> *Give me back my telephone.*
> *Give me back my phone, you bignose slugbrain,*
> *You moldy dollop of poop-trousered monkeysnot.*
> *Give me my phone and answer my questions,*
> *Give me my phone and answer my questions . . ."*

In Twi it sounded pretty bad.

Sid heard his name. He sat there getting more and more scared. After some minutes of this Aneba leaned forward and started to sketch a big circle on the floor, muttering and staring the whole time. He went on and on. "Sid," he repeated, often. "Sid."

He could keep it going for hours. He didn't have to. He looked up and in a quiet but deadly voice in English addressed the two-way mirror.

"You're going to give me my phone now, aren't you, Sid?"

"Yeah," said Sid in a tiny voice, green and sweaty-faced on the other side of the mirror.

And that was how Charlie's parents got his message, which was why his mum was crying, which was how Winner noticed what had happened, which was why he punched Sid, and took the phone off them again, and threw it overboard.

And when the marmalade cat saw that, he knew that he had to act swiftly.

If Charlie had expected the next day to be quiet, from the circus point of view, because of being at sea, he was very wrong. On his way to find Madame Barbue to go to breakfast, he spotted the little Italians swinging around in the rigging. He was right—they were acrobats. The father, wearing a rather worn-looking all-in-one leotard outfit, was hanging by his tremendously muscular little arms from a cross beam, swinging gently to and fro like a piece of laundry. Then suddenly he began to speed up his swinging, going higher and higher until he was flat out at the farthest extent of each swing, then higher than flat, then—If he's not careful he's going to go right over!, thought Charlie. And he did. Right over, holding for a moment at the top, standing on his hands as it were, and then right down the other side and then up again, and he was spinning around and around, his toes pointed, his legs straight, his hands shifting a little on each spin to allow the movement. And then— and it looked even more impressive—he started to slow down again, gradually, bit by bit, until he didn't go over the top, until his body made a flat line again, and until once again he was hanging like a piece of laundry. Charlie couldn't help himself. He burst into applause.

The Italian looked down, saw Charlie, and started to laugh.

"You think that's good?" he said, and when Charlie nodded enthusiastically the Italian grinned, did a little flick or flip of some kind so quick that Charlie hardly saw it, and then he was standing on the cross beam that a moment before he had been hanging from, grinning, foot cocked, arms crossed, and saying, "Ta-dah!"

"How did you do that!" howled Charlie. He was no slouch himself when it came to hanging and swinging, but that was something else. "How did you do it?"

"It's an old family secret," said the Italian. "My father taught me, his father taught him. I teach my boys. You want to learn, first you join my family, then after ten years I show you. If you're good."

"*Could* you teach me?" said Charlie. Suddenly it seemed important—vitally important.

The acrobat jumped down from the beam—a distance of about twenty feet. He landed lightly like a cat, and fixed Charlie with an intent look.

"If I choose," he said.

He stared at Charlie.

"Yes," he said. "Come each day. I see you can learn."

Then the intent look vanished, and he smiled and said: "Sigismondo Lucidi, of the Famiglia Lucidi. Call me Sigi." The rest of his family was in the rigging. He gestured to them vaguely.

"Are you practicing?" said Charlie.

"Every day," said Sigi. "To keep bendy and strong." He lifted his left leg, placed it vertically up the side of the mast, and moved his right foot close in to the bottom of the mast so he was doing a split, with his body sticking out sideways. "And the other side," he said, putting his left leg down again, turning and putting his right one up.

"You do," said Sigi.

Charlie tried. He could do a split on the floor, but not up the mast.

"You certainly are bendy," said Charlie.

"Have you seen Bendy Ben, the India Rubber Boy?" asked Sigi. Charlie hadn't.

"Ties himself in knots," said Sigi. "Gets stuck sometimes. Used to do an act with this big strong sailor, Beppe, and Beppe would tie him in a knot, then pretend he couldn't undo him and get his knife out, saying he just had to cut it, there was no other way."

"Yuck," said Charlie, absolutely fascinated.

"Got to go," said Sigi, and with a bend and a breath he jumped back into the forest of rigging. "Come tomorrow at six. Before eating. You learn."

After breakfast, Charlie found himself staring at his telephone mistrustfully. He'd turned it off after yesterday's message. Now he kind of wanted to turn it on again. And he kind of didn't.

He turned it on.

The little envelope icon flashed.

Charlie screwed up his face for a moment, and then he called up the message.

At first the voice was civil and gentle. "Charlie. Rafi Sadler here. Sorry I was a bit impolite yesterday. Hasty of me. But have no fear I mean what I say, you presumptuous little brat, I'm on my way and you'll be sorry when I arrive, sorry in ways you can't even begin to imagine . . ."

Charlie cut off the message. He didn't need to hear what he was to get ready for. He'd slept badly enough the night before.

He felt shaky again.

Next time he wouldn't listen at all. There was no point.

He was glad when Bikabhai told him to clean out the monkey-cage, which was grubby but not bad. He refilled the monkeys' water bottles and bowls of nuts, and gave them each a banana. The work eased his mind. Then it seemed he was off duty again. He decided to explore: There were zebras, horses, doves, and a Learned Pig to find, and, above all, there were lions. That should keep his mind off Rafi Sadler.

Charlie knew the story about the leopard cub, and the snake, and the jab from the needle and the slashing scratch from the cub's claw. He still had the scar: a thin, pale swooped line on his upper arm. Sometimes he told himself that he remembered the occasion: tottering over on his baby legs to the cuddly little cub, the sharp pain of the slash, and the sting of the leopard's blood in the wound. Sometimes he thought he remembered thinking about his own blood on the jab in the leopard's soft leg, wondering if it stung him too. He knew he remembered the sudden clarity and friendliness of calling out to the leopard, and the leopard calling back. Not that they had said anything in particular. Just that they had understood each other. Baby talk.

Charlie knew that this accidental gift of some drops of leopard blood was why he could talk to the cats. But he knew cats well enough to know that you can't take them for granted, ever. And he was downright nervous about the lions. Lions are different. Lions are wild—even if they are trained. Lions are big. Lions are the King of the Jungle, the King of Beasts. And then there was Maccomo, the unnaturally calm lion tamer. Sorry, trainer. He was quite unnerving, too. Charlie could not keep away from the lionchamber, but he approached it with respect and trepidation.

And that is one reason why he was so surprised to find one of the lions—a male, quite young though no longer a cub—just standing on the deck behind the lionchamber, not far from the door, all alone, gazing out to sea with his whiskers down and a strange expression on his face. Surely the lions would be locked up? Surely the trainer wasn't so powerfully calm that he could let his lions wander about the ship?

Without thinking, Charlie came up beside the lion and said, in Cat: "Hello."

The lion turned swiftly to him, his sad expression changed in an instant to amazement and—yes—fear. How could a lion be scared of me? thought Charlie. I'm just a kid. But the lion was scared of him.

"What?" said the lion.

"I said hello," said Charlie.

"I heard you," said the lion. "It's just—you're talking Cat."

"I know," said Charlie.

"Humans don't talk Cat," said the lion.

Charlie had never come across this before. All the cats he knew at home knew him and knew about his peculiar ability. He'd learned not to mention it to human strangers; but he hadn't thought that a cat stranger—a lion stranger—would be just as surprised.

"I'm sorry," said Charlie. "I didn't mean to surprise you. I've always known Cat."

But his friendly words had the opposite effect. The lion folded his front legs down, lowered his head, and looked as if he were about to cry. Charlie was appalled—"Oh, look, I'm sorry," he said. "Please, I didn't mean to upset you." He bent down and stroked the lion's sad head while murmuring kind words, and after a moment the lion raised his head and said: "Sorry. Haven't heard anyone else speak my language for a long time." But suddenly his voice changed. "Oh, no. Oh, no . . ." he muttered urgently, and began to scowl and growl. Charlie looked up.

They were being watched by an audience of amazed and silent

sailors and circusguys, their mouths open, their faces filled with disbelief.

The lion growled a bit more and pawed the ground a little—for show, Charlie thought, but the audience seemed frightened enough.

"I only came out for a second," hissed the lion. "Didn't mean to stay so long. Now they'll think I've escaped, and it'll all be horrible."

"What can we do?" said Charlie quietly.

"Don't know," said the lion. "I have to carry on being threatening or they'll think I'm weak. GRRRROOAAAWWWWLL!"

"Tell you what," said Charlie, seeing Major Tib forging his way through the crowd. "Let me calm you. I'll take you back in and make something up. Come on, just pretend. I know I couldn't calm you really, unless you wanted me to."

The lion, who had been beginning to enjoy his show of fearsomeness, shot Charlie a sideways look, then said: "All right—in a minute." And he gave a roar—a huge roar, which made everybody jump back and Maccomo, who had just come running up from the hold having heard of the drama, raise his long whip. Then the lion turned to Charlie, laid his head at his feet, and started to purr. A lion's purr is quite something, and for a moment Charlie so enjoyed the heavy, rhythmic reverberations through his feet that he didn't want to move. Then he remembered himself, and put his hand gently first on the lion's head, then on his thick chain collar.

"Come on," he said softly in Cat, too soft for anyone but the lion to hear. "Back inside. Come along. Come along."

The audience, Major Tib and Maccomo included, were dumbstruck. In silence they watched Charlie lead the big cat back to the chamber, in silence they saw the lion padding gently and obediently after him.

Major Maurice stared.

Maccomo rubbed his mouth slowly.

Madame Barbue fainted. (Pirouette grabbed a bucket of water that Hans had been taking to the Learned Pig and threw it over her.) The little Italians burst into cheers—but only once the lion was safely inside the lionchamber.

Maccomo burst through the crowd, into the chamber and right up to Charlie. The moment the lion was through the door of his cage, Maccomo slammed the door shut, locked it, and turned to the boy.

He stared at Charlie. "Explain," he said softly, his eyes dangerous in the dim light.

Charlie, intoxicated by the excitement of the moment, the sweet musty smell of the cabin, and the knowledge that all around him were lions he could talk to, could not think of a single intelligent thing to say.

"Um . . ." he said.

"Not good enough," whispered Maccomo. "Why was my lion obeying you?"

His lion?

"Oh, he didn't, sir, no, not at all," said Charlie quickly. "He, um, I was just there and I saw him, and, er, it didn't seem he should be out there, so he, er, didn't like the crowd I suppose, so, er, he, er . . . went back in." Charlie tried to smile up at Maccomo, but his smile was wobbly. He could feel it wobbling from inside. Maccomo was scary.

The lion trainer didn't answer. He took the two steps that brought him back to the gate of the lions' cage, and stood there, his whip still in his hand. He stared at the young lion, but the young lion did not stare back; instead he lowered his head and laid it on the floor, in a very submissive pose, and made a little mewing noise.

Charlie was worried about this lion. He was behaving so strangely—as if he were confused and upset. Every cat Charlie had ever known had been dignified; had known who and what it was, and had felt all right about it. Even the fattest, laziest, greediest housecat had an attitude that said: "Yes, I am fat, lazy, and greedy, and rather good at it too, don't you think?" But this lion was sad and confused. Charlie didn't like it. It made him feel sad and confused too.

Maccomo made a little noise in his throat, and turned back to Charlie.

"Where are you from?" he asked.

"London," said Charlie.

"No," said Maccomo. "London people are white."

Charlie had heard this said before, and knew that only an ignorant person could say it. Maybe Maccomo just didn't know about London.

"London people are all colors," said Charlie. "People have always come to London from everywhere, so now we are all colors."

"Where is your brown skin from?" said Maccomo.

"My brown skin is from London like the rest of me," said Charlie, trying not to get annoyed. "My father, if that is what you want to know, is African."

"His name and country," said Maccomo.

Perhaps it was Maccomo's rude way of asking, or perhaps it was a natural carefulness, but Charlie didn't want to say. And he didn't have to, because at that moment Major Tib burst in.

"What d'ya think, Maccomo?" he said. "He's got it, don't ya think? I never saw anything like it, and I knew Van Amburgh and

Cooper—ya want him? He's got the knack—you should take him on. You've got to."

Maccomo turned his great black eyes on Charlie, and once again Charlie saw the flash of light reflected in their depths. "I will take him on," he said. "Of course."

"Fine," said Major Tib. "Charlie, you're not the monkeyboy anymore—you're the lionboy."

CHAPTER 9

Charlie was absolutely terrified by the idea of being the lionboy—and at the same time he was delighted and excited and amazed. Lionboy—how cool was that! But working for Maccomo—how frightening was that! And lions . . . real, big, beautiful, strong, wild, golden lions. Charlie's breath came a little short when he thought about it. Remember your big cat blood, he said to himself. Your leopard blood. He imagined that he could feel it hurtling through the tunnels of his veins: strong, brave, agile leopard blood.

"Thank you, Major, sir," he said. And to Maccomo: "Thank you, sir. I'll do my very best for you, sir."

Maccomo's eyes narrowed. He suspected Charlie of something, and Charlie could tell. But he didn't know what Maccomo suspected him of—and nor, if truth be told, did Maccomo know. And actually, Charlie suspected Maccomo too, and he didn't know what of either. So between them was an air of unexplained fear and mistrust: not the best air to have around when starting a new job or taking on a new helper. But funnily enough, each of them resolved to deal with it the same way; in fact, almost exactly the same sentence went through both their heads: "I don't know what's going on with this character, so I'm just going to keep an eye on him and see what happens."

As a boss, Maccomo was extremely civil. For the first three days, Charlie's only work was to fetch water, carry straw, and sweep, and Maccomo always asked him politely to do these chores, and thanked him. His voice was silky and soft: "Thank you, Sharlie," he would say.

There were six lions: the young one, whom Charlie had already met; three lionesses, one very yellow, one silvery, and one bronze-colored, all three calm and silent. There was a younger girl, not much more than a cub, who was restless and bounced around, climbing on her mother's yellow back and nibbling her ears. The leader of the group, father of the youngsters, was an older male with a magnificent mane who sat in silence in his own cage at the back of the chamber, ignoring everyone and everything. The adults were all too quiet and still. As he moved around the cabin, cleaning and tidying under Maccomo's stern eyes, Charlie worried about these poor beasts, stuck in the dark, at sea, when they should be bounding around the plains of Africa, leaping and hunting, or basking under trees among grasses as golden as themselves.

Each morning Charlie went for his pre-breakfast acrobatics session with Sigi. Sigi taught him how to balance, and how to make himself larger or smaller with his breath and his muscles. "If anyone ever ties you up," he said, "make your muscles tense and big, and fill your chest and belly with air. Then when you relax and breathe out, the ropes will be looser around you."

After breakfast the lions were taken down to the ring to exercise and practice. Charlie went with them.

"Pull this handle," said Maccomo to Charlie, gesturing to a shiny, well-used brass pull attached to the chamber wall. As Charlie did so, the bars between the cages lifted, and in the back wall of the middle one a doorway appeared, which opened to a companionway leading down into the heart of the ship. Maccomo watched as the lions quietly and obediently ambled down the companionway. Maccomo pulled the handle again and the door closed behind the lions, and the cage walls fell back into place. Maccomo took a large brass key that was hanging from his belt, and locked the handle into place.

"Come," said Maccomo with his insincere smile. Charlie followed him out onto the deck, down the main stairs, through a hallway lined with mirrors and a doorway hung with crimson, white and gold striped curtains, and into—the most amazing chamber he had ever seen. It was round, as high as three stories; with seats in circles around the edges and galleries of seating rising up around the sides. The roof was like a tent, crimson and white and gold, swooping up to a high point in the middle, from which hung a glorious chandelier, rippling and tinkling with dangling glass prisms and crystals. The seats in the first galleries were of crimson velvet, with gold curved legs; others were long benches of wood. In one or two special boxes among the galleries, Charlie could see what looked like thrones, surrounded by crimson velvet curtains held back by golden cherubs. And in the middle was the circus ring, clean and open and promising, forty-two feet wide, sprinkled all over with clean fresh sawdust. There was a faint and particular circus smell: of animal, sawdust, greasepaint, and the faint leftover aroma of audience—beer and perfume and fish and chips.

Charlie gasped at the size and beauty of it. How could this be on board a ship? He almost laughed, it was so lovely.

Maccomo directed him to another brass handle, one that needed winding. Charlie began to wind it—it was quite heavy, though obviously well-used—and as he did so something extraordinary began to happen. With a shiver and a tinkle high up in the roof of the tent, the chandelier began to divide into sections and pull apart like curtains, and from the center of it began to descend a great silvery-gray mass, a shivering, rustling metal sheet, but metal like chains. It reminded Charlie of something, though he couldn't think what for a moment. Then as it fell it began to billow slowly, and Charlie realized that it was like chain mail—a massive sheet of chain mail with holes the size of ducks' eggs, and it was big enough to cover the entire ring. No, bigger. As the sheet descended it became apparent that it was circular, and the center of the circle was attached to the center of the chandelier. It was hanging like a great awning, or a mosquito net that hasn't been fixed around the edges yet.

Then Maccomo was instructing him again: He was to enter the ring (this alone gave Charlie a shudder of excitement), pick up the edge of the chain-mail curtain, find a hole in the rim, take it to the ring's edge, find the matching hole and tent peg there, and pin the curtain solidly into place; and then do the same again until all holes were pegged and the curtain was spread out, an inner tent of metal, between the audience and the ring.

"And do it carefully, Sharlie," said Maccomo, "for if the lions break out, the world will not be a pretty place for you or me."

The lions! Of course—this metal curtain was nothing but a giant cage to protect the audience, and it was made of chain mail so the audience could see through it.

"During the performance, this will be your job," said Maccomo. "Also to unpin afterward. Now, this one—" He unlocked yet another handle, which Charlie then pulled. As he did so, he heard a sleek rattle on the other side of the ring as a gate went up in the small low wall around the edge, and from it came the lions.

"*Yalla!*" cried Maccomo, and they loped around the ring. "*Shwoyya!*" he called, and they slowed down to a gentle pace. Then he called another word, which you or I would not be able to make out as anything more than a noise, but which Charlie recognized immediately. It was a Cat word, meaning jump. And sure enough the lions began to leap as they ran around the ring.

This set Charlie to thinking furiously. He knew that Maccomo didn't speak Cat, because if he had been able to, the lions would not have been so amazed by Charlie. But he knew this word . . . how? Did he know it was a Cat word? Or had he just picked it up from some other trainer, who had picked it up from another . . . ? Well, however it had come to pass, to Charlie it meant one extraordinary thing.

He was not the only human being to speak Cat. Somebody else, somewhere, at some time, shared his peculiar ability. Once he got used to the idea, he found it rather comforting. As long as it's not Maccomo, he thought, and his mind was brought back to the beauty of the lions. They leaped and frolicked, playing with one another and seeming to enjoy their moments of liberation and light and space, but their tread was too heavy, and every now and then they stopped and stood, staring dumbly as if they didn't know what to do.

Then Maccomo started to order them around again. He had a big nasty-looking whip made (Charlie knew because Maccomo had told him so) of rhinoceros hide. But he didn't use it, he just held it

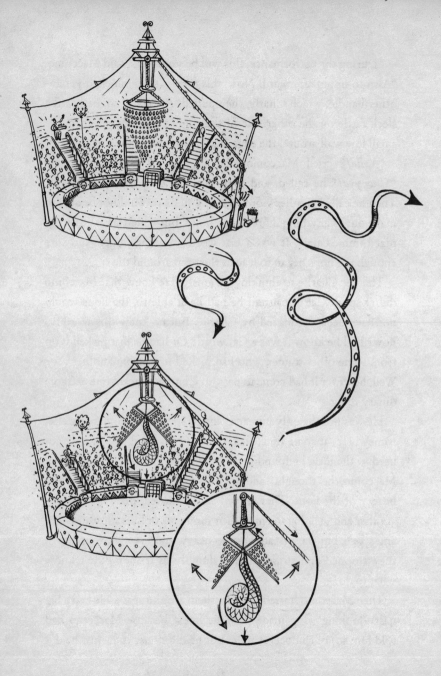

SCALE: |‾from here to here‾| = A LOT OF PEOPLE

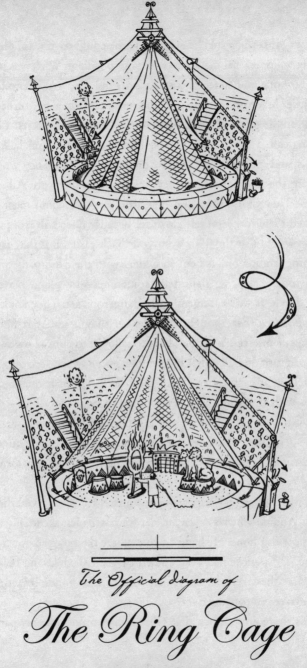

The Official diagram of

The Ring Cage

in a way that suggested he might. Charlie could see it wasn't fear of being whipped that made these lions so obedient. What was it?

The lions and Maccomo started a game that truly astonished Charlie. Maccomo strode into the middle of the ring, turned his back on the pride of lions, flung out his arms, and uttered a loud, strong call. The six creatures lined up behind him, hunched their backs, and sprang at him, one by one, from behind. They wrestled him to the floor, and then they let him fight them off. All six of them. They didn't hurt him one little bit—Maccomo must have trained them to keep their claws in, because one slash from those claws would tear the flesh from your back easily. But they landed on him, landing on his bent shoulders with their footpads spread, sometimes balancing delicately, sometimes—by plan—knocking him down. It was a tremendously dangerous act. They could kill him *just like that,* thought Charlie. Or they could start fighting among themselves. You don't have to talk Cat to notice how swiftly cats can turn on each other in a temper, yowling and scrowling and scratching at each other's faces. Charlie had seen it hundreds of times with the Ruins Cats. Pretending to fight with lions—wow. Was it brave? Or stupid? Charlie didn't think Maccomo was stupid . . . No, there was a reason why the lions were so unnatural, so obedient and calm, and Charlie was going to find out what it was.

Rafi was still angry—especially at himself for letting Charlie get away. And now he was even angrier for having left those silly messages on his phone. He hadn't a clue where the boy had gone. Not a clue. Troy's nose had been addled by the fishstink, and the trail ended at the riverside. So which way had he gone? Inland? Or downriver? Across the river? On a boat?

Was there any chance that Charlie had found out his parents

were heading downriver? Rafi couldn't think of a way. No, Charlie must have jumped a waterbus or hitched a ride, and he could be anywhere in the city, or anywhere on the waterways.

This made Rafi very angry indeed. Having Charlie would have made it much easier to deal with those ridiculous scientists: He'd just have to say "I'm going to pinch your little baby now," and they'd have done what they were told soon enough. Plus he'd promised the Chief Executive . . . So now he'd have to spend money on hiring people to go out and find him—people who would keep their mouths shut, which always costs more. Rafi hated spending money on anything except himself. He really didn't want to spend any on this. It was upsetting his budget. And his pride.

But Rafi was a realist, so he called the best research villain he knew: a young guy he'd met when he was in reform school for stealing phones. He told him: There's a brown boy, in the city or on the waterways. Gave him the name, the description, the details. "He's young and wimpy," said Rafi. "He'll probably just go back home. I want him. Soon."

Then he amused himself by thinking of all the ways in which he would pay Charlie back for the trouble he was making.

At first Maccomo would not leave Charlie alone with the lions. But when he saw that Charlie's knack of calmness around them continued, and that the lions were calm with him too and seemed, if anything, to like him, Maccomo relaxed a little. He wouldn't let Charlie open their cages or feed them, but he did allow him to pour water into their drinking bowls. It was while he was doing this early one morning that Charlie was able to catch the eye of the young lion whom he had led back from the deck. The lion gave a big, distinct, yellow wink, and jerked his head back in a significant fashion.

Charlie made a "What do you mean?" face, and checked over his shoulder to make sure Maccomo wasn't looking. (He wasn't; he was rolling one of his thin black cigarettes.) He made another face that meant: "Come over here and whisper in my ear," and bent his head down to the bars of the cage. The lion padded softly over to him and whispered in his ear with a swoosh of warm breath: "We need to talk to you. Got some news. Important."

Charlie looked up in astonishment.

"What news?" he squeaked in Cat—too loudly, for Maccomo turned, holding the black cigarette now between his even white teeth, and gave him a peculiar look.

Charlie put his finger in his mouth. "Ouch," he said unconvincingly. "Hurt my finger. Sorry to disturb you."

Maccomo stared a little longer, then struck a match on the heel of his boot and lit the cigarette, which began to emit an evil smell. Its tip glowed as he stared at Charlie a little longer, and then he said: "I hope it isn't severe."

Charlie smiled weakly. And then—oh, miracle—Maccomo strolled out of the lionchamber, out onto the deck.

Charlie whirled around to the lions' cage.

"What is it?" he cried excitedly. "What's the news?" Lions, after all, are cats. Cats had been putting the word out to see where his parents had been taken. He should have asked the lions right away.

The young lion glared at him.

"Shh," he said shortly, and turned to face the cage at the back of the chamber, where the biggest, oldest lion lived, and addressed him in the most respectful way—by name. (I would write the name for you, but alas it's not possible to write lion names in the English alphabet.) "Sir," he called quietly—and Charlie noticed that all the lions were facing the oldest lion's cage now—"Sir, may I present the lion-speaking boy."

The oldest lion raised his shaggy head. Charlie had never before had a chance to look into his eyes, and he was shocked by what he saw there. This lion was tired, and sick-looking, and old; his great yellow eyes were cloudy and his movements heavy. Though his mane was large and thick, still it lay flat without movement, and his whiskers hung limp. He looked like a creature without hope. Yet Charlie had seen him leaping about in the ring, healthy-seeming and energetic.

"Hello, sir," said Charlie, recognizing that he should be particularly polite here. He gave a little bow. The lion, with a quiet half-smile, inclined his head.

"Hello, Boy who speaks Lion," he said in a low and courteous voice. He blinked slowly. And again. Charlie thought he might be going back to sleep. It wasn't clear whose turn it was to speak. Charlie sort of expected the lion to say something, but he didn't—perhaps he was waiting for Charlie to speak. The young lion, in the meantime, was looking from one to the other urgently, almost quivering with his desire for them to get on with it. So Charlie spoke.

"The cats at home," he said, "my friends, told me that I should ask a cat, if in doubt . . . My parents, you see, have been stolen away, though I don't know exactly why, or where they are being taken, but the river cats said they were on a ship going out to sea, to France, and I wonder—have you heard anything?"

The oldest lion half-smiled again, in such a sad way that Charlie felt a tweak in his heart.

"I hear nothing, boy," said the lion. "I live in the dark, I go nowhere, I see no one. My wives live in the dark, they go nowhere, they see no one. We eat dead meat; we stay still. From time to time we are taken out by that human and made to do tricks, like a monkey begging for a nut. We are made to pretend to fight. We pretend to fight. We are made to pretend to beg. We pretend to beg. We don't hear anything. Who would tell us anything? We used to be lions, boy. We used to know things. We know nothing now." He gave a soft shivering snort at the end of this speech, and Charlie felt its sadness cold and deep within him. That so beautiful, powerful, and magnificent a creature could say such despondent things—it seemed so wrong. A lion should not be like this.

The young lion hung his head, but there was an angry energy coming off him that he seemed to be trying to squash. The lionesses licked their paws quietly, perhaps pretending not to hear, perhaps too sad to do anything else. The young girl cub had her mouth folded tight, as if she were trying hard not to say anything.

"I'm sorry," said Charlie. "I didn't mean to upset you."

"Oh, we're not upset," said the oldest lion. "That's the problem. We should be—we should be very upset indeed. We should be raging and roaring and plotting and scheming and *escaping*. But we're not. We're just lying about . . ." And at this he rolled over, hiding his face, and the other lions all looked away in shame and embarrassment. Charlie too felt embarrassed.

The sound of Maccomo humming one of his tuneless tunes flickered from the doorway. The lions looked up, and away. The oldest lion turned his back, and went to lie by the wall.

The young lion leaned forward and touched his nose to Charlie's hand. "Come back later," he whispered, just as Maccomo's shadow fell across the doorway. The young lion looked as if he had made up his mind about something. "Come back later and I'll tell you everything."

CHAPTER 10

For the rest of that morning Maccomo kept Charlie busy explaining to him the workings of the equipment in the ring, the ring cage (as the chain-mail tent was called), the lionpassage from the cages to the ring, and the various other bits and pieces involved in the act.

"It is an act *en férocité*," he explained, smoking another of his smelly little cigarettes and looking at Charlie out of the corners of his eyes as he demonstrated the workings of the lionpassage gate. "The lions appear to be ferocious with me, and I with them. But in fact we love each other."

Love? thought Charlie. Hmmm. Not sure about that.

Then it was time to feed them. The meat was kept in the enormous galley fridge, as big as a room, along with the food for the sailors and circus people, and Charlie had to fetch it every couple of days. The lions didn't eat every day. In addition, they had their water, which had to be kept fresh and clean, and their medicine, which they took every day in their water. This Maccomo saw to himself. After they had their medicine, Maccomo went and lay on the floor in the lionchamber, outside the cages, wrapped in his crimson cloth against the cold, and smoked and sang in a peculiar language that Charlie had never heard before.

Every now and then during the morning Charlie and the young lion looked meaningfully at each other, but with Maccomo having his rest, there was no chance to talk. It would have to be later. Charlie was desperately impatient.

The singing put Charlie in mind of the strange, exciting music he had heard the first time he saw the circus ship. As Maccomo was settled in the lionchamber, giving Charlie no opportunity to be alone with the young lion, Charlie decided to go and find Pirouette or Madame Barbue and ask them about the music to take his mind off it. But Madame Barbue was shaving her legs, and told him, from behind the bathroom door, that Pirouette was rehearsing in the big top and mustn't be disturbed. So Charlie wandered back to the ropelocker in search of Julius, but Julius's father had fallen off a stepladder practicing one of the clowns' knockabout scenes with the monkeys, and Julius had to hold ice on his father's leg, otherwise it would never be better by the time they got to Paris.

"So when are we getting there?" asked Charlie, surprised, because as far as he could tell they were miles from land and hadn't even seen France yet. Which was, come to think of it, odd, after three days at sea.

"Oh, that's because we strike a course down the middle of the channel," said Julius. "If we go too close to shore, people yell for us to come in and do the show, and then the monkeys get overexcited and make so much noise whooping and chattering that all the other animals get worked up, so the skipper keeps out to sea. France is just over there to port. We'll be coming in this afternoon, in time to restock in Le Havre and then head up the Seine with the tide tomorrow. We'll make Rouen by tomorrow night, probably. You should talk to the sailorguys, then you'd know what's going on."

As Julius was stuck with his dad's ice pack, he was not available to show Charlie where the music had come from. "Ask Hans," he said. "He'll take you down there."

Charlie found Hans covered in mud as usual, sitting in the Learned Pig's pigsty. He was eating cake and playing with a kitten and looking sad.

"What's the matter?" asked Charlie.

"The Learned Pig is not learned enough," said Hans. "There is a Learned Little Horse in France who is doing algebra, but the Learned Pig only does addition and subtraction and multiplication and division."

"But how can a pig possibly do that?" Charlie burst out. "Or a horse, I mean . . . it's hard enough for human kids. How can animals do it?"

Hans looked up, and for once he seemed happy. He was delighted that Charlie didn't know. "Oh," he said mysteriously. "I can't possibly tell you. Couldn't possibly. You'll have to wait and see—see the show, I mean, and then you'll see that he just is very learned."

Charlie looked at the big, solid, tubular pig that lay snoozing at Hans's feet, his white eyelashes resting on his hairy pink cheek. He looked about as clever as a piece of lard: i.e., about as dumb as a dumb animal can get.

But then, most people don't know that cats talk.

Charlie wondered about the pig. Could he talk? He really didn't look as if he would have anything very interesting to say. Hans leaned forward and scratched him between the ears and he snuffled in his sleep, in a rather endearing way.

Charlie sighed.

"Tell me about the music, Hans," he said. "When I was brought on board there was the most wonderful music going on. Sort of wheezing and droning and pumping and singing, all at once. Like an accordion, only not."

"Ah," said Hans. "That's the Calliope."

"Ca-what-appy?" said Charlie.

"Calliope," said Hans.

"Ah," said Charlie, none the wiser.

"She's a sort of organ," said Hans. "She's fantastic. Do you want to see her? Let's go and look." And in a second, both boys were off down the deck, Hans still clutching the kitten and Charlie hurtling behind, not wanting to lose him.

"Steady on, you two," cried a sailor as they skidded past him, not quite knocking over the elegant coils of rope that he had been laying out.

"*Sorreee!*" they shouted, and dipped down a hatch on the other side of the stern.

This companionway was not like the others Charlie had seen so far. It was not wide and paneled and elegant, for members of the public to come down on their way to the big top. It was not dark and cramped like the low passages leading to the storage areas in the hold, nor slightly smelly of warmth and hay like the ones leading to the animals' quarters. It was quite narrow all right, but it smelled of coal and engine oil, and it was getting noisier and hotter with every step.

"We're right above the engines," said Hans, shouting to make himself heard above the rushing hiss and roar of engine noise, clanging beams and thumping steam.

"Why?" yelled Charlie. "How can they hear the music with all this racket?"

"The music is part of the racket!" shouted Hans, and stopping quickly in the passageway, he banged on a small door, as loudly as so small a boy could. There was no reply, and Hans flung open the door and hauled Charlie inside, slamming the door closed again behind him.

Inside was just as hot but only about half as noisy—which was still, Charlie thought, noisy enough. The room was long but narrow, and the whole length of the long wall was taken up with three great keyboards—like a piano, but longer, and deeper, and colored green and pink instead of the normal black and white. Below were three great pedals of polished iron; above, and in little sections to the side, were a number of curious pegs and handles, each with a label written in old-fashioned writing on a piece of what looked like ivory. Rising above the whole setup were rows of what looked like metal tubes or pipes; the bases visible and the rest disappearing up through the ceiling and goodness knows where.

"What on earth is it?" cried Charlie.

"She's a kind of organ," said Hans. "Those tubes"—he pointed upward—"are her pipes—like whistles—and the steam from the steam engine plays her. Like when a kettle whistles. Then all these handles and pedals make different kinds of noise come out, and the keyboard is for playing the tune."

"Can I try it?" cried Charlie, who quite enjoyed playing the piano, and had once seen a church organ when a cousin got married.

"No way," said Hans. "Major Tib would kill you. It's the loudest thing you ever heard. You'll see when we get to Paris. We always play it so that people can hear that we've arrived—like an ice cream truck. The sound goes for miles. But you know what? It's a horrible noise."

"I heard it on the river," said Charlie. "I remember it." He didn't think it was a horrible noise. He thought it was incredibly exciting. He longed to hear it again.

When Maccomo went to bathe after lunch, Charlie was finally able to speak to the young lion. He pulled up a bale of hay close to the side of the young lion's cage, and they spoke quietly and intently.

"So," said Charlie, "tell me everything."

"There's two things," said the young lion, his yellow eyes aglow. "First, what you want to hear. At Greenwich, before we set sail, one of the dockyard cats came sniffing around and ended up in here. He was looking for you. I didn't realize because I hadn't met you then—but he was talking about the Cat-speaking boy and the missing parents whom all cats love, and saying they were being taken to Paris and the boy must be told. So that's great for you because we *are* going to Paris. So you're on track. Are you pleased?"

Charlie had such a smile on his face. The lion could see that his news had made Charlie so happy that he needed a moment to let it sink in.

"They're on board the *SharkHawk*," he continued. "The *SharkHawk* cat was telling everybody, apparently—he was desperate for the news to get through. His girlfriend's cousin is a Ruins Cat, and was very firm that these humans shouldn't be lost."

Charlie smiled. Good for the Ruins Cats.

"So they're probably just ahead of us," he said. "Do you think?"

"Yes," said the lion. "They can't be far ahead."

"So if I keep my eyes open," said Charlie, "I might see the ship! The *SharkHawk!* Then in Paris will we—"

But the young lion interrupted. "You won't see her," he said.

"Why not?" said Charlie.

"The *SharkHawk* is a submarine."

A submarine! Charlie felt his stomach wobble for a moment. Knowing that his mum and dad were going to the same place as he was great. Knowing they were going by a submarine, under water, with the entire cold, dark sea echoing around them and tons of water on top of them, and perhaps strange pale sea creatures staring in through the submarine's portholes at them with baleful, scary eyes . . . that was . . . not great. But they were nearby: That was good. And they were going to Paris and so was Charlie, and that was the best news in days.

The young lion asked, "Why were they taken, Charlie? Do you know who has them?" He had a warm sympathy in his eyes, and in a rush of understanding Charlie knew why: Because the lions too had been stolen away from their liberty, from their families, from their own lives.

"I believe they were taken because they know something," said Charlie simply. "They are scientists. I think they must have made a discovery, and somebody else wants it, or . . . I don't know. But it must be something like that."

"And what is the discovery?"

"I don't know," said Charlie. "They were working on lots of things."

"Do you miss them a lot?" said the young lion. "I have heard that humans have strong emotions . . ."

Charlie blinked. "Very strong," he said shortly, and lifted his chin.

The young lion watched him thoughtfully. Then he said: "And the other thing . . ." Perhaps he had noticed Charlie's embarrassment.

Charlie turned back to him, meeting his eyes between the thick iron bars of the cage. "Yes, the other thing," he said.

"You have to help us," said the young lion simply. "I have to trust you. If you betray us, then—I don't know. But we can't go on like this. You saw how"—here he said the name of the oldest lion, which I can't write. I shall just say "the oldest lion" when any lion says the name in Cat. Of course they were talking in Cat through-out—"the oldest lion is. How tired and sad. He always used to be planning and dreaming about escape. But now—I don't know. It's as if he's given up. The mothers mostly just follow him—they're so used to obeying him, and not making him angry, that they've for-gotten how to think for themselves. Elsina—the girl—she's brave but she's young. So I have to do something. And you have to help."

"Okay," said Charlie. He didn't even ask what help was needed, or what the lion wanted him to do. He just said okay. This could have been very foolish of him. There are a great many stories about what happens when people promise to do something before check-ing what it is they're promising, and it always turns out to be "Kill your friend" or "Give me your kingdom," and then it's too late to turn back. But Charlie trusted the lion. He remembered the look in the lion's eyes when he first spoke Cat to him. He trusted the lion, and he liked him. If he could, he would help him.

"We need a plan to escape," said the young lion. "We need a hu-man who can help us get off the ship. We need to trick Maccomo and Major Thibaudet. We need help to hide us on our journey. We're going back to Africa."

"Africa!" said Charlie. "Wow."

"Are you African?" asked the lion.

"Yes—my dad is. From West Africa, by the sea."

"We are West African too!" said the lion. "From Morocco,

where the desert and the mountains come to the sea. That's where we are going."

"Dad's from farther south," said Charlie. "From Ghana."

"We are brothers," said the lion. "African brothers. You speak our language. You don't have to come all the way home with us. We'll see where your people are being taken, we'll find a route that works for both of us. We'll help you too."

Charlie liked the sound of that. He liked it very much. It had crossed his mind, the question of how a single boy could rescue grown-ups from other grown-ups—from whoever it was Rafi had hired, or whoever had hired Rafi. He hadn't wanted to think about it, but he wasn't stupid. If the kidnappers had been easy to beat, his parents would have beaten them and escaped already, wouldn't they? (For a moment his heart jumped—perhaps they have! Perhaps they were on their way to rescue him, right now!) But a single boy *with a group of lions* could surely scare off kidnappers, however tough they were. A single boy with a group of lions could give Rafi Sadler the shock of his life . . .

In exchange for helping the lions to escape, Charlie would get them to help his parents escape. Simple and brilliant.

Charlie had an idea.

"Would you do something for me now?" he said to the young lion.

The lion inclined his head to suggest yes, of course.

Charlie smiled to himself as he fished his phone out of his pocket.

He looked up Cocky Slimy Git in the address book and dialed the number.

"When I tell you, roar!" he said to the young lion. "It's the guy who stole my parents!"

The young lion's eyes gleamed.

Charlie had assumed he would get Rafi's voice mail. He didn't—he got Rafi.

For a moment he was shocked into silence. Rafi on the street, at the fountain, with his mum . . . with *Charlie's* mum, maybe. Then as Rafi said "Yeah? Charlieboy?" he launched into action.

"Yeah, you know who I am," he shouted. "You don't know *where* I am, though, do you? You don't know what I'm doing. You know *nothing* and I couldn't be *less* scared of you! If anything I'll be coming to get *you* soon, Mr. Swanky I'm-so-cool jerk! So *you'd* better *watch out*, and you had better *leave me alone!*" He made a frantic face at the young lion, and held the phone out to him.

The young lion, grinning, uttered a low, threatening, echoing, blood-curdling roar. Charlie knew it was a roar of laughing and being naughty; he knew too that Rafi would hear it as any normal human would—absolutely terrifying.

He swiftly pressed the disconnect button and collapsed in laughter. Yes!

Five sailors banged on the door of the lionchamber.

"What's going on?" they shouted. "Are you okay in there?"

Charlie opened the door, still giggling.

"It's fine," he said. "Fine. No trouble. Sorry. Lion's a bit boisterous, that's all. Sorry."

They went away.

Charlie felt good.

Rafi did not.

"You sniking, cheeky little graspole," he said. "What the—how the—what was that!"

He was scared by it. It curdled his stomach. He didn't understand.

"You little . . ." he yelled, and dialed his phone.

Charlie's phone rang.

He stared at it, sitting in his hand. COCKY SLIMY GIT lit up the face.

The young lion stared at it.

Charlie said, "Roar again," and pressed the button.

The young lion really let it rip.

The sailors came back.

The phone didn't ring again after that.

Charlie felt good.

Rafi dropped the phone.

"I don't understand," he whispered. He was shaking now. Fear and anger make a dangerous combination.

"So how about the others?" Charlie said, growing serious again. "Do they agree?"

The young lion flicked his whiskers. "Elsina will agree. She is ready and impatient for the day. The mothers will do what the oldest lion does. And the oldest lion . . . he will agree, if his spirit is not too low."

"So how can we raise his spirit?" asked Charlie, getting straight to the point.

The young lion gave a kind of lionish smile, lifting his whiskers and showing his delicate, ferocious teeth.

"The spirit of an old lion is not for bossing," he said. "But there are ways. And there is something that must be done first of all, and we must start to do it now." Then he drew Charlie closer still to the bars, and whispered in his ear, and Charlie nodded, taking it all in, and together they worked out how Charlie would start the process of raising the oldest lion's spirit and saving the lions from captivity. After that, Charlie went back to his ropeshelf and thought about his parents, and Rafi, and planned ways of righting what was wrong.

Ahead of them, approaching Le Havre, the marmalade cat on board the *SharkHawk* had managed to swipe a pen from Winner's jacket pocket, and was attempting to push it under the door of the cabin in which Aneba and Magdalen were incarcerated. The paper had been easy—he had ripped it from Winner's ship's logbook, with one vicious swipe of his claws, and carried it in his teeth. The pen was a little harder. It was difficult to get a grip on, and kept rolling away when he dropped it. Plus now it didn't want to fit under the door.

The cat thought. The cat had an idea. The cat took the pen in his mouth, and crunched down on it with his sharp, strong little teeth. The plastic casing split and shattered, and the little central cartridge full of ink fell away. Quickly, with his paw, like a kitten batting a ball of wool, the cat batted the ink cartridge under the door. Then he started up a horrible yowling and meowing, aimed through the same crack.

It was Magdalen, who liked the cat, who woke, and stretched, and said: "Oh shut up, puss." And when he didn't, it was Magdalen who said: "I can't let you in, sweets, the door is locked, as you may have noticed." It was Magdalen who came to the door, to speak kindly to the distraught-seeming cat, and it was Magdalen who stepped on the ink cartridge, noticed the piece of paper, picked them both up, and set to wondering.

The next morning, when Sid brought in the prisoners' breakfast, and the cat swerved in swiftly between his legs, it was Magdalen whom the cat started bothering, pushing the pen toward her, rolling on the paper in a meaningful fashion, and saying "Meow! Meow! Meow!" over and over again, and, it must be said, rather irritatingly. At least, that's what Magdalen heard. Actually, the cat was saying: "*Write. The. Letter. Write. The. Letter.* Oh for goodness' sake, woman, get a move on. How hard is it to work out? Pen. Paper. *Write the letter!*"

And Magdalen murmured: "This cat's trying to tell me something." ("Yes dear, bravo," sighed the cat.) Which made her think of Charlie, not that she ever *wasn't* thinking about him, but it made her think about cats telling *him* things, and him telling cats things, and she looked at the marmalade cat's face, staring at her so intently, as if willing her to understand . . .

And she understood. Sitting with her back to the two-way mirror, she wrote:

> *Dear Charles,*
>
> (How proud she had been of his telephone message! How cleverly he had picked up the clues she had left in her first letter, how cleverly he had left his own clues!)
>
> *I'm sorry to hear you are out sailing all the time instead of being in class: You know too much sea air is bad for you. Daddy and I are enjoying our boat trip, though it's still a bit of a mystery tour. The food is good and there's a lovely marmalade cat who is very friendly. I hope this gets through to you. Will let you know where we'll be staying when we get there;*

please also tell me which field trips Brother Jerome is
planning for you. Love you so much and miss you.
Be a good little boy! I know you will.

Your ever-loving mummy

Aneba was looking over her shoulder.

"That's good," he said. "But how are you going to get it to him?"

The marmalade cat leaped onto her lap and stretched out his furry orange neck with its little purple flea collar. Magdalen folded the scrap of paper small, and tucked it firmly into the buckle, held in place by the pin.

"Looks secure, I think," she said.

Aneba was looking at her.

"Sweetheart," he said, a note of doubt in his voice. But at that moment the door opened as Winner came to take their breakfast away, and the cat, pausing only to give them a tiny but definite wink, zapped through it.

"What?" said Aneba. "What? Really?"

"He brought me the paper and pen," whispered Magdalen. "If he can be the stationery shop, why shouldn't he be the postman too?"

Aneba smiled. Magdalen smiled. He gave her a big kiss. For the first time in days, they felt almost a little bit happy.

"Don't know what you're looking so sniking chirpy about," said Winner. "You're soon going to be reaching your destination. Not much for you to laugh about, I wouldn't of thought. All right for me an' 'im, we'll just be handing you over and getting our fee, and then I have a plan for a week or two in the sun with Mrs. Winner. But you, now, you'll be meeting the gentlemen from Personnel, and they're not very nice gentlemen, frankly, and then if I'm not mistaken you'll be hauled up to meet the Chief Executive . . . Oh, dear," he said exaggeratedly. "There was me about to let slip about the Chief Exec . . . Ooops! There I go again. When he'll be so keen to explain your new duties to you 'imself. He's a very particular man, from what I hear. A very particular man. I'm particularly glad that I don't work for him. Sooner you than me any day."

Winner went off with a nasty look on his face.

"Personnel?" said Magdalen.

"Duties?" said Aneba.

"I don't like the sound of that," said Magdalen.

Charlie was kicking himself. How stupid to have called Rafi! How self-indulgent! And twice! Now that Rafi knew Charlie had received his messages, he might send more. Now that Rafi knew that Charlie was in a place with lions—well, that narrowed the field. And now Rafi would be even more annoyed with him. Stupid!

It had been fun, though.

CHAPTER 11

It was mid-afternoon when the great crimson ship came through the electricity farm—ranks of ocean windmills, like an army of giant propellers on sticks—into the harbor at Le Havre. Charlie found that he was very glad to see land again, although he had hardly noticed missing it. As soon as they were docked he ran down the gangplank onto the big concrete quay, desperate to find a cat with some news. As he landed, his legs jarred horribly—how very solid the ground seemed after his days at sea!

"Hey there, Lionboy!" called a voice from the deck behind him. It was Major Tib. "Y'all better get back on board right now. We don't do shore leave without leave. Get back in here and help Maccomo. There's plenty of work to be done."

Turning back, disappointed, to the ship, Charlie saw a most peculiar sight. A great crane had been waiting for them on the quay when they cruised in, looming red and white against the sky. It had now sort of leaned in toward the ship, where the entire crew seemed to be scurrying around on deck at the foot of one of the masts. A huge chain hung from the crane, and was, Charlie realized, being attached near the base of the mast. Another chain hung in midair—no, it was moving. Halfway up the mast another knot of sailors were busying themselves with something.

Suddenly a cry went up, the sailors all moved away at once, and the mast was uprooted like a great tree in a high wind, or a giant weed in the hand of a giant gardener. Where it had stood tall and proud, it now lay flat in the air, hanging from the chains, flying slowly and ponderously toward the quay.

"What's happening?" cried Charlie to one of the harborguys standing near him.

"Stand back!" shouted the man as the mast lurched through the air in their direction. "Way back!"

Charlie gawked. Then as soon as the mast was laid down, and unlikely to knock anyone's head off, he scampered back up the gangplank onto the deck.

"What's going on?" he said to one of the sailors.

"Unstepping the masts," replied the sailor briefly—he was on his way to the base of the second mast. "Didn't think they'd fit under the bridges of the Seine, did you? We leave 'em here in storage. Pick up the other set at Port St. Louis. Get over, now, I'm busy."

Charlie gazed in amazement as the second and then the third mast were lifted from their roots, flown through the air, and put down on the quay. That is, until Maccomo called him, wanting him to go to the bursar and remind him that they had been promised extra fresh meat for the lions but hadn't received the money yet, and telling him to make sure the quartermaster had arranged for the meat to arrive before dawn the next morning, because it was an early start and a long run down to Rouen, and when he'd done that he was to run ashore and get some of Maccomo's cigarette papers because he was running out.

Charlie was happy as could be to go ashore. The quay was frantic with activity: fresh bread and vegetables coming aboard, sailors refilling the water tanks in the hold through massive hose pipes like gigantic pythons, which flexed and leaped as the water poured through. He found a Tabac—a small shop selling all kinds of smoking things—a street away from the harbor, and found that his French was quite good enough to buy Maccomo's horrid little papers. All the while he had his eye open for a cat—but nothing. He took a roundabout route back to the quay, but without luck. Where were they all? Surely a harbor should be full of cats? But he could delay no longer—Maccomo would yell at him if he were too late, and Charlie wanted to keep him sweet.

Behind a crate full of sardines, although Charlie didn't know it, Claudine, a very fat little pink-nosed French cat, lay fast asleep with a scrap of paper under her paw. Claudine had accepted half of the marmalade cat's dinner (on top of her own dinner) in exchange for agreeing to deliver the note to the brown English boy on the crimson ship, but she had eaten so much that she had dozed off. The marmalade cat, having seen his human friends transfered in the dead of night onto a sleek little motorboat, was already heading back to England, happy to know that the letter was on its way.

Claudine was very lazy. Having been up late with the marmalade cat, she slept all day.

That evening, as the mad activity of restocking a boat with so many people and animals on board began to wind down, Charlie joined

Maccomo in the dining room and drank hot chocolate with him, being friendly and listening to tales of the lion trainers of old. He made a point of thanking Major Thibaudet for taking him on board and giving him the job of lionboy. He chatted with the twins, with Hans and Julius and some of the Italians, who after supper sang and played the mandolin, and everyone joined in. Later he curled up in the ropelocker. Through it all he thought and thought about what would be the best way to handle the job with which the lion had charged him.

All the while, Claudine slept on.

Just before dawn, the engines started to shudder and rumble, and the tide turned that would carry the *Circe* up the great, broad, gleaming Seine to Paris. Charlie smelled the bacon frying in the galley, and heard the gulls cawing in the pale first light. With cries and calls and a great churning of water, *Circe* pulled out into the river.

Behind them, a fat little cat rushed to the waterside. Seeing the great ship moving inexorably upriver, a look of great guilt and sadness appeared on her face and she started to cry. Beside her, a scrawny, moldy-looking black dockyard cat, with bald patches on its bottom and sharp blue eyes, told her rudely to stop her yowling.

"Don't you talk to me!" she said prissily. "The likes of you shouldn't talk to the likes of me."

"Well, the likes of you shouldn't be screeching the whole bliddy place down," said the rude cat. "Why don't you just go back to your palace, Madame de bliddy Precious?" Whereupon she stopped yowling, started sniveling instead, and told him at great length and with a lot of repetition that she had every right to be there—which was more than could be said for some who by rights wouldn't exist at all—and she'd promised to get a message to the boy with the missing parents, and he was sailing away on that boat right there, and if the rude cat had done such a thing he too would be yowling and screeching the place down, and she was so upset about it that she didn't know what to do.

Then the moldy-looking cat screeched.

"It'll be *them!*" he exclaimed. "It'll be *that* boy. We've to get that epistle to him at once! You dingwit! How bliddy stupid can yer get! Gimme that!"

Once he had taken the letter from her he was no longer interested in her. He looked after the ship, estimated her speed, looked around at the early-morning traffic, and raced straight to the bus station. With the letter in his teeth, speared on one of his canines, he leaped onto the roof rack of the first electrobus heading south, where he sat and complained without ceasing to the other cats up there about how incompetent the French were. His French was execrable—he was a north of England cat, on his travels—but at least he made the effort to be rude to them in their own language.

Charlie, with no knowledge of any of this, had decided what he had to do.

When Maccomo fed the lions that morning, Charlie watched closely, without being observed, to see what he did with the medicine. Five drops in the oldest lion's water, three for each of the mothers, one for Elsina, and five for the young lion. He watched closely where Maccomo put the medicine (in a small locker in the lionchamber), and he watched closely where Maccomo put the key to that small locker. Then when, after lunch, Maccomo lay down with his crimson cloak around him to smoke his cigarette and doze, Charlie silently tiptoed into the chamber. Once he was certain that Maccomo was asleep, quietly and with great fear in his heart Charlie took Maccomo's own water flask from where it stood on the floor beside him, emptied it out, and refilled it from the oldest lion's water bottle—the bottle with the most medicine added. He replaced the bottle by the lion trainer's side, then he tipped out the rest of the medicined water in the lions' bottles. The low gurgling sound as the water poured out made Charlie start, but Maccomo didn't stir.

Most of it went on the floor—it couldn't be helped. He just hoped Maccomo wouldn't notice—and he might well not, because it was Charlie who cleaned the cages. Swiftly and silently, he refilled the lions' drinking bottles with fresh clean water. All the while the young lion and Elsina watched him, and they purred quietly, and Elsina growled gentle phrases of encouragement.

Then they all just had to wait and see what happened. Charlie lay back on his bale of hay and despite everything, began to doze a little himself.

It wasn't long before Maccomo woke up, thirsty, reached for his flask, and took a long swig. So far so good! Disturbed by the noise, the oldest lion woke up, also thirsty, and took a long swig of his own water. Neither of them seemed to notice any difference.

Julius had said they expected to reach Paris in six days' time. That meant there were six more opportunities to make and keep Maccomo dopey, and six more days to clear the mind of the oldest lion. If Charlie could pull off this trick again and again, and if the young lion had been right about what was in the medicine, then by the time they reached Paris, the oldest lion would have his spirit back and Maccomo would be constantly tired and dull.

Charlie grinned at the young lion. The young lion whisked his whiskers at Charlie. Step one had been accomplished.

Maccomo yawned, rolled over in his cloak, and went back to sleep.

"Yay!" whispered Charlie, in triumph but trying to be very quiet.

Maccomo began to snore gently. Charlie and the younger lions began to relax. (The lionesses looked on, silently.)

"Charlie," said Elsina. "Why were your parents taken away? Have they been taken to a circus, like us?"

"Don't be stupid," the young lion began. "Humans join circuses because they want to, not because anyone makes them."

"But, in a way, it's the same," Charlie said. "Someone wants them to work for them, perform tricks they don't want to perform, to hand over their specialness and their skills . . ."

Elsina looked shocked. The lionesses blinked. They understood this, and they felt for Charlie.

Charlie didn't notice. He had just thought of something.

"Ahh," he sighed.

The young lion cocked an ear.

"I know what it is," said Charlie. "At least—I don't know exactly what it is, but I know . . ." But he stopped himself from telling the lions. He'd twice let his mouth run away from him: giving his name to Major Tib and calling Rafi to be rude and proud. He very much wanted a friend to confide in, but it was too dangerous. Only if he needed to would he tell the lions about the series of letters and numbers written in his mother's blood. It wasn't that he didn't trust them. He just had to be self-controlled about this.

"If you know," said the lion, "won't they come after you too?"

Charlie felt cold.

Could Rafi know that he had the formula? Could Rafi know what it was for?

Surely not.

But Charlie knew so little about what was going on . . .

And if Rafi knew, maybe he'd think it was easier to get it out of Charlie than out of his parents.

Why would Rafi want it? He's just a—no, Charlie, he's not just an anything. He's in this up to his ears. Probably he thinks he can sell it or something. He's your enemy.

Rafi hadn't called again since the young lion had roared at him— so in that sense, the roaring had worked. But Charlie really had to keep his head down. The circus was a good place to hide, and he should never have risked it by making that phone call!

"You need to talk to a cat," said the young lion. "Find someone coming the other way and see what's being said."

"I can't go and start yelling in Cat over the side of the ship to some passerby," said Charlie. "The circusguys and the sailors will think I'm crazy."

"True," said the young lion. "Wait till we pull in for the night at Rouen, then you can go and sniff around."

Charlie nodded, and went back to the ropelocker. He wanted to try the telephones again, just to see if by some miracle someone had called him. But he didn't. In case Rafi had. "Cocky Slimy Git," he muttered, but it didn't work.

He felt very alone.

"My only friends are lions," he said, trying the idea on for size, and liking it, but finding it quite scary. He wondered if he could confide in Julius, or Hans. He'd like to. Nothing against the lions, but sometimes a boy just wants to talk to another boy. But he couldn't risk it.

Everyone was banned from both the big top and the rehearsal cabins when anybody else was rehearsing, so Charlie hadn't seen any of the other acts yet, and he longed to. Hans's kitten apparently did a parachute jump. Whatever plan developed for the lions' escape, Charlie decided, it would happen *after* the big show in Paris. He might never again have the opportunity to run away with the circus, and he absolutely insisted that he was going to get to see the Show at least.

Of course, what he really wanted was to be *in* it. Flying through the air on the trapeze; topmounter in the Lucidis' human pyramid, or human cannonball even, in a little velvet suit, landing way over yonder with his face covered in soot and his ears ringing. He wanted to see the Learned Pig being learned. And Madame Barbue—did she just walk in and be bearded? Or did she do tricks too? Tricks with her beard? Julius and Hans and the twins had made it clear that there was a big difference between Acts—people with skills, who did amazing things, and belonged to the circus— and what they called Freaks—people who just sat there looking weird or strange, like a three-legged calf, or the fattest person in the world. If a freaky-looking person had an act, then that was great, they could—and should—be with a circus. But not if they were just there for people to stare at. "It's easy to feel alone and weird when people are just staring at you," said the twins in unison. "But if you're doing something to amuse and amaze them, then you feel good."

There was so much that Charlie wanted to see. He wanted to watch the audiences' faces when the ring cage came down, as he scurried from one hole to another, pegging it safely into place so the lions couldn't escape. He wanted to hear the Calliope whistling and droning down the canal, and through the streets of Paris, so that all the Parisians would be saying "What is that?" and widening their eyes and dropping their shopping bags.

For a moment, Charlie seriously thought that perhaps he should not help the lions to escape after all.

Then he thought about his parents, and about the Ruins Cats, and about Rafi and his sneaky mother, and about lions lying around under the African sun, being free and happy, and he sighed.

It's 234 miles from Le Havre to Paris. They would be passing through six locks, and the journey would take six days. It could be done quicker, but because the *Circe* was so huge, she had to move quite slowly once they were past Rouen. If they went too fast, their wake could capsize smaller vessels, or wash away the banks of the river. There were speed limits to respect, and the locks took time to pass through . . . But this first section of the journey had to be done as fast as possible. They had actually set off just before the tide had turned, because there was a low bridge at Honfleur, and they had to get there during low tide so the ship could pass under it.

"We're on the road to Rouen!" cried Julius, giggling. "There's no hope for us now!"

"What?" said Maccomo, who didn't have a sense of humor.

"Rouen," said Hans. "You know, like Ruin. The Road to Ruin."

Maccomo still didn't get it, or if he did, he didn't think much of it.

They soon left the open bleakness of the estuary behind, and were moving quickly past pretty wooded cliffs that gave way to swampy-looking sandy banks. Stuck on one of them, a little way ahead, Charlie and Julius could see a small boat at a strange angle. It looked as if it had been washed up there and just left hanging. There were some people on it, shouting and waving. They could just make them out.

"Oh, hang on," said Julius. "This'll be good!"

"What?" said Charlie, and as he said it he felt a strong, firm increase in the rumble of the *Circe*'s engines, and a sudden forceful surge in her power. They were speeding up.

It was a bit like the moment before an airplane takes off—though of course Julius and Charlie had never been in an airplane. It was a moment of pure power, and it thrilled the boys.

"What's happening?" yelled Charlie. "We're going to drown that boat!"

"Quite the opposite!" cried Julius, grinning and hanging over the side. "Look! Look!"

The people in the boat had stopped waving. As the *Circe* drew nearer, Charlie could see that they were very busy: They were up on deck, facing the shore, and they had poles and boat hooks. A couple of people were on shore too, also holding poles out, as if they were expecting something. And so they were.

As the *Circe* came careening past, she steered dramatically in toward the bank. Charlie thought she was going to collide with the boat. "What are they doing?" he yelled, but then, rather later than Charlie found comfortable, the *Circe* swerved suddenly back out into the middle of the river. The great wave of her wake spread in a huge V behind her, whooshing toward the bank, and the little boat that hung so precariously upon it.

"Alley-oop!" came a shout from the Lucidi family, who were hanging off the rails like Julius and Charlie, watching the action.

Charlie was terrified for the little boat, but as the wash came upon it, a cry went up aboard and ashore, and there was suddenly a great pushing and shoving with the poles and boat hooks, as those ashore tried to push the boat into the river, and those aboard tried to push off from the riverbank. And with the arrival of all that extra water underneath them, it worked—the *Circe*'s wake snatched the little ship from the muddy bank where she had been stranded, and pulled her back into the main flow of the river—right side up, shaky, its occupants cheering.

"Wow!" cried Charlie.

"Ai ai ai ai ai!" cheered the Lucidi family.

"Caramba!" yelled Julius.

The circus ship gradually slowed down again. Capsizing the little boat she had just rescued was not part of the plan.

"Do you often do that?" asked Charlie.

"Hardly ever," said Julius. "I've only seen it done once before, by another ship, and it didn't work. The little boat got shoved even farther up the bank, and on its side too. This was fantastic. Fantastic."

Charlie and Julius careened around the deck, pretending to be small boats stuck on mudflats and big boats rescuing them, until Julius suddenly found that he *was* stuck in a mudflat: a big pile of Learned Pig poo. Charlie got the giggles. Julius, however, was annoyed—he felt Hans should pay more attention to where his pig pooped. So he went and jumped on him, which annoyed Hans—he felt Julius shouldn't jump on him and wallop him when he hadn't even known that his pig *had* pooped.

Charlie left them to it, and went quietly back on deck to think about the lions.

That night when Maccomo had gone to dinner, Charlie said to the young lion: "What I don't understand is why *you* aren't affected by the medicine. It was in your water too, but you're not dopey and tired. You haven't given up."

"He's been sharing my water," said Elsina quietly. "I get fewer drops because Maccomo is hoping I will have cubs one day, and the drops are bad for a young lioness's health. So I get one drop just to calm me down a little. Of course one drop had hardly any effect on *him* because he's much bigger than me." She gestured to the young lion, who smiled and looked rather pleased with himself.

Charlie nodded. He was glad that these creatures he had fallen in with were intelligent. It was reassuring.

Later, just as Charlie was preparing to sneak off the ship and find a cat, Maccomo said: "Don't imagine that you are going ashore. Tonight you sleep here and guard the lions. Do not leave them alone. French people are not honest."

Charlie was torn between anger at not being able to leave and the urge to say: "That's stupid. You can't say people aren't honest just because of where they come from—some are and some aren't, like everybody." Instead he just sat there, fuming, in the lionchamber. He made himself angrier still by calling his dad's phone over and over, even though it had been unobtainable for days now. He was furious that he had to do as Maccomo said, to avoid making him suspicious. He *had* to be sensible and keep out of trouble. If it hadn't been for that, he would have been over the side in a second, no matter what the old bigot said. He was getting desperate for news.

He didn't feel like being sensible. He felt like *doing* something, running somewhere, punching someone, throwing something out the window.

He looked at his phone.

He looked up Cocky Slimy Git.

Before he could stop himself, he'd pressed the button.

Voice mail.

"Hi, Rafi," he said in an insolent way. "I hope my trip to the zoo amused you. And what a shame it is you haven't called again. I'd be so interested to learn how you sleep at night—" And then he hung up quickly, because in his mind the sentence was continuing "you greasy bully slimeball . . ." and his purpose was not to make Rafi angry again. It was to put him off the scent.

There. Done it.

Charlie smiled dangerously.

It worked—for about five minutes. The zoo, eh? thought Rafi, gliding along in the silver car. Which zoo, he wondered, and why?

Then he thought: And why would he be telling me—calling me especially to tell me—that he's been on a trip to the zoo? . . . Because he hasn't!

Here, for the moment, Rafi took a wrong turn. He wants me to think it was just a trip. He's at a zoo now! He's staying in a zoo!

So he called his research villain, and as a result wasted another couple of days and quite a lot of money having him locate and visit all the zoos in the country reachable by water.

CHAPTER 12

After Rouen they had to slow down even more: The river was narrower and the water shallower, with islands and sandbars to negotiate. From time to time the *Circe* had to cross from one side of the river to the other to find the deep channel. Crossing was quite a palaver because all the other boats around had to know what the big ship was going to do, so the skipper would hang a large blue board out to starboard, with a flashing white light at its center, to warn them. When boats were planning to overtake one another they had to communicate that too. Charlie hung over the deck railings next to the figurehead trying to figure out if there was a pattern in all the hooting and tooting, but just when he thought he was getting it, Maccomo would call him in to do some job, or a sailor would tell him to get out of the way.

Charlie had never been to France before and, between fretting, planning, stealing conversations with the lions, and all the extra jobs involved as Paris and the Show grew closer, he had time to admire it. A pale path followed much of the bank of the river, for horses to tow barges, with every now and then an emergency recharging point for electro-barges that hadn't charged up properly overnight at the electric berths. The towpath was lined by tall straight trees, set as regular as soldiers, and beyond them lay wide, flat green fields, and occasionally a golden-gray farmhouse, with black-and-white cows, and apple trees. In the distance, Charlie could see the silvery towers of faraway towns, and the occasional gleaming line of a main road. The river itself was quite isolated and quiet and beautiful. From time to time he could sit and enjoy the calm movement of the ship after the bumpy sea passage and the speed of the race to Rouen, and feel the warmth of the sun on his cheek. All the while, he watched out for any cat who might be able to give him any information.

The day they left Rouen, the locks started: Amfreville was the first, and it took two hours to maneuver *Circe* into the great chamber on the river, close the gates behind her, wait for the box to fill up with water beneath her, bringing her up to the level of the section of river they were moving on to. Charlie had seen locks on canals before, small ones taking in the whole canal and operated by hand. This was something else: For a start, it only occupied a small amount of the river, which was busy erupting in rapids and little waterfalls all around. It was as if a section of canal had been built in the middle of the river, and when the *Circe* came out the other end of it she was higher up, beyond the rapids and waterfalls, and sailing along smoothly again, leaving all peril behind.

"You'd never get a big boat up here without all this," he observed.

"Ah," said Julius. "But the Seine was never as bad as the Ourcq."

"The what?" asked Charlie, intrigued. He liked to hear Julius explain things. He was amazed that such a young boy knew so much. Sometimes Julius gave him a look that seemed to say "I hope I'm not boring you." Julius knew that not everybody was interested. It made him shy sometimes. But not with Charlie.

"On the Ourcq—" began Julius.

"Sorry, what is the Ourcq?" interrupted Charlie.

Julius gave him a pitying look. "It's one of the other rivers that goes to Paris," he said. "And in the old days, the old, old days"— by which Charlie knew he meant not just before the gasoline ran out, but before the gasoline was discovered in the first place— "they brought wood and stone down it, from the countryside into Paris for building. It was a really quick wild river, and the boats just came hurtling down on the current, which was very, very fast, and then when they got to a weir they would just shoot over the top and plunge down into the waters below. So loads of people drowned, and half the boats were broken and wrecked, and even if they weren't, when they got to Paris they were destroyed anyway, because there was no way back up."

Charlie gave a little shiver. Half of him found it quite exciting. The other half thought it sounded extremely scary.

Each time they passed an electro-barge, tooting as they went (one long, one short definitely meant "I am going to overtake," but one long and two short seemed to mean it too—he couldn't get the hang of it), Charlie scoured the decks for a cat. No luck. Why were there so few? He saw one asleep under the trees, and one in the basket of a bicycle being ridden along the pale path under the trees, but none he could talk to. Then, approaching the lock at Notre Dame de la Garenne, they came upon a barge going their own way, towed by horse in the old-fashioned way. In the flurry of communications and negotiations involved in locking in and out, Charlie spotted the barge's cat, a fat cheerful-looking tabby, coiled like a rope on the barge roof.

"Excuse me, Monsieur Cat!" he called.

"*Mademoiselle Chatte,* if you please," replied the tabby, sticking her leg out and stretching it a bit, lazily.

"Sorry, mademoiselle," cried Charlie. "Look, could you come and talk to me a moment?"

The cat, opening her sleepy eyes, realized she was being addressed by a human, and was so surprised that she rolled right off the roof and started to hiss.

"Yes, I know, I'm very unusual, sorry," said Charlie. "But please. Just for a moment, then we can drop you on the bank and you can regain your own boat later when it comes up. Please, come now, please."

The tabby gave him a very baleful stare, but her curiosity overcame her (cats are very curious, as you may know), and she was not too proud to leap from the roof to one of the circusship's fenders, which she caught with her claws before easing herself elegantly over the side, with a grace that suggested it had been no effort whatsoever, and whoever thought it had been was simply rude.

"And your point is?" she said.

Charlie, with great courtesy and some charming compliments (because he had read somewhere that French people are gallant) explained that he desperately needed to hear if there was any talk or gossip on the canal about a pair of English humans, one black, one white, one male, one female, who had been stolen away and taken to Paris, in a submarine.

"You look like a lady who would know everything that was worth knowing, mademoiselle," he said suavely.

"I look like a monsieur," she replied. "You said so yourself."

"I was momentarily blinded," he replied, which was a phrase he had heard his father use once when he mistook a cardinal in his fine scarlet robes for a beautiful lady in a red dress. "Confused by your glamour." He seriously hoped that it was all right to say this sort of thing to a French canal cat. It had gone down fine with the cardinal, but you never can tell how those people you don't know are going to take things.

The cat laughed. (A cat's laugh is quite something—especially a French one.)

"It doesn't matter," she said. "I do know everything. Are you the boy?"

Charlie looked around. "I'm *a* boy," he agreed cautiously.

"But are you *the* boy?" the tabby asked again.

"In what sense?" asked Charlie. He really didn't know if he was *the* boy, from the cat's point of view, and he didn't want to claim to be some boy that he wasn't.

"The boy who has lost his parents and is following in search of them."

Ah. *That* boy.

"Yes," said Charlie, "I think I must be. I mean, I have lost my parents and I am following in search of them."

The cat looked at him with sympathy.

"They are way ahead. They'll be there tomorrow morning easily, I heard."

"Tomorrow morning!" Charlie wanted to swear, but he remembered his father telling him that one reason you shouldn't swear is because then when you *really* needed a strong word to express a strong feeling, you would have none strong enough left. But tomorrow morning! If they were that far ahead, how could he ever find them in Paris? He was days behind them! Would the cats there know to keep track of them? How would he get any more news?

Charlie was a brave boy and quite a tough one, tougher than he thought he was, but when he heard this bad news he sat down on a coil of rope and tears sprang to his eyes. In this moment of disappointment, thoughts that so far he had managed to keep away from himself began to sneak into his mind. Thoughts like "How are they feeling?" And "Are they worrying about me?" And "How could anyone ever have overpowered my great strong dad in the first place?" And "When will I see them again?" And even—"*Will* I see them again?"

The deck was quiet because most people had gone in to eat, but even so he was not, not, *not* going to cry anywhere anyone might see him. He jumped up to rush into the ropelocker, but as he did so Mademoiselle Cat, in a sudden burst of pity, said: "Don't worry—everybody is looking for them. Everybody will help you. Everyone knows the story."

Charlie looked up, blinking. "What story?" he asked.

Mademoiselle Cat twitched her whiskers and said, "The story of your parents. Who they are."

"What is their story?" said Charlie. He had a sudden very strong feeling that this story might fill in the gaps for him—why they had been taken, by whom, maybe even where to. "Tell me," he said urgently. "Tell me!"

"If you don't know," said Mademoiselle Cat, "then maybe you are not the boy . . ." She looked doubtful rather than suspicious, but even so Charlie was now filled with a burning need to hear this story immediately. How could he find and rescue them if he didn't know everything there was to know?

"Tell me," he said furiously. "I have to know. They're my parents. What's the story?"

"I can't say," she said, quietly. "Just because . . . in case . . . but if you are you, don't be afraid." Before Charlie could stop her, she leaped swiftly from the deck of the circusship into the water.

"Come back!" shouted Charlie, not caring now who saw him yelling in Cat from the deck. "Come back! Cats don't swim! Come back!"

But she didn't. Charlie stared furiously after her, then furiously kicked a pile of coiled ropes, knocking them over and earning himself an earful from the sailor who had just coiled them up. Charlie didn't even hear him. He was livid.

If you're you, don't be afraid.

Well, of course he was he, and of course he was afraid: He'd just been told his parents would be in Paris long before him and he'd probably lose them, and there was some great mystery going on, about *his* mum and dad, which he, apparently, was the only person not to know, and now some blooming cat was suggesting that he wasn't even himself.

"Rats!" he shouted—which gave the cross sailor a shock, and sent him scurrying off, saying: "Where? Where? I'll get my gun; I must tell the cook . . ."

Charlie leaned over the side, scratching his head—it seemed ages ago that his mum had cut his hair, and his beautiful crocodiles were growing out already—and staring out over France. Gradually his anger slipped away, leaving only one question in his mind: Should he try to leave the circusboat and get to Paris quicker by some other means?

It didn't take long to realize that this idea was not a keeper. For a start, what other means? Unless he was intending to ride a tall silvery tree into Paris, he'd be walking, because the floating circus was the fastest craft on the canal, and there was nobody using the path at all—let alone anybody in a nice quick gas-powered car. And then— he had promised the lions, and he didn't break promises, and even if he were the kind of person who did, he didn't think breaking promises to lions could ever be a good idea. No, he'd just have to bite his lip and continue gliding up this wide and windy river.

Charlie knew that worrying about something you can't change is pointless, but he couldn't stop himself. He was miserable about his parents. He didn't think he could bear this delay.

All the next few days, as he fetched and carried, swept and yanked, tipped out drugged water and filled it up with clean, he pondered the two questions: Lion Escape and Parental Mystery. Lion Escape was easier to think about, because it had some answers, and it didn't make him want to cry. So he chatted innocently to everyone about the Show, and who would be where, and what happened when; and he wandered the ship, looking for ways on and off, for gangplanks and hatches that would give easy access to the shore.

The public gangplank was on the starboard side of the ship: It was broad and open and led to the grand staircase down to the foyer and the big top. Could they make it along the public gangplank? Perhaps, if they ran during the show—say after the lions did their act but before the show was over—because nobody would be there. Perhaps they should go in the dead of night—but with Maccomo sleeping in the lionchamber, Charlie didn't like their chances. No, it seemed to Charlie that the time to run away was *after* the show, when there would be a lot of people to-ing and fro-ing and everyone would be excited about how well it had gone, and nobody—except Maccomo—would notice that the lions weren't there. Perhaps he could persuade Maccomo to let him put the lions to bed after the show. Perhaps if someone were to invite Maccomo out after the show, then Charlie would be left in charge, and they would have some hours before they'd be missed. But whom would Maccomo want to go out with in Paris?

Charlie thought and thought and thought and thought, and gradually his plan started to fall into shape—but he needed help.

Then at Andresy, when Maccomo went out to the Moroccan restaurant, a mangy, travel-stained, bald-bottomed black cat came aboard the *Circe*, carrying a chewed and grubby bit of paper in his yellow teeth, and Charlie was knocked sideways with happiness.

CHAPTER 13

The mangy cat leaped onto the arm of the beautiful figurehead, stalked straight down the deck, not caring who saw him, twitching his nose and following the smell of the lions. When he reached the lionchamber he lay down in the shade and waited for Charlie.

When Charlie saw the mangled piece of paper between his teeth, his heart skipped.

The cat opened one eye, and then opened his mouth hugely. His breath was horrible. Charlie delicately took the piece of paper, unskewering it from a sharp little cat tooth. He stared at the cat, and then they quietly slipped behind the lionchamber.

He unfolded the paper.

He read it.

His eyes filled with tears and his heart filled with joy. They were alive, they were okay, they were being fed, they had a clever cat looking out for them. They'd received his message. They'd understood his code, they knew he was looking for them, they didn't think he should have done it, but they accepted it, they were going to keep in touch with him.

Charlie stood up, his face almost breaking from the strength of his smile. His face was all twisted with joy, his eyes like diamonds stuck in. There behind the lionchamber he did a little dance, clenching his fists and jumping from foot to foot with joy, trying not to make any noise, bursting with happiness.

The mangy black cat was gazing at him patiently.

Charlie stopped jumping for a moment.

"Thank you," he said simply. "This is the best thing that has ever happened to me. You have done the kindest thing anybody has ever done for me."

"Good," said the cat. "So do I get a refreshing beverage as a demonstration of yer appreciation then, or what?"

"Oh—oh yes!" cried Charlie, and he tucked the letter into his pocket and raced to the galley to scrounge milk, fish, and a small piece of cake—on principle, because cake was a treat, though he didn't know if the cat would like it.

The cat wolfed down the cake, and a tin of anchovies, then looked up.

"Do you—do you want some more?" asked Charlie.

"Yeah," said the cat. Charlie fetched him more.

Then he said: "Can you wait? Can you take a reply? Can you find them in Paris?"

"No," said the cat.

"Oh," said Charlie, his face fallen. "Oh—I . . ." He couldn't think what to say. It was like being shown a bicycle on Christmas Day and then being told, "Oh, no, it's not for *you*."

The cat looked up.

"Well, maybe I could," he said. "I wasn't planning it. But if it's entirely necessary for your intellectual and emotional peace of mind, I suppose I could. Seeing as it's you. And them." The cat was, to be honest, thinking about all the restaurants in Paris, all the fish heads and half-eaten lobster shells and bags full of bits of deliciousness that would be waiting for him in the compost heaps behind those restaurants.

"If you insist," he said. "If you twist my forelimb. I don't suppose I've much choice." His mouth was watering already.

"Fantastic," said Charlie. "Fantastic. Because I'll need to know where they are, and where they're heading, and if you can take messages between us . . . then have you seen my mum and dad?"

"No," said the cat. "I got the message off some bliddy posh girl at Le Havre, and she got it off a marmalade." Charlie smiled. That would be the one they mentioned. It seemed to bring his parents closer: This cat knew a cat who knew a cat who'd been with his parents.

"But, yeah, I'm acquainted with the history of who they are, yeah, and you being their appendage. 'Course I am," the cat was saying.

Charlie jerked his head up. He was about to say "Who are they, then?" when he remembered how he had scared off the French canal-boat cat, who had become worried that he might not be himself. Take it easy, Charlie, he told himself.

"I was wondering," he said casually, "why they seem to be so famous here. Of course at home everybody knows them, but I didn't realize cats in France would know them too . . ."

"Because what they've done, they've done for all cats," said the cat, dropping his slightly sneery, half-joking tone, and becoming suddenly quite serious. Charlie was genuinely surprised, because this cat was so mangy and bald-bottomed, and had so far shown no manners to speak of. "They're not proud. They're not saying this kind of cat's better than that kind. Ever since the Allergenies started apparating, your parents have been on their side an' all. What they've done, their work, has been the best thing any humans have ever done for us. Obviously they've not succeeded yet, but their professional enterprises—well, it could be the saving of us. All of us. We don't want humans to hate us. Your parents are single-handedly—*mono-digitally*—saving the whole relationship between cats and humans. And between cats and Allergenies, if it goes right. Of course cats all over the world know about 'em. And honor 'em. Plus there's you, of course."

Charlie was dumbstruck.

Allergenies? Work to save the cat/human relationship? "You, of course"?

This was the mystery, no doubt about it.

How to find out more without giving away that he knew so little?

"Ah, yes," he said, trying to sound intelligent and well-informed.

"There's been very few humans capable and willing to talk Cat, and I'm very honored to meet you," said the black cat in quite a humble way. "Very honored to be of service. Any cat would be. Even, um, the Allergenies. I know a lot of cats hate 'em, but it's not their fault, is it?" He looked a little embarrassed. He seemed to be waiting for some kind of reaction from Charlie, and a little as if he wasn't sure what that reaction would be, or indeed if he really wanted a reaction at all. In fact, he looked as if he now realized that of course it would be a bad reaction, so he was off down the pub and forget he ever asked. All this in about five seconds.

"Er, no," said Charlie, hoping this was the answer that the cat wanted. His mind was racing.

"Allergenies are not all bad," the cat continued. "I know some who've gone off to live wild in the country, so as not to do any harm. Some of 'em are miserable about what they've to do. And about what's been done to them. Miserable." He spoke with passion, but then he seemed to notice that Charlie was having trouble following. He sighed. "Anyway, look," he said. "You better appraise your reply so I can get on my *bicyclette*."

Charlie liked the way he talked.

"Give me a few minutes," he said, and went into the ropelocker.

He thought very hard about what to say to his parents. He had a lot of questions to ask, and he thought it better to ask his parents directly than to question the cat. But he couldn't phrase it *directly*. He had to ask in their special code.

"Darling Mummy and Daddy," he started.

"It was really good to get your letter. Everything's going okay for me. Brother Jerome is going to take me to Paris, which is I think where you are going too . . ."

He stopped to think. He didn't want to say Paris, in case anyone read the letter and would learn that he was coming after them. How could he put it?

He thought hard.

Of course! There was a girl on their block named Paris. Her sister was named Rita. He started again.

"Brother Jerome is taking me to visit Rita's sister, and I know you are expected there too. If you get there first, try not to leave too soon, as I hope I can see you there . . ."

How to ask about the Allergenies? He strongly felt that his mum and dad would know what they were. But who else knew? And how risky would it be to ask about them? And, come to think of it, how could his parents explain them in a reply, in code?

Perhaps he should just ask the cat after all.

Or—no! He thought of something.

"I am doing a project on pet cats. I wish I could ask you about it. Please tell me all you can when you reply." He couldn't think of anything better. He hoped they'd get it.

Was there anything else he needed to tell them? Could he risk saying something about the circus? In case they were able to escape and come to him?

No. He didn't want the baddies, whoever they were, seeing "circus" and mentioning it to Rafi, then Rafi putting it together with the roaring on the telephone . . . And he and the lions would be leaving anyway.

He finished off: "I am being a very good little boy like you said. Hope to see you very soon. I will bring some friends—bigger kids—to Rita's sister's. Lots and lots of love from Charles."

He folded it tiny, returned to the back of the lionchamber, and tucked the note into the black cat's collar.

"Crike of a lot easier than carrying it in me gob," said the black cat gratefully.

"What's your name?" asked Charlie.

"Sergei," said the cat.

"Why?" asked Charlie. He didn't mean to be rude; the name just didn't seem quite—this cat looked like he should be called Bandit or Alias.

"Me dad liked Rachmaninoff," said Sergei. "I'll be off now."

Charlie said: "Um, Sergei—who else—human—speaks Cat?"

"Well, nobody at the moment, only you. Van Amburgh did—the lion trainer—and King Solomon, obviously, St. Francis, the patron saint of animals. And St. Jerome, who extricated the thorn out of some lion's paw some centuries ago—no one understood how he could do it, and that's one reason he got sainted. You could be a saint maybe, Charlie—ha ha! And, erm, Hugh Lofting, who wrote those books . . . you know . . . Dr. Doolittle . . . erm . . . Daniel, of course, in the Bible, in the lions' den. Some others who just thought they were off their rockers. Not everybody knows what to do with it. You're one of a rare and honored tradition, you know . . . There's not a lot like you."

Charlie was touched by this mangy cat's goodwill.

"So when Maccomo used Cat words to the lions, he probably got them off Van Amburgh."

"More likely off Daniel or the gladiators," said Sergei. "Ask those lions. Lions are big on history."

"Thanks, Sergei," said Charlie. "Come back soon!" Sergei flicked his ear and was gone, off on the road to Paris, to ask all the Parisian cats where the famous English couple, the black man and the white woman, whose son was *that* boy, were being held prisoner.

I don't think Rafi knows where I am, Charlie thought on his way to lunch. If he did, he'd be here by now. He's got a car!

He didn't imagine that even if Rafi didn't yet know where he was, he might at any moment find out.

Charlie ate his lunch with Julius and Hans.

"Julius," he said. "What's an Allergeny?"

"Don't know," said Julius—not a phrase he used very often. He looked a bit surprised. "What is it?"

"I don't know either," said Charlie, and then, realizing that Julius would ask about where Charlie had heard the word, and so on, he decided to change the subject.

"Tell me about the famous circus people in Paris," he said. "Are there any?"

"Are there any!" exclaimed Julius. "There are bucketloads. All the best circus people live in Paris. They've got the best halls, except for in the Empire homelands, of course: there's the Cirque Fernando on Boulevard Rochechouart, and the Cirque d'Hiver on Boulevard des Filles du Calvaire—that's really fine, with twelve sides and Corinthian columns at each corner, and equestrian statues by the entrance, and oil lamps, and a frieze of horses and a cupola on top with a winged figure . . ." It occurred to Charlie that if he had been planning to stay any longer on the *Circe,* he'd have had to get a dictionary for talking to Julius. (Sergei used long words as well—*bicyclette!* appendage!—but Charlie had the feeling he just used them for fun, whereas Julius was pretty serious.)

He really wanted to talk to Julius about the lions' escape. He just knew that Julius would be full of useful knowledge and good ideas. But he couldn't tell him. It wasn't safe, and it wasn't fair to Julius, because just by knowing, Julius would have to betray either his new friend or his circus.

So Charlie would just have to get Julius to answer his questions without arousing any suspicion about why he was asking them. This did make him a little uncomfortable, but he had no choice.

"Wow," said Charlie, sounding impressed (which was easy, because he *was* impressed). "And tell me about the people." He was just keeping the conversation going while he worked out how to drop in the questions he needed answers to.

"Well, there are some fabulous clowns—there's Popov, Charlie Cairoli, Coco, the Fratellini Brothers, Scaramouche. Van Amburgh was there with his lions before he died, you know about him, of course, and John Cooper, and Jacob Dreisbach—he more or less invented the *férocité* acts. Van Amburgh was fantastic, but Dreisbach just thought it was all too gentle, the audience would like some more whip-cracking and fighty stuff. Maccomo hates Dreisbach—did you know?"

"No, why?"

"Because of Mabel Stark," continued Julius.

"Who?"

"You *must* know Mabel Stark—everybody knows about her! You really don't know anything, do you, Charlie? She's this fantastic tiger trainer, she's amazing, she does all the things the men do and more. She really loves her tigers—*all* the trainers say it's about love, but here you can see it is. It's like she's the tiger's mum or something—it licks her hair and hugs her. And she's really beautiful and wears white leather costumes and everybody's in love with her, including Dreisbach, and Maccomo—"

"Maccomo's in love with a lady!" squeaked Charlie, amazed. He couldn't imagine it.

"Yes!" cried Julius. "It is funny, isn't it? And he was going to marry her, only then Dreisbach—he was her teacher—told her not to and she didn't, and so Maccomo hates him."

"Why did Dreisbach tell her not to marry him?" said Charlie.

Julius's face changed and he looked suddenly embarrassed.

"Um," he said.

"Why?" said Charlie.

Julius frowned, gathered up his courage, and then said quickly: "Because he's one of those stupid people who think black and white people shouldn't marry each other." He didn't look at Charlie as he said it, so he didn't see Charlie's face begin to burn with a blush. Of course Charlie knew there were people like that, and of course he didn't like to hear about it. But he also knew that Julius was upset at having to bring up the subject, and he appreciated him for being straightforward about it.

"Stupid pig," said Charlie, trying to sound cheerful, and Julius looked up gratefully and said, "Yeah, stupid pig. So we hate him." Charlie smiled at Julius, and Hans, who had stood nervously on the sidelines of this bit of the conversation, said quietly: "I hate him too."

There was a small pause, and then Charlie said, "So where's Mabel now?"

"Oh, she's in Paris," said Julius, glad to change the subject. "That's why everyone's so nervous about the show, because all the top Parisian circus people will come, or they won't come, and they'll like it, or they won't like it, so everyone's in a tizzy."

"Do you think Mabel will come?" asked Charlie.

"Bound to! And she'll bring Louis Roth—that's her boyfriend. He's a lion trainer, and he's Hungarian and wears these boots almost up to his bottom."

Charlie was thinking furiously. A brilliant idea had dropped into his lap like a ripe fruit off a tree. Mabel must lose her boyfriend in boots and invite Maccomo out after the show, then he would be out of the way for the lions to escape.

So how to get a woman he didn't know to invite out a man she hadn't seen since . . .

"How long ago was the Mabel-Maccomo thing?" he asked Julius.

"A year or two, I suppose," said Julius. "Maccomo still looks thunderous if her name comes up."

"But he loves her, right?"

"Oh, yeah."

"So why would he look thunderous? Wouldn't he be pleased to see her?"

"I dunno—I suppose he thinks she doesn't like him anymore."

Charlie knew, from listening when his mum and her friends were discussing grown-ups' love lives, that there was no logic when it came to grown-ups being in love. But he was pretty sure that if Maccomo were to get a message from Mabel saying "I miss you and I want to see you," he would go along.

But how to get her to send such a message?

Charlie was halfway through his sticky toffee pudding when he had his most brilliant idea. Mabel didn't have to send the message. As long as the message had Mabel's name on it, it didn't matter who actually sent it. And then—he almost laughed, he was so pleased with his brilliance—Mabel could receive a message from Maccomo too—only it wouldn't be from Maccomo. And each of them would think the other had invited them! And each would be flattered, and curious, and go along, and it would be ages before they realized that they had been tricked! By which time, Charlie and the lions would be off rescuing Mum and Dad.

Charlie actually did start giggling.

"What is it?" said Hans, with a bit of sticky toffee sauce trickling down his chin.

"Oh, I'm just happy," said Charlie.

"Really?" said Julius. "But what about your parents?"

"Can't be sad all the time," said Charlie. "You get tired of it."

Julius looked at him consideringly, and Charlie wondered if he suspected something. But how could he?

"What's the swankiest restaurant in Paris?" Charlie asked.

"Oh, it's full of swanky restaurants. One of Dad's favorites is Chez Billy in the Marais, but he can't afford to go there—it's very expensive and you always have to book . . ."

Thinking about it, Charlie realized he was going to have to work fast. Get their phone numbers and text-message them, then there'd be no problems with either of them saying "But that's not his/her handwriting." Then he'd have to call the restaurant and book a table. What time does the show end? How long would it take them to get there from the ship? It would be good if it wasn't too close, because that would give him and the lions more time. Charlie felt like a criminal, making sure all the details were right, and that he would not be suspected.

"Is the Marais near where we dock?" Charlie asked innocently.

"Why?" demanded Hans, and Charlie realized he'd better start asking his questions to different people, if he didn't want to have questions asked of *him*.

So—phone numbers. He could start that night.

First he had to run the plan by the lions. It was easy because Maccomo was snoozing—the medicine must have been working. As the trainer snored on the floor in his crimson cloak, Charlie started to tell the young lion and Elsina what he planned. But before he could do so, the young lion hissed at him: "About time! Venice!"

"What do you mean, Venice?" said Charlie.

"A nasty-looking black cat turned up and said he was sorry he couldn't stay—'wasn't able to delay his perusal of your business' was his exact phrase—and to tell you Venice!"

Sergei. Charlie smiled. Venice! He'd seen pictures. The streets were full of water. Venice was beautiful and strange.

He thought quickly. So would his parents get his letter? Well, Sergei would take it to them.

Would he? Yes, Charlie thought. He was rude and mangy, but Charlie was pretty sure he wasn't dishonest, and he had really

144

seemed to care about Charlie's parents. Why else would he have taken the trouble to bring the first letter all this way?

"Have they left yet?" he asked.

"He didn't say," said the young lion.

Well, thought Charlie, if I don't get to them in time in Paris, I'll just have to go to Venice. Which was south, more or less, and closer to Africa. So the lions could come with him. There was no point in wondering why Mum and Dad were being taken there. He only hoped they'd stay long enough for him to catch up.

He was pretty sure you could get a train to Venice from Paris. In the old days there was one called the Orient Express that went from Paris to Venice to Istanbul.

He made a note in his head: train from Paris to Venice?

Then he told the lions his plan about Mabel. They were delighted.

"It's a great idea," said the young lion.

"Brilliant," said Elsina.

"And it may just work," said a third voice. They all turned to look. It was the oldest lion, standing up in his cage and looking over at them. "He's crazy about that woman, always was. He'd do anything for her. Certainly go and have dinner with her in a restaurant. And I think she would too."

Charlie and the young lion grinned at each other. Maccomo was dopey, the oldest lion had perked up, and the plan had his agreement.

"Best get on the telephone then, Boy who speaks Cat!"

Charlie's brain was ticking away, thinking through all possibilities. He felt wonderful, intelligent, and in control. Details! That was what you needed. Knowing what was what. For example:

"Where's the key now?" he asked.

The young lion nodded. "Over there," he said.

There it was. Big old key, on a hook. Plain, old-fashioned, couldn't be simpler.

"Well, that's all right then," said Charlie. "And we need to think about where we go next."

He had made a decision. He and the lions, once they'd escaped, could not hang around where the circus was. They'd be followed and caught. If he didn't hear back from his parents, or a cat, telling him where they were in Paris, he would go straight on to Venice.

In the back of his mind he heard Rafi's tight, angry, violent voice: "Just stay there and I'll be along to get you soon. Along. To get you. Soon." He doesn't know, Charlie told himself firmly. He couldn't. But *couldn't* and *doesn't* are two different things.

Worry about something you can do something about! he told himself. In a very short time he'd be standing on a French street corner with six lions to look after, and he'd need to know which way to turn. Plans in general had to become plans in particular.

The oldest lion smiled down at him. "I have some ideas, boy. Go and telephone now."

"Yes, sir," said Charlie. "By the way—does anyone know what an Allergeny is?"

The lions all just gazed at him. "No," they said. "What is it?"

Huddled and stiff in the hold of a motorboat, Magdalen was whispering. "I think we have to try to escape," she murmured. "In the submarine we couldn't do anything, but next time we're transferred, we should just knock them down and run. We can't go on like this. Well. Maybe you can, but I can't. Charlie's out there somewhere, he needs us. He's not safe if he has . . . And I'm going mad here, doing nothing. We must do something!"

Aneba was sitting beside her, holding his knees. It was cramped in there; warmer than the sub, but hardly more comfortable. They couldn't stand up, and were instead half-lying on sacks of something that felt like rice.

"If we run," he said, his voice strained by whispering and by trying to be patient—they seemed to have had this conversation many times before. "If we run, assuming we get away, how will we find out who hired these fools to kidnap us? How will we find out what they want? We couldn't go home; they could just come back for us again—or for Charlie. We wouldn't be safe. We have to stay, to find out what it's all about. Assuming—let's assume—that it's about the asthma cure. Do we assume that?"

"Yes," said Magdalen in a small voice.

"So who wants it? Who wants us? Or is scared of us?"

"Or thinks us so important?" said Magdalen. "I know, love, but . . ." She was thinking about Charlie.

"I know," said Aneba. "But he'll be no safer than us until this thing is sorted out. So that's what we are going to do. Get there—wherever it is. Identify our enemy. Deal with it. Sort it out."

"Sort it out," said Magdalen sadly. "Yes. If only."

Suddenly the boat jolted. Boxes fell on their heads—"Yow!" cried Magdalen as a crate of sardines fell against her.

"Shut up in there," came a voice from outside—Winner's voice.

The boat was docking.

Charlie was extremely relieved to hear that the oldest lion had some ideas, because he didn't. However, he did know what to do when short of them. His mum and dad had both drummed it into him: "When you don't know what to do, get more information!" So after the lions' afternoon rehearsal, and setting up and putting away the ring cage, and having a discussion with Maccomo about the final details of the performance, Charlie went to see Signor Lucidi, to find out exactly what would happen once they were in Paris.

He found him lying on his stomach on the floor of his cabin, with the youngest of his children walking along his backbone.

"Gosh!" cried Charlie. "Is this part of the act? Use your dad's spine as a low-wire?"

"Ah, no," groaned the acrobat. "I wish it was, but it is not. It is for the pain of my back. Carrying so many of my family makes me hurt, and if I am to hold the Tukul for twenty seconds in Paris, then I must be strong and not aching . . . We are practicing too much and I hurt. That is all."

"What's the Tukul?" asked Charlie.

"Most difficult human pyramid," said Sigi. "Everybody up on Daddy. On Daddy's legs, four people, plus on Daddy's shoulders, five people, plus on Daddy's head, my bambino here. On Daddy's head too—the pride of the family name, because if I don't hold it twenty seconds at least, all Paris will laugh at the name of Lucidi."

"Gosh," said Charlie again. Standing upright with ten people on top of you. That must be hard.

"So tell me, what happens when we get to Paris?" Charlie asked.

"Well, tomorrow morning we go into the Canal St. Denis, and we should get to our stopping place near the Bastille a few hours later," said Sigi, between grunts of pleasure as his little boy's heels dug in along his spine. "It's convenient—the canal joins on to the river. We dock, we parade, we get everything ready, then the next day everybody comes, we perform, we all go out and get drunk to celebrate. We stay three weeks, then we are back to normal, following the canals down to the Mediterranean Sea, performing all the way. Then we perform the Italian coast, all the holiday towns and fishing villages down to Rome and Naples, then over to North Africa for the winter and up the Spanish coast and back to Marseilles, and who knows where—maybe around Britain again, maybe to the Caribbean and the Empire Homelands. We can go anywhere on this boat—anywhere Major Tib wants to take us."

Listening to this list of places, Charlie wished and wished that his parents were safely at home where parents ought to be, and that the lions could be happy in captivity, and that he could stay with the circus forever and ever.

But he couldn't.

"Is the Bastille near the Marais?" asked Charlie.

"Yes, it's very close," said Sigi. "It's close to everywhere. The university, the station, the menagerie, the river, the canal, the police, the courts of justice . . ."

Charlie ticked all these off in his head. Police and courts of justice—oh, dear. The station—aha!

He was just about to ask Signor Lucidi if the train was the best way to Italy from Paris, when he realized that this would be a very stupid thing to do. After he and the lions were gone, Maccomo and Major Tib would ask everybody if they knew anything about it, and if Lucidi said that Charlie had been inquiring about routes to Italy, then everybody would know that's where they'd gone. And they'd come after them, and they'd be extremely angry.

Charlie resolved to get a map of the area.

Back out on deck, the little envelope was flashing on his telephone.

He pressed the button. COCKY SLIMY GIT.

He took a breath, and retrieved the message.

"You stupid little kid, Charlie. You're on completely the wrong track. You haven't got a clue, have you? I'm here with your parents now—your mum's really ugly, isn't she?—and you know what? You're not going to find them. And you know what else? They don't want you. Why do you think they left without you? 'Cause they don't want you. Who would? Little squit like you. Uppity little squit at that. Stupid uppity little squit who couldn't find his stupid uppity parents if they were squashed on the motorway under his nose. So as you're obviously not going to get here on your own, I'll be along to get you soon, like I said . . ."

The voice was low and vicious and went on and on. Charlie listened in a frozen, horrified fascination, unable to hang up, for just a little too long.

The next night they were due to enter Paris. They stopped early at a place called Chatou, found the dock, and rested up for an early start in the morning. Charlie went about his duties, chanting, "You don't fool me, you don't fool me, you don't fool me" under his breath, trying to drown out the echo of Rafi's nasty voice and nastier words. "I'll beat you, Rafi," he repeated over and over. "I've got lions. I've got six beautiful, strong, huge, killer lions, with massive teeth and sharp hard claws that could cut you in half. Have you seen how big a lion's claw is, Rafi? Do you know how many they have? They're like carving knives, Rafi, and they keep them tucked into their paws so they stay good and *sharp!* I've got lions, Rafi, and all you've got is a nasty tongue . . ."

"What are you muttering?" demanded Maccomo. "I have a headache. Quiet down."

Charlie was glad he had a headache. He hoped the drugs had caused it.

Later on, sitting on the deck with his sleeping bag around his shoulders and Pirouette's old street map of Paris on his knee, Charlie discovered that the Canal St. Denis would take them to the Canal St. Martin, which would take them back to the Seine, in the center of Paris, at the Port de Plaisance de Paris Arsenal, Bastille for short because it was very close to where the old prison called the Bastille used to be, and the Marais, he saw, was close enough to be a sensible choice of area for Maccomo and Mabel to go out to dinner, but not so close as to make it risky. Also, it was in the opposite direction to the station. Things were beginning to fall into place.

Above him the small, high moon sailed across the night sky. Below, it made a still, gleaming path toward him across the river's waters. He tried hard to still his jumping mind. And for a few minutes he let himself wonder about what the barge cat had said. About the story, the Allergenies, his parents' work—the great mystery.

He couldn't bear to look at the telephones. The possibility of more of Rafi's threats, plus the inevitable emptiness of his mother's phone—no, it was too depressing. Why wasn't anyone calling his mum? Any of her colleagues or her friends? People to say "Come over and visit," or Brother Jerome saying "Why isn't Charlie coming to lessons?" Charlie didn't know that Rafi had told all his family's friends and relations that they had had to leave suddenly for Africa. He felt as if he and his family had dropped off the edge of the world, and nobody cared.

Not that the circus people didn't care, but . . . they were all new friends, and apart from the lions he couldn't tell them what was on his mind. And he couldn't tell the lions how scared he was, and how he wished he didn't have to do this. Late in the evenings he wanted someone he had always known. Someone from home.

He read his letter again. Thought of the friendly cats who had helped. Wondered again if he could trust Sergei—well, he had no choice. Wondered again about the Allergenies. Wondered for the thousandth time what his parents were working on that made them heroes to cats. Well, he was working to find them. So let's get on with it, he said to himself toughly, before the moon started to look too sad, and the night grew too lonely. Get on with it.

So he started to track down the phone numbers he needed—and very complicated it was too. Then the phone at the restaurant was constantly busy. Charlie really hoped he wouldn't have to find another excuse to ask Julius about swanky restaurants. It was such an unlikely thing for someone like Charlie to need to know about.

By the time he went to bed he'd sent two text messages, booked a restaurant reservation, and found out that trains to Venice left from the Gare d'Austerlitz, which was the station right across the river from the Bastille, and that the train left at half past midnight.

Here are the messages he sent:

> MABEL, SUCH A LONG TIME PLS
> COME TO SHOW ON FRIDAY, AND
> AFTERWARD TO CHEZ BILLY, I WILL
> MEET YOU THERE. AFFECTUEUSE-
> MENT, MACCOMO.

And to Maccomo he sent:

> MACCOMO, SUCH A LONG TIME, I
> AM COMING TO SHOW ON FRIDAY,
> PLS JOIN ME AFTERWARD CHEZ
> BILLY. MABEL.

He really hoped he had the tone right. Who knew what grown-ups wrote to each other? But he had seen invitations with things like "afterward" and "please join me" written on them. Oh, well. Either it would work or it wouldn't. And if it didn't, they'd just have to think of something else. He felt a little sick at the thought.

CHAPTER 14

The next morning dawned misty and damp. While Charlie was out practicing with the acrobats, each of the electric lightbulbs that adorned the ship's rigging and smokestacks was itself adorned with drips of misty rain, drops of water through which light shone and refracted, each reflecting off all the others and glowing in the mist. Charlie had not seen the lights illuminated before. The entire ship gleamed like a ghost. The raindrops flew, shattering rainbows, as the acrobats jumped and swung. Charlie felt like a ghost himself—a flying, silent ghost.

"Whaddaya think, Lionboy?" It was Major Tib, looming out of the mist in his green velvet jacket, tall and suave as Captain Hook.

"It's gorgeous, sir," said Charlie, coming down from a handstand on the edge of a smokestack, and wishing he were somewhere else. He didn't want to look the major in the face when he was about to trick him out of his lions.

"Looking forward to the parade tonight?"

"Oh yes, sir," said Charlie.

"And the show tomorrow?"

"Oh yes, sir."

"Know what you've got to do?"

"Yes, sir, and looking forward to it!" said Charlie bravely.

"Mighty glad, mighty glad," said Major Tib, but his attention had wandered and Charlie could escape.

He did know what he had to do—more than Major Tib could dream of. Not only did he know how to lower and raise the ring cage, and pin it in place, and let the lions in and out of the ring, he also knew how he was going to get the lions away from their life of captivity and tricks, off the boat and if necessary onto the train to Venice and freedom, en route to Africa. The night before he had sat late into the night with the lions, hatching their plan. Tonight he would be in the parade, and tomorrow would be his first and last day with the show, the day he would steal the lions.

"I wonder where we are," murmured Aneba. He wished he had his phone, with its global tracking device, which would have told them immediately. Well, before Winner had taken the phone from him again they had been heading southeast, and they had been traveling, quite slowly he felt, for days. France, he thought, and river. The sea would be a rougher ride, and deeper.

Their door flung open. There was Winner, with a hat pulled down over his head.

"Put these on," he snapped, throwing a pair of what looked like giant socks at them.

"Even *my* feet aren't that big," said Aneba. He liked annoying Winner with jokes.

"Shut up," said Winner. "On your heads."

Magdalen and Aneba pulled the socks over their heads (Magdalen giving Aneba a last beseeching look—a "Please can we wallop them and run?" look) and allowed themselves to be handcuffed and pushed out the door.

Darkness and stumbling. The giant socks smelled moldy and damp, but through them came an unmistakable smell of outdoors. It was cold, but they both breathed deeply, glad of the fresh air at last.

Winner tripped over something—they could hear him cursing.

Something brushed Magdalen's legs.

A noise—"Mraow!"—and Winner complaining and standing up.

There was something under Magdalen's hand—warm, furry.

She knew exactly what to do. The cat was moving into position beneath her bound hand.

No, wrong end—tail. Rather a bald tail, by the feel.

Head. She stroked it swiftly, wanting to convey kindness and gratitude. Neck. Collar. Yes! Piece of paper! Yes!

She whispered "Thank you!" under her breath and got a rough "Mraow!" in response, before the cat disappeared. She held tightly to the scrap of paper, as tightly as if it had been her son himself, rather than a letter from him.

Two hours later, in the back of a truck parked on the side of one of the few remaining European motorways, Magdalen and Aneba read the letter from Charlie. Magdalen managed to unfold it, and Aneba wriggled into a position where he could read it aloud. A lone streetlight sent its weak gleam in through the grubby window of the truck.

"It's upside down," Aneba said very quietly. He didn't want Winner overhearing. "Turn it to the left a bit so it's in the light."

Darling Mummy and Daddy,

It was really good to get your letter. Everything's going okay for me. Brother Jerome is taking me to visit Rita's sister, and I know you are expected there too. If you get there first, try not to leave too soon, as I hope I can see you there. I am doing a project on pet cats. I wish I could ask you about it. Please tell me all you can when you reply. I am being a very good little boy like you said. Hope to see you very soon. I will bring some friends—bigger kids—to Rita's sister's.

Lots and lots of love from Charles

"Rita's sister!" said Aneba. "What's that about?"

"Rita's sister is named Paris," said Magdalen, smiling broadly in the dimness. "Clever little blighter."

"So that's where we're heading. How does he know?"

"Cats," said Magdalen. "It's got to be. And the project on pet cats . . ."

"Yes," said Aneba.

Magdalen folded the letter up again and held it firmly in her fist.

"He's finding out about the whole thing, presumably," she murmured.

"I suppose. I suppose the cats are telling him."

"The Allergenies and everything?"

"I suppose," said Aneba quietly.

"We were right not to tell him, though, weren't we?"

"Of course. What do you think they'd do with him if they thought he knew about it? And if they knew what he can do?"

"I hate to think," she said very quietly.

"Sorry," said Aneba.

"Yeah," she said.

They sat in silence for a moment.

"You know," she said. "I wrote out the formula—the basic formula—and told him that if he ever had to go anywhere, he should take it with him."

"You *WHAT!*" shouted Aneba, so loud that Winner wondered for a moment what was up in the back. "You *what?*" More quietly and intently.

"I don't know why. I suppose so that . . . if anything happened to us, at least one honest person would have that knowledge."

"One honest *child*," hissed Aneba. "One honest ignorant kid, who if they knew what he had would be totally at the mercy of these people. And if they knew what he can do as well . . ."

"Yes." She sat miserably. "Should I not have?"

"No, you shouldn't have," he whispered furiously. "Now not only is he the only Cat-speaker, he's also got the formula—did he take it with him when he set out into the world, all alone, totally unprepared? We don't know, of course. Oh, God . . ."

Magdalen was crying, softly. Aneba didn't hear because he was too angry.

"Keep your voice down," she murmured. "Don't tell everybody. It's bad enough."

"He's out there, on his own, with the formula *and* the language, and he doesn't have a clue about the Allergenies or how they came about, or anything."

"No," said Magdalen. "But *we* don't know how they came about either. And he's learning. Remember? His 'project on pet cats'? He's a clever kid, Aneba, and he's finding out what he needs to know, and telling us he's doing it. We must get a letter back to him telling him as much as we can. But how's that cat going to find us again? And where *are* we?"

"Heading to Paris," murmured Aneba. "If Charlie's right."

But they weren't. They had passed Paris, and as soon as Winner had had his breakfast they would be moving on again. Not with Winner and Sid, though. Three large men from the Personnel Department arrived, punched Sid and Winner, just because they could, and then bound and gagged Aneba and Magdalen, who, being handcuffed, couldn't fight back. Magdalen had hidden the note in her boot, so that was all right. Not much else was, though. "You have an appointment with the Chief Executive," was all the men would say, and they said it with a sneer. "He'll tell you all you need to know about the position."

Rafi was getting very frustrated. He'd had no luck with the zoos. No luck with the waterways. No luck in the city.

He decided to go back to the fish stalls to bully Mr. Ubsworth. He felt like hitting someone, and in the absence of Charlie, Mr. Ubsworth would do.

By noon, the great crimson ship was swanning slowly along the Canal St. Martin in the warm sunshine. It would have been a graceful sight, but for the noise it was making: The Calliope was in full voice. What a racket! It had been loud enough the time before, on the river in London, but here, with the buildings all around, it blared and farted out like a troupe of carnivals on a summer's day, a noise full of fun and nostalgia at the same time—an irresistible noise. Charlie noticed that a lot of the circusguys were down on the banks of the canal, handing out fliers with the details of the circus on them. The people were looking at the ship, laughing at the Calliope, reading the leaflets and putting them in their bags and pockets. They all wanted to come to the circus.

Then there were four more locks to negotiate on the Canal St. Martin. Charlie was again amazed by how snugly a ship fits into a lock: like a fat man in a bath, it's a wonder there's any room for the water. But there is—just enough to allow that curious, staggering, slightly nauseating motion as the boat tries to keep still and not bang against the edges. The locks sprayed their smelly foam as the water tumbled and flooded in and out, the metal bars set in the lock walls gleamed beneath their green weed, the lock-keepers called *Bonjour!*, and the lock bells rang. Pale green footbridges arched over the water, so high that the people who stopped at the top to admire the circusship seemed to be standing on the branches of the trees, in among their sweet green leaves.

Charlie was just getting used to it all, knowing that they were nearly at their destination, when the Calliope, which had been cranking away, suddenly wheezed and hiccuped to silence, and the ship drew into the Temple lock. The smell of her fumes wafted back over them as she drew to a halt and idled. It was here that a cat called out to Charlie from the bank.

"You're to be told they've gone on!" she called.

"What?" called Charlie. "Come here—come on board!"

The cat shrugged. With a great rush and tumble the water began to flood out of the lock chamber, and the *Circe* began to sink down beneath him. Charlie rushed to the side nearest to the cat and cried back: "Gone on? When? Where to? Is it Venice?"

"Bof," said the cat. "I suppose. Only you're to be told they have gone on. I don't know more."

Ahead, the ship was facing a brick wall. At the top of it Charlie could see the back of a statue's head, with a pigeon sitting on it, and a formally clipped dark green hedge. At the base, he noticed, way down beneath him when he peered over, a low stone arch.

"Come here," he called to the cat urgently. "Please! Come and tell me more. When did they leave?" If only he knew how they were traveling and for how long, perhaps he could work out how to catch up with them.

"Please!" he called. Hissing, so that he wouldn't be noticed.

"I don't know nothing more," said the cat, and as the ship sank down into the lock, she sauntered off.

Cursing the cat, Charlie spun on his heels. Julius was giving him a most peculiar look.

"Why were you yelling and spitting at that cat?" he asked.

"For luck," said Charlie quickly. Then: "Oh, my—look! What's going on?" He found himself looking down at the tiny arch ahead of them. They were heading right for it.

"We can't go in there!" he cried. "It's tiny!"

It wasn't so much tiny as far away, far down. It looked like a manhole. Charlie had a moment of panic. It was too steep! How could they go down so far in such a short distance? They seemed to be tumbling and sinking into the bowels of the earth.

Even when the lock chamber was empty and the gates at the other end opened, the ship was still way too big and the arch still way too low. It would be like crawling into a small cave, a dark little entrance to the Underworld. But as they edged out of the lock chamber, he realized they were just entering another. This was a double lock, a steep set of watery stairs, and they were now going even deeper into this dark, wet hole. Charlie couldn't help thinking about the story of Orpheus, who went down to the Underworld to get his wife, Eurydice, back from the land of the dead. But his parents weren't here to get. They'd already left.

The damp, wet, dangerous hole matched his mood precisely.

Suddenly all the sunlight was gone. In place of the lovely spring day they had just been enjoying with its blue sky and fluffy clouds, its red geraniums on wrought-iron balconies, the white shutters and black lampposts of Paris, they were surrounded now by slimy green walls and foaming yellow water. Looking back, Charlie could see the beautiful day disappearing behind them. A few wet, green ferns framed it as it slid away through the curved arch astern. They were going into a huge, dark, damp tunnel.

At first Charlie could see by the strong, beautiful stonework that it was really old, but then he could hardly see anything. There was a path along the right-hand edge, cobwebs dangling from the roof, and strange-looking skinny stalactites, black with white tips. He could feel the wetness, and smell the mildewy, watery old smell of it, and it chilled his bones. But he couldn't see much. He felt he was plunging into a wrong direction, a further journey, new problems. He had thought he had taken on the idea of Venice, but now he just felt as if he had no idea how to get there, what to do when he got there . . .

In front of the *Circe* the water was smooth and black; behind, it was dirty and foamy with their wake.

"Tunnel!" whispered Julius beside him. His voice echoed spookily, up to the roof, down to the water. "Napoleon built the canals, and then . . ." But Charlie wasn't listening to him. He was shivering. He didn't like it at all.

Then up ahead he saw an oval shaft of greenish-gold light drop from the roof to the surface of the water—and indeed through the ce: It lit up the smooth green water and transformed it into a milky column. For a moment it made Charlie think about the water was, and what it would be like on the bottom

162

of this underground canal. If the light had been at all comforting, this thought took all comfort away.

"What's that?" he whispered urgently to Julius. He didn't feel like hearing the echo again.

"Skylight to the road above," he said. "There's traffic and everything going on up there. The canal used to be open to the air like the first part, but they covered it over."

The skylight drifted away above them. As they passed under it Charlie craned his neck to look up: High above he could see sky through a metal grille, and a framing of leaves—the skylight must have been positioned in a garden or a park.

"Is it very long?" asked Charlie warily. He wanted to be outside again.

"Nope," said Julius. "Nearly there." The tunnel seemed to be curving. Charlie felt as if his stomach were being left behind, and maybe other parts of him too. He could see now that in fact the *Circe* herself was shining a light, up ahead, to see her way. Another weird, faded-looking skylight appeared in the roof, letting loose its spooky, glowing shaft before dropping away astern. The darkness closed around him again. And stayed.

Nearly there, Charlie thought. If only. And anyway, when I get there, then what?

Then another shaft of light. And another.

Looking back and forward, Charlie could see a pattern of arches and shafts of light, darkness and reflection, where the columns of light fell through from the outside world to the dim, smooth green water. It was beautiful, like molten glass ahead, and a rushing river behind. There were immense iron rings set into the stonework of the curved walls. If he'd reached up, he could have touched the crumbly stone ceiling.

"How nearly there?" asked Charlie softly.

Suddenly, a completely different kind of light, bright, electric, and colorful, appeared in the dank wall beside them: a panel, modern and shiny, flashing the words BIENVENUES AUX CANAUX DE PARIS. Welcome to the canals of Paris.

"Ha!" thought Charlie, not feeling at all welcome.

Above his head pigeons were cooing and pooing and nesting on iron girders. Then there was a brassy, glassy tunnel crossing their path overhead, with a train rushing through it—Bastille metro station.

And then they were spat out into the sunlight again—real, full, glorious, shining, warm, beautiful sunlight. Charlie was happy to be in it and out of the tunnel, but his low mood clung to him.

They were there: Port de Plaisance de Paris Arsenal, once the moat of the Bastille prison, where aristocrats went in the French Revolution to await having their heads chopped off, where prisoners trained rats to carry messages for them, and where people were jailed and forgotten about for years and years and years. The high wall on the right was the remains of that great fortress. It was pretty different now, crowded with pleasureboats and marketboats and cruisers and masses of people, and a park with playgrounds. But Charlie felt like a prisoner, a scared and desperate prisoner who has sworn to escape but . . . actually . . . doesn't know if he dares.

The crowds seemed to be expecting them. Residents came running out from their boats, popping their heads up out of their cockpits like gophers from their holes. The Lucidi family swung down to the quay even before the ship had docked, scattering fliers, and the Calliope started up again, wheezing and grunting like a senti- old man singing the dance tunes of his youth. Everybody on deck, waving and making a big noise to show that the circus was in town. Major Tib's voice came back to Charlie: "We are not *a* circus, boy—we are *the* circus, the finest and best, the most daring and the most astounding, the most magnificent show on earth! We are Thibaudet's Royal Floating Circus and Equestrian Philharmonic Academy!"

Later, everyone would eat, and rest, then they'd prepare themselves and their animals for the parade to take place that evening. All the work of the past few days—the mending and cleaning and practicing—was about to come to fruition.

The *Circe* swung around to dock. Looking back to the canal tunnel, Charlie could see, way above, beyond the metro platform in its glass tunnel and beyond the stone wall and the treetops, a golden winged figure that seemed to have landed with one elegant leg on top of a great tall column. With arms outstretched and wings flaring, it looked as if it might take off again at any moment.

"What's that?" he asked Julius.

"It's a monument to the French revolutions," said Julius. "That square is the Place de la Bastille, where the prison was, and that statue is in the middle."

"But what's the statue of?" said Charlie.

"Liberty," Julius replied.

Liberty. His parents' liberty seemed further off than ever. (It was lucky he could not see them at that moment, tied up in the back of the personnel department's van, racing south, bouncing down the highway.) The lions' liberty was a scary challenge to be achieved. Charlie felt hollow inside. For everyone else, all was fuss and excitement. For him, it was more work and more worry and more fear.

So Venice it was. They'd leave after the performance and head straight for the train. After lunch, Charlie was about to go and check out the lay of the land, and work out their route to the station, when Maccomo called him back to the lionchamber. "Here, boy," he said. "Put these on."

He tossed Charlie a bundle of clothes. A red velvet suit, with gold braid at the shoulders and down the front, and twisted gold down the side of the pants, and a pair of black boots too big for him. Charlie stared, and then he put them on.

Charlie had continued to give Maccomo some of the lions' medicine each day, and the trainer had changed visibly. He was less controlled, less quietly intelligent. Before, he had looked as if nothing in the world would ever worry him; now he was moody and inconsistent. It didn't make him less frightening.

Maccomo looked at him in the outfit. "Good enough," he said, and then taking Charlie roughly by the head, he swiftly wrapped something around him, twisting and tucking, and when Charlie stood straight again, he found he was wearing a turban.

"Good," he said. "In the parade you ride your friend."

There was silence for a moment.

"I what?" said Charlie, bewildered.

"You ride your friend," said Maccomo simply.

"What friend?" said Charlie, hoping very much that Maccomo did not mean what he thought he meant.

"Your friend the lion," said Maccomo. "Him." He gestured shortly. The young lion stared sleepily ahead, his nose on his paws. He seemed not to notice that he was being gestured at.

"But I . . . I can't," stuttered Charlie. "I can't ride a . . ." When he'd said to Major Tib that he could do a handstand on a lion's back, he'd been joking, of course. You can't do things like that. A lion is a wild animal. A creature of strength and dignity who could, and quite possibly would, rip you to shreds and eat you. Just because these lions were in a circus didn't wipe out their lion instincts.

"I know," said Maccomo, "what you can do." His face was as still as stone and his expression blank, but his eyes were twitching.

Charlie's knees went a little weak.

"I know exactly," said Maccomo. "I have heard you."

What had he heard? And had he understood?

"So you say to your friend that you are riding him today," said Maccomo. "And then you ride him. In the parade. And then for the show, I will tell you later what you are to do."

"But—" said Charlie. He didn't know what to say.

Maccomo suddenly moved close to him. "Do you think," he said, very quietly, "that you are the first ever to have spoken to them? Do you really think some little London boy would be the only person ever in the history of the entire world to have that gift? Why would it be you, little boy? Why? *Why?!*"

And Charlie knew, suddenly, that Maccomo was jealous; that when he said "Why you?" he was really saying "Why wasn't it I, Maccomo, who was given this gift?"

Maccomo gave himself a little shake and was calm again. "You will be my translator, little boy. We will make the finest lionshow the world has ever seen. And it starts tonight." He narrowed his eyes a little. "I did not believe for a while that you had this thing," he said, "or I would have started work sooner with you. But when I saw you this afternoon, calling to that alleycat by the canal . . . well. Tomorrow—we will come up with something fabulous for tomorrow. Or after tomorrow. I have plans, little Lionboy. We can . . . we can . . . oh—and after the show, you will put the lions to bed. I'm going out."

His eyes were gleaming, and Charlie knew in that moment that Maccomo had received the message from Mabel. The message not from Mabel. And he knew that whether or not Mabel went to Chez Billy after the show, Maccomo would go, and that was all that Charlie needed.

And with that knowledge, Charlie didn't care what Maccomo thought. After all, after tomorrow night, they wouldn't be here.

"Okay," he said, very quietly.

"So tell him," said Maccomo with a little smile.

Charlie looked up at him nervously. "What?"

"Any reason why not?"

Charlie was silent. It felt very peculiar, after hiding from Maccomo so long, and hiding the fact that he could speak to cats for so long, to be suddenly ordered to talk in this way.

He couldn't, just couldn't, admit his ability to Maccomo. Everything in him shrieked "No!" But he had to do something.

He swallowed, and then he went over to the young lion and spoke, very quietly so that Maccomo would not see or hear him, into the lion's ear.

Then, "Young lion," he said, in English.

The young lion did not respond. He didn't even flicker a whisker.

"Young lion," Charlie said, "Monsieur Maccomo believes I can talk to you. I don't know what to do—how to show him it's a crazy idea. Anyway, he said to tell you I'm supposed to ride you in the parade this evening. I, er . . ."

"Speak Lion, boy!" shouted Maccomo. "Don't try to make a fool of me!" He was rubbing his temple. Charlie hoped he still had a headache.

"Er, roarrr!" said Charlie. "Meow, roaarrr—I can't, sir! I don't know what you want from me!" He tried to look as if he were about to burst into tears.

The young lion yawned, and covered his nose with his paw.

Maccomo was watching them intently.

"And?" he said.

"And what?" said Charlie, trying not to let it sound rude.

"And what did he say?"

"Mr. Maccomo, sir," said Charlie desperately, "I don't know what—I can't talk to lions, sir! Why would I? How could I?"

"You can," said Maccomo shortly. He fingered his rhinoceros-skin whip. "And you are going to teach me."

At that moment, Charlie became heartily glad that he was leaving the circus, and realized that he would have no regrets at all.

Of course, the moment Maccomo left the chamber, Charlie and the lions had a great deal to say to one another: on the urgency of their having to leave, on going directly to the station to get the train to Venice, on whether Sergei would reappear before they left, and on the precise plans.

"The people will leave after the show from the gangplank amidship," said Charlie. "The one opposite the grand staircase. Everybody will be up there, or below, cleaning up. Now, if we come out of this chamber and immediately cut around behind it, we can leave the ship by the stern."

"How do you suggest we get ashore?" asked the oldest lion. Now that he was back in form, the young lion was far less chatty. The lionesses still just stared and lounged around. Charlie had no idea what was going on in their heads, but he was beginning to suspect that maybe a great deal was, and they just weren't letting on.

"I've been thinking about that," he said respectfully. "And

knowing your great physical skills and circus experience, I was wondering whether . . . whether you would be able to walk the rope that attaches the ship to the quayside. It's not very far, I checked, and the rope is tight . . ."

The yellow lioness flicked her whiskers.

"You want us to walk the tightrope?" said the oldest lion with a note of amusement in his voice.

"Yes, sir," said Charlie. "If—if it's not too . . ." He meant to say something about "if it's not too undignified," but it seemed disrespectful even to mention the lions' dignity.

The oldest lion gave what would from anybody else be a little giggle. "I imagine we can do it," he said. He looked around at the others. His mane was thicker, his eyes brighter, the black of his lips shinier than before. He was better. The lionesses yawned disdainfully, and the younger lions just raised their elegant lion eyebrows and twitched their whiskers back and then forward again. Walking a little bit of tightrope was not the slightest problem to them.

"Excellent," said Charlie. "Then, once on the quayside, just follow me down the towpath to the river, across the bridge to the station, and we'll find the train. It'll be dark, and late. There'll be no one on the towpath or by the riverbanks, and it's hardly lit anyway. The bridge'll be the risky bit, but again, it should be empty by then . . ."

His heart sank. Look at them! They're huge! How was he going to get six lions across a bridge in the center of a city without being seen, even in the middle of the night? Yikes! He hoped everybody in Paris would be drunk, or in bed—or at the circus.

"Then at the station, I've thought about that, if we come in on the tracks rather than the platforms, we shouldn't see anybody, but we'll still reach the train. If we lose each other, we can make our own way . . . and we've got an hour to get over there, before it leaves at half past midnight. Most of the passengers will already be on board, because it opens at ten so they can go to bed early and all that . . ." He ground to a halt.

"And have you booked our seats? Isn't that what humans do?" said the oldest lion with a smile.

"No, sir," said Charlie, worried for a moment, before he realized the lion was teasing him. "No, sir," he said again, smiling, "but I have got a plan for where we'll travel . . ."

And Charlie and the lions talked, softly, late into the night, finalizing their plans.

The plan was full of pitfalls. Charlie was terrified.

CHAPTER 15

~

Charlie led the circus parade that evening.

When, at Maccomo's insistence, he had pretended to try to get on the young lion's back, the young lion had turned around and swiped at him viciously, leaving a great scratch down the side of his face. It hurt a lot (later the lion had apologized—he hadn't meant to do it so hard), but it put Maccomo off—for the moment—and that was what mattered.

So instead, clad in red velvet, gold braid, and black boots that shone like polished licorice, Charlie walked beside the lions, who were tethered with heavy, heavy chains to a great metal bar that rolled behind them. Ringboys danced ahead to clear the way, and the rest of the circus gave them plenty of room behind. The crowds gasped and flinched when they saw the six great beasts and the brown boy walking among them.

They led the entire circus along the riverbank past the island with the great cathedral of Notre Dame where the hunchback lived, down the Rue de Rivoli past the Tuilerie Gardens to the Place de la Concorde, down the Champs Elysees to the Arc de Triomphe, and then back again, followed by the zebras and the horses, the Learned Pig pulling the twins in a little chariot, the Hungarian wearing his performing bees as a beard, the dancing girls and the bearded lady, Pirouette and the cowboys and Major Tib on his fancy black stallion, the Lucidi family turning somersaults and cartwheels, and the band in their pale blue suits playing all the show tunes and marches in their repertoire, drums rolling and saxophones parping and glinting in the sun. They all called out and sang and handed out fliers. They were pretty tired when they got back to the ship, but as Major Tib said in his speech when they returned, "Now everybody in Paris knows we're here, and they'll come, and they'll all bring their friends."

Then, when everyone went to bed, Charlie tried again to go out and check the route to the station—but again Maccomo called him back.

"I'm tense, boy," he said. "I've been throwing up. Massage my neck." So Charlie had to rub Maccomo's strong, wiry neck and shoulders.

Everyone was tense. Tomorrow, the Premiere, the Big One, the first night. Excitement and anticipation roiled and coiled around the ship like vines, like smoke. Tomorrow, at last, they'd be doing the Show.

Charlie was tense too. But he knew what he had to do, and that made him calm. And in the meantime, despite everything—Rafi, his parents, Maccomo, the Allergenies, the imminent escape—he was really, really looking forward to seeing the Show.

Because he had never seen the Show before, Charlie was allowed by Major Tib to join the ringboys, who crouched right at the ringside, at the bottom of the aisles, ready to jump up and clear up between acts. Of course when the lions came on, Charlie would have his own work to do, but in the meantime he could just squat down there and watch.

First came the audience. What a crowd! They came rolling down the cobbled ramp from the Place de la Bastille to the quayside, and they were glorious: swanky ladies in big skirts, fat men in white waistcoats with sashes and medals, dangerous-looking fellows in long dark coats and high boots, children and mothers and fathers, skaters and punks, tough-looking big boys in worn leather pants, a gaggle of beautiful young girls carrying balloons and flowers and presents, laughing and obviously celebrating something, red-faced people up from the country, soldiers, a priest. They were of all colors, and spoke all languages: Some Charlie recognized—English and French of course, and some Arabic—but others might have come from Mars. Charlie peered around, looking for a lady who might be a tiger trainer, who even if she wasn't actually wearing white leather looked as if she might, but no one stood out.

The Imperial Ambassador's party had taken over the Great Box, and were the grandest and sharpest of all. Major Tib was up there with them, shaking their hands and clicking his heels and kissing the hands of the ladies. With the Calliope creaking away (luckily it was not so noisy inside the ship) and the gabbling of the crowd as they settled into their seats, the smell of the fresh sawdust from the ring, and the gentle glow of the yellow lights shining down, Charlie wished that he had no troubles—that he could just be an excited kid at a circus.

The music from the Calliope was fading now, and the chattering of the crowd faded too. The lights began to dim and a hush fell over the ring, over the ranks of people looking down on it and over the performers waiting beyond the curtains for their moment to come on and dazzle the crowd.

As darkness fell in the big top, there was a long moment of silence. The audience seemed to breathe as one in the dark.

Then a drumroll broke out, loud and bright:

Trumdada
dumdada dumdada
DUMDUMDUM
dada
DUM DUM DUM!

At the exact moment that the band broke into a gay gallop, swirling, sweeping spotlights in different colors appeared way up above and cast their rays around the ring, garlands and paper streamers fell from the roof in twirls of color and a troupe of scarlet-and yellow-clad tumblers began to leap and vault from the four entrances of the ring into the center. One by one they hurtled in from different directions, lit by the spotlights, bouncing off their hidden springboards and somersaulting onto the mattresses in the middle. They missed one another by inches, it seemed, then leaped up, bowing and grinning, and ran back into the shadows at the edge of the ring to come bouncing in again. Some beautiful piebald ponies were brought in, and the tumblers bounced right over them, landing safe as cats, arching their bodies and flinging their arms back in delight at their own skill.

As the acrobats took their bows, bending in the middle and dropping their heads to their knees, or doing splits as if they were pieces of rubber, Major Tib came striding into the ring in a bright spotlight of his own, gorgeously costumed in a midnight blue tailcoat with shining gold buttons, white buckskin breeches, and black leather riding boots. He was holding his long elegant whip, and in ringing tones he proclaimed: "Ladies and gentlemen, *meine damen und herren, mesdames et messieurs,* welcome to Thibaudet's Royal Floating Circus and Equestrian Philharmonic Academy, the Show of Shows, the Night of Nights: Tonight for your education, your delectation, your temporary perturbation, and your ultimate satisfaction we have the pleasure, the honor, the unparalleled ardor to bring you the show you have all been waiting for . . ."

His honeyed voice was as fine and round as a bell. He told the crowd what acts would appear, and how fabulous they would be, he cracked his whip, he blew his whistle, he threw back his manly shoulders and twirled his dashing mustache, and all the men in the audience rather wished they were a bit more like Major Thibaudet, while all the ladies in the audience rather wished their boyfriends and husbands were. Charlie could see that the ringboys meanwhile were sweeping up the streamers and garlands, and pulling the leapers' mattresses out of the ring, in the darkness, while from the spotlight Major Tib extolled the magnificence of the show that was about to start.

It began with twelve zebras waltzing in rows of three to a beautiful tune called "Zizu's Waltz," their plump little bodies glossy and fat, and their strangely ancient-looking heads adorned with black and white plumes. They bent their striped knees, to-ing and fro-ing, making the prettiest striped black-and-white patterns as they crossed and recrossed one another. Then the lighting changed color, which changed the color of their white stripes, and they made pink patterns, then blue, then green, and then a mist slid out over the ring from the dry ice machines, and the zebras arranged themselves in a circle, all facing inward, bowed to one another, and carefully lay down as the mist rose up to cover them, for all the world as if they were going to sleep, and the beautiful sad tune was taken up by a lonely saxophone.

The lights turned to the inside of the great striped roof of the big top. Snow was falling from the roof—but going up too—swirling—only it wasn't snow, the flakes were too big: It was fluttering doves, all different colors. And rose petals. Falling and floating. Everyone gazed, entranced, as the doves and petals swirled and settled around the sleeping zebras.

Not even Charlie had noticed what was going on meanwhile up in the flies: The wireguys had been preparing the next act, which Major Tib came back out to introduce.

"Ladeeeez and gentlemen," he roared, "tonight, *ce soir,* here in Paris at Thibaudet's Royal Floating Circus and Equestrian Philharmonic Academy you are about to witness the wonderful, you are about to experience the exceptional, you are about to be implicated in the impossible, for tonight, *mesdames et messieurs,* we have with us for your amusement and astoundment the one, the only, the world-famous, unique and irreplaceable Devil of the Air, el Diablo Aero, *funambuliste extraordinaire,* the man who can live his entire life on a wire as thin as your neckchain, madam"—here he gestured magnificently to a lady in the front row—"and as high as the regard in which the Imperial Ambassador holds his wife"—here he gestured magnificently toward the Great Box, and carried on without taking a breath. "In short, ladeeeeeeeez and gentlemen, without further ado, I give you—el Diablo Aero!"

Way up in the big top the wire was stretched taut as a guitar string across the expanse of empty space, and at one end there was Aero, looking quite superb in a silver leotard with silver legs, holding his long, drooping balancing pole, and pointing one of his toes with inexpressible elegance.

First he just stood there for a while, looking fabulous. Then he ran along the wire, just to show it who was boss. Then he danced along it, hopping and skipping, and he kicked off his shoes. Then two girls came out to join him, also in silver leotards: the twins! They tied a blindfold around his head, and blindfolded, he trotted across the wire. Then he put the twins in a wheelbarrow and wheeled them across. Then he got out a little stove and cooked an omelet up there, flicking it like a pancake; then they made a big hoo-ha of inviting a fellow up from the audience. In fact, one of the Imperial Ambassador's party was very keen to come, so he was helped into the ring, trying to look tough and confident, and then he climbed up the rope ladder to the flies, and then when he reached the platform, el Diablo Aero had a word with him, then lifted him up on his back, and carefully, gently carried him piggyback over the high wire to the tiny platform on the other side. Charlie was consumed with envy.

But now what?! Instead of bringing him back again, el Diablo had scampered back across the high wire, leaving the fellow stranded! There were no rope ladders on the other side; indeed there was no way down . . . El Diablo and the twins were laughing, but goodness knows what the Imperial Ambassador's guest thought. Charlie bit his knuckle.

El Diablo was gesturing to the man to walk back across, but the fellow, seemingly in good humor, was shaking his head and gesturing "no way." El Diablo beckoned to his reluctant guest, but he would not be moved. Finally he took hold of a violin and began to play a sad and beautiful tune, full of minor chords crunched against one another like the beating of a broken heart. Indeed he played so tragically that people nearly forgot he was standing on a high wire way, way up in the air, trying to tempt a member of the audience to walk the wire himself.

Even danger itself is dazzled by how beautiful and clever the circusguys are, thought Charlie, and so it forgets to knock them down, or break their necks, or have a tiger bite their heads off.

By now a clown had entered the ring, imitating el Diablo Aero: Julius's dad! There he was, elegant in whiteface, Pierrot clothes, and a mischievous manner. He was playing his gigantic fiddle behind his back, doing somersaults with it, playing it between his legs—then running up to the top of a ten-foot ladder to play a duet with Aero, still up on his high wire trying to lure the man across.

By the time they were all down in the ring again, the music had turned bright and parping, and suddenly Bikabhai and the monkeys came in on bicycles. They were all wearing beautiful, white silky pajamas and white turbans with a peacock feather attached by a jewel at the front, and their bicycles were peacock blue. They did somersaults and carried one another around, waving parasols and pretending to smoke pipes. They picked up the rose petals from the ground and gave them to Bikabhai, and then to members of the audience, and then two of them got in an argument and began eating the roses.

The clowns were still acting foolish like nobody's business. "Here we are again, all of a lump!" they cried. "How are you?" Major Tib came in after them: "If you please, Major Tib," said one of the fat ones, "he says that you said that I said that they said that nobody had said nothing to nobody!" Julius's dad had meanwhile set up a tiny little high wire and had rats running along it, dancing, and stopping to eat the chocolates he was feeding them. "Who needs to cook?" he was saying. "Cooking's fancy. Cooking's showing off." And he gave one of the rats his cell phone and said it was calling for takeout, and then he was trying to invite one of the ladies from the audience to join him for dinner, paying her extravagant compliments.

When it's not being dangerous, it's just silly, Charlie thought. What a funny mixture. And then in a rush he remembered that this, the rats on the high wire, was his cue. He leaped to his feet, heart pumping like a piston, and, feeling proud and glad, he vaulted into the ring. He knew exactly what to do, and so like a professional he began to pull the polished levers and wind the well-worn handles that would bring down the ring cage, for the next act was Maccomo and the lions.

Charlie had wondered how he would feel about watching the

lions perform. He knew what they would do—he'd seen it often enough in rehearsal. But it would be different to see them do it in front of a crowd, as if it were all they could do, and as if Maccomo were incredibly brave and clever to have "taught" them to roll on the floor, and let him pick up their paws, and to roar when he told them to. As if they weren't really incredibly much cleverer than this and only humoring Maccomo because he fed them—and because he had fed them drugs, more to the point. Charlie had thought he would find the whole thing a bit humiliating for them, and a bit embarrassing.

But he didn't—far from it. He was enchanted by how strong and graceful his friends were as they entered the ring, staring down their snooty noses, and as they leaped around the ring. Maccomo looked wonderfully stern and brave in his long African robe with his rhino whip, taking the lions by the paws and making them roar, throwing their strong bodies down on the ground and lying on them. When he turned his back on the young lion for a moment, Charlie genuinely feared for his safety; when he harnessed the old lion to a small chariot, and stepped into it to drive him, for a moment Charlie feared even more, because he knew what Maccomo did not, that the old lion had regained his dignity and would not care for this humiliating treatment any longer. But the old lion had also regained his intelligence, and he knew that in order to escape later, he had to be obedient now, so he put up with it even though he hated it—all this Charlie could see in his beautiful old furry face.

Then the lions pretended to fight, and Maccomo separated them, to gasps and shrieks from the more nervous members of the audience, and finally the lionesses did a magnificently effective trick called the Bounce, which used to be done in the old days before there were ring cages. In those days, wagon cages had to be rolled into the ring, and the trainer would go inside the cage with the lions, and they would bounce around on the cage's walls, running up one wall and down the other and so on. Now the band broke into the special lion tune—"Esprit du Corp" by Sousa—and the lionesses leaped up the side of the ring cage, not holding on with their claws, but bouncing from cage to ground and up the wall of the cage again, like a kitten on the back of a sofa. The audience shrieked to have the great cats leap toward them, and to hear the metal rattle and shake as the great weight of the animals crashed against it, to hear the growls and see the lionesses' great paws and sleek creamy bellies—it was fantastic, it was terrifying, it was magnificent. It was the circus.

And then came the intermission. Charlie was mighty glad. Between being in the audience and being in the show, and being constantly, silently, nervously aware of what he had to do later, he was already exhausted and exhilarated and overwhelmed—and it was only halfway through. And after that—well, he couldn't think about afterward yet.

As soon as he had stowed the ring cage and helped Maccomo to settle the lions, he just had time to sit quietly for a moment or two on the deck, breathing deeply, watching the moon with her calming stare, and reassuring himself that yes, that rope attached to the bow was the one down which they were going to run to avoid any crowds at the gangplank. And yes, they could get to the bridge quickly, and yes, it was all dimly lit, and the moon was not so big as to cast too much light, and yes, it was doable and they were going to do it. He wished he had been able to check the route all the way, but he had seen how the towpath led all the way to the river, so as long as they weren't spotted, how complicated could it be?

When Maccomo went to get himself a cup of coffee from the refreshment stand, Charlie got his bag from the ropelocker and made sure his few possessions were in there: the phones, the letter in blood, his medicine, his tiger, his knife, his mum's little ball of lapis lazuli . . . He looked at his phone. Ha ha, Rafi, he thought. You didn't know where I was. Did you? You didn't come and get me. He stowed as well the bits of food he had been saving from the last few meals and the packages of meat he had purloined for the lions. He just hoped it wouldn't leak in his bag. It was all quite heavy, but the lions could help carry.

He was very, very excited.

CHAPTER 16

❧

On his way back to the ring for the second half, Charlie saw Maccomo, who had showered and changed out of his circus robe into an exceptionally clean and well-ironed pair of stiff white African pajamas—up-and-downs, as Charlie's dad called them. He was on the grand staircase with a woman.

She had red hair piled up on her head and escaping in curls down the sides, and her skin was like a pearl. Charlie could easily imagine her in a white leather suit.

Mabel!

They seemed to be getting along just fine. Mabel was doing something with her eyes that Charlie thought might be what was called "batting her eyelashes"—he'd heard the phrase but he didn't think he'd ever seen it done before. It was rather nice actually. Charlie stared at her for a while. He wondered if they were going to go off now, before the show had ended. Would it matter if they did? He didn't know. Might they finish eating early and come back too soon?

On a whim, he rushed up to them.

"Good evening, Maccomo, sir," he said. "Good evening, madam."

Maccomo looked at him as if he were insane.

"The show is so wonderful, isn't it? You must get back to your seats—you don't want to miss the second half. It's starting any minute. You should really be getting back, madam!" He grinned idiotically and sort of shepherded Mabel back toward the ring. Maccomo was confused. The old Maccomo would have responded immediately, sending Charlie off with a scolding, but this new, dopey Maccomo just sort of watched, and then followed as Mabel, with an amused look, allowed herself to be led back into the big top and toward her seat. No sign of a Hungarian in tall boots. Charlie smiled madly. Maccomo seemed to be going to sit with Mabel. Good. Mabel said, and her voice was low and beautiful: "Thank you so much. You're a considerate child."

Charlie thought it must be rather nice to be one of her tigers.

Once he was certain they were sitting down and staying put, he hurried around to the narrow, crowded back stairway to get back to his ringside position.

Once again the band fell silent.

Once again the big top fell dark.

Once again the drums rolled—

And the spotlight fell on Major Tib, who—well, you know what he does by now, and he did it magnificently, of course, and then he leaped swiftly out of the way as Hans came prancing out with his little Learned Pig. First they did math: Hans would ask "What is five minus three?" and the Learned Pig would stamp his foot twice; Hans would say "What is two times two?" and the Learned Pig would stamp four times. "Stamp once for yes, and twice for no," said Hans. "Am I very clever?" The pig stamped twice. The audience laughed and laughed.

After a bit of this, Hans said: "So, Learned Pig, who is the most beautiful lady in the audience?" The Learned Pig immediately ran over to a smiling dark girl—one of the ones with the flowers and balloons—and bowed down in front of her. The girls giggled and whispered. They thought it very funny that the pig thought she was beautiful.

Someone else didn't find it funny, though: Julius's father, the clown, who had been quietly watching the math, was offended.

"My lady is much more beautiful!" he cried, waving to his dinner date, but adding "No offense, signorina" to the Learned Pig's lady and blowing her a kiss. The Learned Pig didn't like that at all—he squealed and rushed at Julius's dad, trying to knock him over. Julius's dad didn't like *that:* He made Hans go and fetch Major Tib, who thought about the problem very picturesquely, holding his folded whip to his brow in deep thought, and finally suggested that they fight a duel to settle the matter. He gave the clown and the pig a pistol each (the pig took his in his mouth), then he blindfolded the clown, and Hans blindfolded the Learned Pig. Julius's dad complained that the pig was peeking. The pig squealed in indignation at the suggestion. Then they lined up, back to back, and Major Tib counted to ten for them to walk away from each other. Finally there were two shots, and both clown and pig fell down. The clown jumped up again, but the pig didn't.

"Are you dead?" the clown asked the pig. The pig quietly opened his eyes and looked around, then got up very gently and stamped once, then lay down again with his eyes closed. "You don't mean it, you don't mean it!" cried the clown. "Say you don't mean it! Stamp again! Make it two for no!" Hans joined in the pleading, and so did Major Tib, but to no avail—the pig insisted he was dead.

"Well then, Signor Pennacorrente," said Major Tib. "That's murder! You'll go to court and be sent to jail forever and ever! Or longer!"

Julius's dad rolled over onto his knees and wrung his hands and wept; Hans was blowing his nose and weeping too, and stroking his poor "dead" pig.

"You'd better run away," said Major Tib, "and take the body with you!" So they rolled the pig into a sack and the clown started dragging it across the ring—quite a heavy job, you can imagine.

Suddenly the end fell out of the sack—and there was the pig in a flowery bonnet, looking furious, bouncing with good health, and chasing after Julius's dad until he caught his shirttails between his teeth. The shirttails turned out to be about forty feet long, and each time the pig pulled more out, it was a different color. By now most of the audience, including Charlie, were laughing so hard, they couldn't breathe properly, and at least four people had fallen off their seats.

Major Tib had to give them a little while to calm down before introducing the next act. Charlie was completely seduced. For a moment, he was just a kid at the circus.

As the people gradually stopped laughing and caught their breath, the lights dimmed, and a long, pure, high note was heard, as if from a distant trumpet. Major Tib, in a calm and almost trance-like tone, called out like a voice from way above: "There's magic in the air tonight—here—can you feel it? There's magic in the air!" The trumpet note was still playing—it sounded like a shaft of light—and then an actual shaft of light flew out and lit up one of the high-wire platforms up in the flies, and there was the trumpeter, dressed in white, but though the note could be heard, he wasn't playing. A second shaft of light appeared—and in its pool was caught the other platform, and there stood another trumpeter, identical to the first, playing the long and slow note. Then he took his trumpet from his lips, and the note continued—it was the first trumpeter, who now was playing. The note passed between the two of them and it was impossible to tell which one was making the sound. . . . Golden pricks of light appeared like stars on the great rounded ceiling of the big top, and the two platforms rolled back toward the edges of the ring, leaving a third standing empty and spotlit way up among the stars.

"MAGIC, LADIES AND GENTLEMEN!" cried Major Tib, and the lights flared up to reveal a huge green-bronze cannon in the ring below, with a bunch of men fussing urgently around it, a flash of fire, a cry, a crashing explosion, a cloud of smoke shooting out, and flying through the air toward the platform, a streak of gold, a zooming bird, a figure—

And then, landing on the platform, clutching the rope supports with a gasp and a flex of golden muscles, was a beautiful girl with sleek brown skin and sleek black curls pulled back tight from her intent, alert face. She was dressed in a sleek gold suit and was smiling broadly, looking for all the world as if being shot from a cannon and landing on a small platform a hundred feet up in the air was her idea of perfect fun.

Charlie barely recognized her.

"The one and only, the beautiful and magical, mystical, adorable—Miss Isabel Andart, known to her phalanxes of fascinated fans as the fabulous, the fearless PIROUETTE!" cried Major Tib. "Ladies and gentlemen, this girl can *fly!*"

The band broke into a fine habañera, trapezes fell from the roof, and Pirouette focused her mind, filled her lungs, bent her knees a little, flung her strong arms up to heaven, and leaped out into the abyss.

Well, she caught her first trapeze and twirled around on it for a while; then she stood on her hands, wedged her legs against the ropes, and brought the trapeze to a standstill. Another trapeze flew toward her out of the darkness—someone must have been up there controlling them—and she flipped over and caught it with her legs, so she was hanging upside down again by her knees and swinging gently, like a flower on a tree in a gentle breeze. How beautiful and hypnotic it was. The music slowed. She looked so comfortable and calm. Everybody sighed.

And then the habañera started up again, trapezes began to fly at her—some with people hanging from them by the knees—and she began to fly around the roof of the tent, from one trapeze to another, caught here by a catcher's hands, being flung there to another, catching herself with arms and hands or knees and feet. She flew through hoops, and through hoops covered with paper (how could she know where she was going to end up? She couldn't see!). Charlie could see the sweat on her face, and the tension, and the look of absolute joy as she swung away again and the hands released her to fly on to another trapeze below, where she built up more swing, until it was reaching the horizontal and higher, and she took another great leap, somersaulting in midair as she went, to yet another trapeze. She was fabulous. She *could* fly!

Then she and the catchers were swinging and leaping around the roof in a giant game of trapeze tag, and each time she caught one of the men—for she was by far the quickest—they tumbled and somersaulted down, down, down from the Kingdom of the Flying

Trapeze to the solid ground below, like angels falling from heaven, or birds banned from the sky. Pirouette alone remained on high, swooping more slowly now, until she raised herself to stand on the big central trapeze, beautiful and exhausted, her curls escaping and sweat streaming down her face, looking as gloriously happy as anyone Charlie had ever seen in his life.

The trapeze rose up, and she disappeared into the shadows of the roof. Charlie gazed, dumbstruck. He couldn't say a word.

She seemed to have had the same effect on the next act. Three clowns came in, gazing upward in adoration, calling to her, waving and beckoning, jumping up to be with her, crashing down again, bumping into one another and finally all lying down on the floor in paroxysms of unrequited love.

Then a big green-and-gold cage-wagon full of snakes rolled in, and a belly dancer took a couple out and danced with them. The clowns got scared, and then she let out a huge snake, so the clowns ran away, in a very comical manner. The huge snake was dancing along the ground, rippling and sinewy, and then suddenly it started flexing and thrashing about—what was it doing? It was a powerful mover—and then Charlie realized what was happening. It was shedding its skin. The whole patterned slinky surface was shimmying and rippling down from the snake's body.

So what was underneath?

For a moment Charlie was scared.

Something pale was emerging.

"Arrghhh!" cried Charlie, before he could stop himself. And he wasn't the only one to yell, not at all.

The shivery snakeskin fell away. The pale, naked snake body slithered on the ground for a moment, then with one last great thrash it reared its head and rose up to its—feet?

It was standing up.

On legs.

Waving to the crowd.

With its arm.

It was Bendy Ben, the India rubber boy.

The crowd cheered as only a crowd that had been genuinely frightened and was now genuinely relieved could cheer.

So then Bendy Ben did his bendy act, during which, among other things, he sat on his own head and fed himself with his feet, using a knife and fork. Julius had told Charlie that Bendy Ben had sold his skeleton to a clinic in the Empire Homelands for a hundred thousand pounds. Charlie had assumed that the clinic would get it after Bendy Ben died, but looking at him now Charlie wondered if he had had his skeleton surgically removed, and was held together inside with bits of elastic.

Charlie glanced across to where Mabel and Maccomo were sitting.

Oh dear, where were they?

He looked around. He couldn't see them.

His heart thudded.

No, stay calm. Search the crowd. Look carefully, scan across.

Scanning. Looking.

He found them. Maccomo was in his seat. He must have been bending down. Mabel was working her way back down the row of seats. She'd been to the restroom or something. That was okay. Charlie would have been more worried if it had been Maccomo who'd left.

But he could do without that kind of fright.

Meanwhile the Icarus Games had started, where Sigi Lucidi lay on his back and little Beppe Lucidi did acrobatics on his dad's feet, including a handspring, and then the Lucidi men lay on their backs in a circle, each with his hips propped up on a wedge-shaped thing called a trinka, and they juggled their children between them so that the kids flew from one set of feet to another, rolled up like little bundles as they flew. Then Hans came on with his kitten. It ran up a very tall pole and leaped off the top, with a parachute, floating sweetly back down to earth, meowing and twinkling its whiskers.

How sweet, Charlie was thinking, but then the air went out of his lungs and he gasped and froze.

Sitting with Maccomo and Mabel was a dark figure. Shaven-headed. Leather-coated.

Rafi.

Francis the cowboy rode in on a white horse, his monkey on his shoulder, guns blazing, and tried to kidnap Major Tib, shouting that he was Paul Pennacorrente's brother and he would have his revenge!

Charlie squatted like a frozen toad at the ringside. He couldn't move. He couldn't even think. He kept his face turned down, away from the circus lights, away from any chance of being recognized.

The trick riders were all riding in at once on their strong piebald horses, galloping after Francis and trying to catch him. The band was going crazy. But Charlie wasn't watching. He was hiding under his turban, desperately trying to gather his thoughts, desperate to look up again and check. Perhaps it's not Rafi. Perhaps it's some other young guy with a sleek shaved head and a black leather coat. And the same shape face, and the same cool look . . .

The ring lights dimmed for a moment as the rest of the trick riders disappeared and Francis took charge of their horses. Charlie risked looking up.

It was Rafi all right. Maccomo was talking to him and he was smiling, his eyes flickering around. Was he looking for something? Or someone?

The audience was cheering. The drumming of the hooves and the sweet salty smell of the horses came strong from the ring, and another smell, like pine—the smell of the sticky rosin that was rubbed on the horses' backs to keep the riders from slipping. Charlie felt sick. He stared down at the sawdust, breathed in the smell, and felt sick. Why was Rafi here? And if he had come for Charlie, why was he wasting time watching the circus? What was Rafi doing with Maccomo? How did they know each other? How long had he been there? Had he seen Charlie? Charlie had to assume he hadn't, because otherwise all hell would have broken loose . . .

Down in the ring, two trick riders were standing on horseback, leaping, driving banks of fine horses, doing laps and calling out how clever they were. Charlie was frozen in position, the cheering of the audience ringing in his ears. He wanted desperately to sneak away, but he didn't want to draw any attention to himself, and he wanted to keep an eye on Rafi too.

Oh—was his horrible dog with him? Was Troy going to come slobbering and snarling . . . No, Charlie remembered with relief. Dogs had to stay outside during performances.

The audience was cheering again. All except one person.

"What d'you call that? That's pathetic," this man called out.

Charlie stared dazedly at him. He seemed mad, or more likely drunk.

"I could do better," called the drunk, and, heaving himself up from his seat, he staggered down the aisle toward the ring. All around him people frowned and pursed their lips and cried "Oi! Behave!" The riders ignored him to start with, but as the pest started down to the ring and began shouting even louder, they reined in their horses, looked over to where the pest was, and started laughing.

Charlie wondered. Could this disturbance be an opportunity for him?

Think, Charlie, think! he urged himself silently, but his mind was too confused.

"I could do better than the lot of you!" shouted the drunk unclearly. He was rather bundled up, with a scarf and a hat he hadn't taken off, and a big beard.

The riders looked at him and laughed even harder. "All right!" cried one of them, Fabien. "Come on then, big boy! You catch Francis the sharpshooter, and we'll find a lovely reward for you!" Francis, laughing, took off around the ring, backward on his saddle for a better view.

Charlie, still frozen in position, was realizing miserably that there was nothing he could do. He put his hand to his eyes, and glanced up to the seats beyond. Maccomo and Mabel were watching the show with professional interest. Rafi was looking vaguely amused.

Fabien was sneering at the pest. He unhitched one of his pretty rosinbacks and handed over the reins, saying, "Here, why don't you start the easy way?" Whereupon the pest clambered up the horse—and toppled straight over it and down the other side. It would have been pretty funny . . . Then the pest managed to get up, but the moment the horse started moving, he fell down the side again and was hanging by one leg from the saddle. When he tried to hoist himself up, he went down the other side again, then he fell off completely. Fabien and Francis could hardly control their laughter.

Maccomo was leaning in toward Rafi, as if he were trying to interest him in something. Rafi was looking as if it was all a bit childish, really.

Well, thought Charlie, he's not looking at me, or for me, which means he doesn't know I'm here, because if he knew, he'd be looking. So that means Maccomo hasn't told him.

The pest, angry now, was tearing off his coat and jumping back on the horse, galloping halfway around the ring, and falling off again. This time he tore off his suit jacket, jumped back on, and fell off again immediately. His vest came off: He tried getting on from the other side, and failed, galloping around hanging over the saddle on his stomach like a sack of flour. The horse drew to a halt again, then took off again, rearing up so that the pest slid off backward and landed on his bottom.

So perhaps, thought Charlie, it's a coincidence.

Could it be?

Could it?

At that moment, Maccomo and Rafi both looked up and scanned the ringside. Maccomo pointed. Rafi stared and focused. On Charlie.

It seemed as if it was the weight of his heart lurching that flung Charlie back into the shadows just beyond the circle of ring lights. Had Rafi seen him?

Charlie's breath got short. He felt his shoulders tightening and his lungs shrinking.

Not now, he told himself. Not now, please . . . Keeping himself carefully in the shadows he reached for his inhaler and started doing his breath-control exercises.

Charlie's eyes were closed, counting his breaths. Calming himself, calming the asthma attack. He didn't notice when the pest threw himself up to stand on the horse's back. The horse looked as if it were about to take off again, but the pest uttered a great cry, tore off his hat and his long baggy shirt, and—

Charlie opened his eyes.

It was Madame Barbue standing on the horse, beautiful in a tiny, pale green sequined ballet outfit and tights, her beard curled and oiled, her arms bare and her toes pointed in their pretty slippers. "Alley-oop!" she cried with a gay laugh, and the horse, which seemed to be laughing too, took off around the ring, Madame Barbue balanced on its back, throwing her arms out and looking as elegant as you please.

Charlie breathed, slowly and gently. He kept his face well back. Nothing was happening over on the other side of the ring. No one had leaped across, shouting: "You uppity little squit, I'll get you . . ." Rafi, Mabel, and Maccomo were still in their seats, still watching the show.

Madame Barbue was gathering together all the horses that Fabien had been driving, and doing a tour of honor around the ring before scooping Francis up onto the horse behind her, and delivering him to Fabien with a flourish.

Charlie's breath began to settle. He seemed to have edged back up the aisle without even meaning to.

I will stick with my plan, thought Charlie. I have to. There's nothing else I can do. It's too complicated to try to change it. *I* have a lot of horses to keep in line too. An image sprang into his mind: the lions all hitched up in reins, and him driving them across the Seine to the station.

He smiled, and his smile made him brave.

And then it was the end of the show. All the horses and the zebras came into the ring, with colored lanterns on their backs, and took up their positions. They were forming, Charlie realized, a giant carousel: circling, dipping, and jumping in concentric rings going opposite ways, each one level up from the one outside it, so the form seemed to rise to a pyramid in the center like a wedding cake.

And there at the top, where the bride and groom would be, tiny white ponies circled a rearing black stallion. Garlands and balloons and streamers of all colors fell from the ceiling, glittering and glinting in the shaft of colored swirling light. Rose petals flurried about, the band played on, and the big top roof opened to the sky and fireworks streamed up into the starry darkness. Charlie would have been beyond delight, but instead he was on his feet and running.

CHAPTER 17

The lights came up, the applause died down, the audience was drifting up the grand staircase saying, "Wasn't that fantastic? Wasn't that wonderful? That bit when the . . . And how about when the . . . And that girl! I've never seen anything like it . . ." The last sparks of the fireworks were drifting back down to sink in the murky waters of the canal basin. Charlie, out on the deck, invisible in the shadows, heard them plop and fizz.

He saw Mabel and Maccomo, heads together, emerging from the main entrance with the crowd. Rafi was with them. He sauntered a step or two behind, with the dog Troy on a leash. Every now and again he leaned forward to say something. When he did, Maccomo turned back to him with an ingratiating smile. Charlie, keeping himself invisible in the crowd behind them, got the impression that Maccomo had arranged to meet Rafi, but didn't want him hanging around. He was being polite, though. It wasn't often that Maccomo took the trouble to be polite.

The trio headed out on to the gangplank.

"Go on, go on," breathed Charlie.

They were leaving.

Charlie ducked through the crowd and out into the gardens, where he was able to overtake them. Lurking in the shadow of the shrubbery, he could see their faces in the crowd. Mabel looked annoyed—she had wanted to be alone with Maccomo. Rafi had moved up, between her and the lion trainer, and was saying something. As they passed by Charlie's hiding place, Charlie strained to hear, but couldn't make anything out.

Then the men turned and, excusing themselves from Mabel, moved away from the path, the light, and the crowd. Charlie melted into the darkness. They were coming toward him. His heart pounding, he slipped behind a tree.

Rafi and Maccomo, in the shadows, hidden from the crowded path by a bush, were standing and pretending to pee. Charlie could see and hear them clearly. He could only hope that they could not see or hear him. He breathed lightly. His asthma attack had passed, and he felt fit and strong and ready.

"So, Maccomo," Rafi was saying. "If your lionboy can do what you say, then obviously I have clients who would be interested in that. Any genuine unusual talent, genetic variation, skills—that kind of thing can always sell. You know that. But I've got to know that it's genuine. I can't turn up with some trick—this is science, not the circus, know what I mean? So you enjoy your dinner with your young lady"—here Rafi seemed to suppress a laugh—"and tomorrow I'll come and have a look at him, and we'll see what we can do. All right?"

Charlie, deep in the shadows, gave a dark smile. So that was it. Maccomo had told Rafi about the Cat-speaking. Rafi sells skills and talent—so Rafi had stolen his parents in order to sell them. And now Rafi wanted to sell him too. Whom to? The same people who have his parents? That would be one way of getting to where they were . . .

Stupid . . .

But Rafi obviously didn't know that the Cat-speaking lionboy is Charlie Ashanti. How long before Maccomo lets slip Charlie's name, and Rafi realizes that the boy with the talent is also the boy he was after anyway?

The moment Maccomo tells Rafi my name, thought Charlie, I am in deep doo-doo.

Rafi was still talking. "So my compliments to Ms. Stark," he said smoothly, "and I'll see you tomorrow."

They started to move away, toward the bright lights. "By the way," said Rafi. "Where is he now?"

"What, the lionboy?" said Maccomo, in his soft voice. "He'll be back on the boat somewhere, maybe with the lions . . ."

"What's his name?" said Rafi.

"Sharlie. Ch—arlie."

"Charlie what?" said Rafi with a sudden alert look.

Charlie turned.

He heard Mabel's voice behind him, calling, "Come on, Maccomo, what's keeping you?"

He ran. Quicker than Rafi, because only Charlie knew that the race was on.

Straight to the ship, straight to the lionchamber.

Six sets of yellow eyes greeted him in the darkness of the cabin, and a new kind of energy awoke in him. He took the big, heavy old key from its hook, and unlocked the cages.

"How goes it, Lionboy?" came the voice of the oldest lion.

"Fine," said Charlie shortly. "Rafi is here. We're off. *Now!*"

The oldest lion heard the urgency in his voice. "Ride the young lion," he said. "Quicker."

Charlie didn't hesitate. It was true that a lion could not hide so well in the shadows with a boy on his back, but it was even truer that a boy is slower than a lion.

He grabbed his jacket, shouldered his bag, gave the youngest lion a grin, and slipped out the door of the chamber. All was quiet outside, just as he had expected.

But Rafi was out there somewhere, and coming for him.

Charlie made himself look around carefully, before letting the lions slide out, then closed the door behind them and locked it. He remembered his mum's lab door, open when it should have been shut, right at the beginning of this adventure: his first warning of danger. His heart was pounding like a woodpecker: quick, light, relentless.

Charlie could hardly see the lions as they slunk against the walls of the cabins, in the dark areas where neither moonlight nor lamplight fell. Over by the gangplank, the sounds of voices and activity bustled and hummed. Laughter came over the water, and the lights twinkled. Way above, along the boulevard above the basin, streetlights and people and traffic were going about their business. Behind them lay the ship, and the canal, and the way they had traveled so far. Ahead of them lay the run down to where the canal met the river, then the river itself, which they had to cross to get to the station.

The rest of the night was dark and quiet, cool and damp and rivery. The moon was still low.

The lions hooded their eyes and disappeared—no more than

dark shadows as they glided along the stern, breathing fresh air for the first time in months. It took no more than seconds for them to slide over the balustrade onto the rope, a few seconds more to slither across the rope to the shore. They didn't give a second glance to the dark space between the ship and the quayside, to the gleaming cold water at the bottom of the abyss, or the slimy green weed shining on the wall of the quay. Charlie, for a horrible moment, wondered how *he* was supposed to get over. Could he clamber across the horrible gap, clutching the nasty, rough, slippery, salty rope?

The young lion was beside him.

"On," he whispered urgently, his breath warm in the darkness, and Charlie was glad to climb onto his long back and lie clasped to him, smelling the warm, sweet, furry smell and feeling the muscles move beneath him as the lion, like a river made flesh, slid over the railings and across the rope.

"Go! Go!" urged Charlie, his hands caught up in the young lion's shaggy mane, his legs clutching tight to the golden back. Rafi could be under any tree, behind any bush. With luck he was on the ship, trying and failing to get into the lionchamber. But who could count on luck?

The young lion began to run, and Charlie realized he was panting. There was the shrubbery, and the shadows. He had counted on being safe hiding in the shadows, but now the shadows themselves held danger.

There was a shout behind them—angry, violent. His name: "Charlie! Charlie, you little graspole—"

Rafi. Definitely.

"Ignore it!" Charlie cried. "Go on!" The lions were quicker than Rafi—best to race ahead.

"Faster!" he hissed in the young lion's ear, and the young lion ran. So did the oldest lion. So did Elsina.

The lionesses did not.

They growled.

Behind him, as he hurtled through the damp night air, Charlie heard another shout, a human cry—a scream. A dreadful scream. And a splash. It chilled his soul.

He tried to look over his shoulder. "What was that?" he yelled. The young lion didn't slacken.

"Stop!" Charlie shrieked. "Don't!"

He didn't even know quite whom he was yelling to, or what he was telling them to stop.

All he knew, deep inside him, was the dreadfulness of that scream. Until he heard it, it had not occurred to him that the lions might not agree with him, might not obey him. Now that single sound reminded him: These are wild animals. They hunt for food. They've been locked up for years. That's an enemy chasing after them.

"Shut up," panted the young lion. "Shut up. Never mind."

Never mind?

Charlie closed his eyes and hung on for dear life. He had never seen the lions out in the open, with room enough to pick up their pace. They were quick. They were in the park alongside the Port de Plaisance in no time, hugging the walls and sprinting through the gaps. Rosebushes dangled their flowers above them; the high wall was to their left and the moored boats down to their right. In moments, they reached the end of the park. We have to go back, Charlie thought. We have to go back—that was a human being—

Yes, but it was Rafi—and Rafi wounded and in the water was better than Rafi strong and angry and coming after them.

Of course they couldn't go back.

Under the high walls at the far end of the basin, the lions ran swift and silent over the cobblestones, avoiding iron mooring rings and posts. The noise of the traffic drifted down to them from the boulevard as they lurched along in the damp basin. The old stone wall was set with iron gates and mysterious doorways; racing past, Charlie had no time to wonder where they led. He just held on tight. A flurry of ducks, disturbed and quacking, scurried into the water with an unnaturally loud splashing.

The final lock before the canal met the River Seine was under a bridge. Signs said no entry, *Pas de Pietons.* The lions swiftly sneaked under the bar and brought themselves to a halt in the silent darkness on the narrow footpath beside the canal, under the bridge.

"What happened?" gasped Charlie. "What have they done?"

The oldest lion gave him a curious look. "That was your enemy!" he said. "The one who stole your parents, you said. The one who threatens you."

"Yes," said Charlie, puzzled. It didn't seem that simple, though. "Yes, but . . ."

What if Rafi were dead? He didn't want to say it out loud.

The young lion cocked his head. Elsina was breathing fast and smooth, looking back to where her mother must be.

And where were the lionesses?

They all stared back the way they had come. No sound. Nothing to be seen.

The lock was right beside them: horribly deep, and horribly dark, and shiny, and close. The drop into the river, beyond the pale green metal lock gates, was even deeper and darker. Trickles of water seeped through the metal plates, making a small echoing noise. On one side of the thin-looking gates was high dark water; on the other a deep drop into blackness. Charlie, rolling from the young lion's back, kept himself close to the wall. He was grateful to find a cold, narrow metal handrail to hold on to. All they needed now was for someone to fall into that black abyss. He was glad they only had to go alongside the canal. Crossing it would have been even worse.

They breathed and rested for a moment. Above them, beyond the bridge, there was a second bridge over the canal, and then, almost immediately, another. They had to pass under all three before they got to the river, wide and swift and dark.

"Charlie?" said the oldest lion.

At that moment a thundering dragon roared across the next bridge. Instinctively, they all flattened against the damp wall, staring wildly at the monster as it passed. A few of the monster's eyes stared back—it was a metro train, full of people going home late. Some of them, staring out the window into the night, saw the reflective gleam of six yellow eyes, but they would never guess what it was that they had seen.

"Before another one comes," the oldest lion hissed.

"But the lionesses!" cried Charlie, his voice tangled.

"Trust them," said the oldest lion. "They're hunters. You mustn't be caught."

Charlie was not comforted to hear that they were hunters.

"Have they eaten him?" he whispered. Though Rafi was his enemy and meant him nothing but harm, he couldn't bear the thought . . .

"We are lions, Charlie," the oldest lion said softly. "We hunt. We eat."

Charlie stared at him.

Everywhere he looked in himself, he found fear.

"But we are not stupid," the oldest lion continued. "We eat at leisure. Not when we are escaping with our lives. We do not eat humans, on human territory. We are not stupid."

Charlie gulped. He was fooling himself if he thought he was in charge of anything here.

"Onward," said the oldest lion.

Just by the stern of the *Circe*, a lumbering, spitting shape was emerging from the dark, cold water, shattering the reflections of streetlights and circus lights into a thousand wet shards across the surface. His white hands clutched the stone blocks lining the quay, and he pulled himself heavily out of the water. His leather coat was soaked, and his face furious. His movements were stilted: One of his arms was weak, and in its hand he clutched a small clump of something wet and dark . . . a tiny handful of golden fur, sodden with the canal water.

As he came to standing, he wiped his pale face with his good arm, and then touched the bad arm. Even in the dim light, he could see on his fingers that the water dripping off him was mixed with blood.

"Troy!" he bellowed. A big slathery dog lolloped up to him, whimpering and limping from a wounded back leg.

He held out the clump of soggy fur to the animal's twitching nose. "Fetch," he said, and his voice was grim.

Charlie climbed slowly back onto the young lion's back. Though the lion was sure-footed, the towpath was narrowing and the water seemed just too close now. As the lion loped along, the black water raced past, just beneath his right legs.

Between the road bridge and the metro bridge a metal spiral staircase led up to street level to the left. A group of people went past on the road up there, laughing and playing around. Charlie and the lions ducked swiftly under the black, industrial-looking girders of the metro bridge. Had they been seen? A pigeon, confused by their presence there so late at night, flew suddenly out, flapping and flustering. Some small, black, fluttery shapes moved in the darkness. Bats.

Another small gap of sky, and then there was the third and final bridge over the canal: much bigger, more modern-looking—more of an overpass, a great concrete construction, twentieth-century probably, and the noise from it was thunderous as vehicles roared by overhead. The towpath continued underneath, and as they followed it out to the river, Charlie realized that he had made a big mistake.

The young lion and Elsina stopped abruptly.

The oldest lion, just behind, caught up with them.

The towpath, when they finally turned the corner and emerged from under the concrete overpass, led to a narrow ledge at the base of the great, high wall that separated the overpass from the river, and the ledge led not to the bridge over the river, the bridge they had to cross, but on and on as far as the eye could see, stuck between the deep mobile water of the Seine on the right and the forty-foot sheer wall sloping up to the left.

It was about a foot wide.

The bridge they needed, the bridge that crossed the river, was only a couple hundred yards away, but it was also a couple hundred yards above them, and there was no way up.

Charlie stared at it. The lions stared at it.

Charlie remembered again how his dad said it was good not to swear, because that way you kept the swear words for when you really needed them.

Charlie swore.

The mothers knew exactly what they were doing. The silvery lioness headed back the way they had come: onto the *Circe* and off down the mooring rope on the bow, then along the water's edge to the tunnel leading under the Bastille metro, back into the Canal St. Martin. When she reached the third skylight, only dimly lit by the streetlights from above, she paused, and breathed, and waited.

The bronze lioness went across the park until she came to the high wall. She sloped alongside it, passing the mysterious iron gates and doorways till she came to one that was open. She slunk in, and from within she climbed carefully onto the top of the door, where she paused, and breathed, and waited.

The yellow lioness, with blood on her claws, raced down to the lock, but she was too late to reach Charlie and the others. They had been here: She could smell them. And if *she* could, that dog would too. The yellow lioness flicked her whiskers, squatted down, and then she peed, a lot. She stared through the gloom, trying to make out the other side of the canal, but she couldn't see clearly. Then, elegantly, carefully, she picked her way across the slender top of the lock gate: cold, deep water on one side, twenty-foot drop into cold, deep water on the other. At the other side she checked—yes, a huge, rusty, spiked metal barrier bolted into the wall blocked the towpath on that side. Clearly, people were not meant to use this side. She flicked her whiskers again.

She had seen locks before. Her plan would work. She shivered, and she paused, and breathed, and waited.

They couldn't go back. They couldn't stay here. They couldn't do nothing. There was no time to think.

So were they going to swim? Charlie looked out at the Seine: wide, rushing, and undoubtedly cold.

He looked at the wall.

He looked at the ledge.

He thought of all that Sigi had taught him about balance and agility and trusting your body.

I have done handstands in the rigging of the *Circe,* he thought. I can do this.

"Come on," he said, and he started to lead the lions out.

"One moment," said the young lion. "Take my tail."

So the young lion led, and Charlie held on to his strong, wiry tail. Elsina and the oldest lion followed behind, treading carefully on their sensitive cat feet and using their tails to balance. Way above and beyond them the whole of the great city of Paris was carrying on, its lights and its people, its busy roads and its chattering restaurants, its trees and its late-night shopping, its cars and bars and trains and parties, its hospitals and stations and harbors and circuses, and all alone, in the heart of the city, this little procession of lions and boy walked slowly, carefully, invisibly along an eight-inch ledge between the water and the wall, and nobody knew they were there.

Way beyond Paris, at this very moment, though Charlie could not know it, his parents were being taken from a huge parking lot, through a beautiful, moonlit subtropical garden full of palm trees and huge rounded rocks with a stream trickling over them, into a large, complex low-lying building. Not that Magdalen and Aneba could see it—they were still blindfolded.

"Hi there!" exclaimed a pretty, smiling receptionist in the entrance hall. She had a plant on her desk and her eyes were blue and round, and her clothes extremely clean. She didn't seem to notice that the two guests were handcuffed and blindfolded, or that the three men from the personnel department were propelling them at gunpoint. She didn't even seem to know that it was the middle of the night.

"Hi there! We have an appointment with the Chief Executive," smiled one of the personnelguys. "New staff arriving!"

"Hey, welcome to the Corporacy Gated Village Community, where we embrace our aspirations!" the receptionist said cheerfully. "And you are . . . ?"

Aneba and Magdalen said nothing. They couldn't—they were still gagged.

"It's Professor Start and Dr. Ashanti!" said the other personnelguy.

Magdalen was wondering why they were talking in exclamation points, why the air smelled so sweet and cold, why such cheerful people didn't care about blindfolds and gags and guns, and what they were all doing at work at this time . . .

Aneba was trying to identify the smell in the air. His nose twitched and his brain ran through its enormous knowledge of chemicals, plants, and aromas.

"Great! The asthmaguys!" the receptionist cried, and picked up the phone.

"He'll see you now!" she trilled. "He sounds so pleased to know that you're here!"

The lights twinkled above and far away.

The lion's tail was firm and rough and warm in Charlie's hand.

The cold river air rose up to his right. The hard, cold, steep concrete wall stood immovably to his left.

The dark water was right there beside him.

Step by step, carefully, slowly.

He looked at the young lion's back. Not at anything else.

Not the necklaces of light on the far, far riverbank.

Not the great, high bridge, growing in height as they drew nearer to it.

Step by step.

He wanted desperately, desperately, to look behind him and see if the mothers had caught up with them. But he couldn't. If he looked anywhere other than at the lion's back, he would fall. It was that simple.

Step by step.

He had to place his feet a little closer together on each pace than he would naturally, because the ledge was so narrow. It made him feel slightly as if he were going to lose his balance.

Step by step.

Watching the lion's back.

Breathing.

Tall.

Strong.

The bridge loomed up in front of them, white and calm. The overpass to his left had swooped down now behind its great wall. The ledge continued, and so Charlie and the lions continued as well, under the bridge they so longed to cross.

As they came out the other side, the ledge widened a little and Charlie found the courage to look back up at the bridge. There was nothing they could climb to get onto it. How were they going to get up there?

There was another bridge, way ahead upriver. Even if they could get onto that one, it was too far away. They had a train to catch, and maybe an angry guy with a big dog chasing them. Now Charlie could see the great iron and glass curve of the roof of the station, just there across the river. So near—only a few hundred yards. For a second he looked down at the water that separated him from the station. He shivered.

Then the young lion stopped. Charlie let go of his tail in surprise. The lion flicked it, once this way, once that.

"Charlie," he hissed, over his shoulder.

"Yes," whispered Charlie.

"There's an entrance here—a small tunnel. We could go in. What do you think?"

Troy was at first confused by the scents of the three lionesses going in three different directions.

Rafi stood dripping on the quayside by the *Circe*, glaring at him.

"Find the scent, Troy," he said in a dangerously polite tone. Some last stragglers from the audience noticed him, and stood for a moment looking on in curiosity at the sodden, angry youth. He jerked his head back and gave them such a filthy look that they fled, chattering.

Troy ran to and fro, whining and snuffling at the ground. Here, there . . . Then he picked up the scent of the yellow lioness, whose fur he had been given to smell, and raced swiftly down the basin after her. When he came to the lock, he balked at following the scent across the narrow gate-tops, but with Rafi yelling at him from behind, he had little choice. Rafi followed him, nimbly, considering he couldn't move his arm.

The lioness was perched motionless on top of the remote lock control. In the dark she just looked like a lump. Troy knew he was close, but he had no idea how close.

The beam that passing boats had to trip to operate the lock shone out invisibly just beneath her.

As Rafi and Troy reached the safety—as they thought it—of the other side, she let her tail droop.

Flicked it slowly across the beam.

Yes.

A creak and a shudder warned that the lockgates were beginning to open. A growl and a leap and a thwack in the face with a golden tail were enough to confuse Rafi and Troy. Another leap—onto the gates as they began to swing open, and from one gate to the other— yes—just before they swung too far open for the gap to be leaped.

And there they were. Rafi and Troy on the far side of the canal, with no way back till the slow-moving lock closed again in, oh, twenty minutes. The yellow lioness gleaming her teeth at them from this side.

She gave a short, sharp roar.

The silvery lioness heard her, and using the same trick, set off the lock at the other end of the basin. It wouldn't start to work till the first lock was closed again, but for now Rafi and Troy were cut off, and however they tried to cross back, it would take much longer. Then the silvery lioness and the bronze lioness left their hiding places and swiftly, quietly hurtled down to join their friend.

"We should go in," said the young lion. "It might lead somewhere, and anywhere is better than here."

"Okay," said Charlie, glad that someone else had made the decision. He called back to the others what they were going to do, and then took the lion's tail again as they plunged into the darkness of this tiny riverside tunnel. It led directly into the bank.

Inside it was dark, and the water in there was smelly and scummy—plastic bottles bobbed and Charlie could tell from the smell that there was litter and dirty caked-up foam. That meant that the water stopped somewhere up ahead of them—moving water would not smell this bad. If only the path would continue . . .

It did. Twenty yards inside the tunnel, the ledge suddenly widened out into a stone quay like the ones by the Canal St. Martin, and the water came to an end. Charlie could just make out what looked like a big, round pipe sticking out of the wall ahead of them, dripping weed and smelling disgusting. Drains, Charlie thought. Sewage, maybe. Old, old drains.

An open doorway led into the wall behind the quay. Again, the stonework was old and finely made, but by the look of it, nobody ever came here.

"Stay here a moment," Charlie whispered to the lions. "I'll go and see where it leads." He hoped that the lionesses would catch up to them while they stopped. Catch up and say that the splash was just someone falling in, that the scream was just a scream of getting wet.

Wrinkling their noses and flaring their whiskers at the smell, the lions prepared to wait.

Concentrate, thought Charlie. Be grateful—if he's in the canal, or if they've wounded him, he won't be following, at least not so quickly . . .

"I'll be as fast as I can," he said.

"Thanks," said Elsina, whose little nose was as wrinkled up as a prune. She lay down on the stone pavement and buried it in her paws.

Through the door was a staircase, cut into the stone.

Up the staircase was another doorway. Through that doorway was a chamber. Charlie silently peered through to see what was there.

It was mostly dark, but there was a dim light coming from somewhere, just enough to show him that the chamber was smallish, grubby, and absolutely filled with trash. But it was not just a dump. It was organized. Three supermarket carts stood in a row, full of bits of old-fashioned wires and plugs and the insides of electrical devices. One corner was piled high with big black plastic bags, some of which spilled pieces of cloth. Also, there was a small, low folding table with a mug on it, and some cushions put there as if two or three people might sit on them to talk to one another. And there was what could have been a bed.

And on that bed was what could have been a person.

And what could have been a person rolled over, and snored deeply, and flung out an arm, which knocked over a tall, ornate glass water pipe. The top fell off and some of the water spilled, and some last embers of tobacco fell out on the floor, sending the aromatic smell of apple tobacco out into the room, and reminding Charlie of the Arab cafés in London, and the delicious pastries made of nuts and honey . . .

Concentrate!

Across the room was a metal gate. Beyond it, the night sky, with the huge road beneath it.

Whoever brings this stuff in here must bring it in from somewhere; must have access to the outside. Access on foot—something other than the overpass, which no one could walk on.

Charlie turned back down the stairs. Maybe the mothers would be there. Maybe they'd have caught up.

They weren't. They hadn't.

He said to the lions: "Come on. There's someone up there, but he's asleep. Wait in the doorway and I'll see if I can open the gate to the outside."

His heart was beating fast as he led the lions back up the stairs. They coiled themselves in the doorway, just out of the light, and silently waited for him, their eyes lazy but their whiskers alert. As he stepped out into the dim, grubby room, Charlie felt very strongly his responsibility to them.

It was difficult to cross that room in silence. There were things all over the floor, and there were dark corners and curious shadows, and there was the scary snoring figure, and there was very little light. It wasn't really Charlie's fault that he stepped on an old rollerskate, then fell into a pile of scrap metal and hit his head, and yelled, and that the sleeping man woke up screeching. And it certainly wasn't Charlie's fault that the lions glanced at one another, and then leaped as one from the doorway to the man's bedside, where they surrounded him, staring down at him, their claws out, their eyes intent, their fang-filled jaws hanging open, growling, ready to pounce.

"Stop it!" yelled Charlie.

The poor man shrieked and shrieked. The oldest lion put his paw on the man's chest and roared. It worked. He stopped shrieking and started gibbering instead, but this was at least quieter.

"Stop it," said Charlie. "Please."

The lions looked around.

"You're scaring—" He had meant to say "You're scaring him." It came out as "You're scaring me."

Elsina looked at him sideways.

The oldest lion flicked his whiskers.

"Sorry," said the young lion.

Charlie thought quickly.

Then he went over to the mangy bed.

"*Taisez-vous,*" he said. It means shut up, but he hoped by putting in the polite form of "*Taisez-vous*" instead of "*Tais-toi,*" the man might realize that he didn't mean to be rude.

How silly. There with three lions on his chest, the man would not be worrying about manners.

"We are a nightmare," he said. "You mustn't tell anyone about us. Do you want to get rid of us? Tell us where the road is. Then we can go there. How do we get to the bridge?"

The man, who was not very old, and had a pleasant face as far as could be seen beneath his abject terror, could not speak. He tried to—he seemed to want to, but though his mouth moved and his tongue flapped, no noise emerged.

"Lions," murmured Charlie, "perhaps you should get off him for a bit."

The lions withdrew, and lay like a circle of sphinxes a few feet from the man.

He looked up at Charlie and blinked and swallowed.

"Take your time," said Charlie. "But not too long. We're in a hurry."

The man looked back at the lions. And back at Charlie. When he spoke, finally, it was in Arabic.

"But they're Moroccan!" he shouted.

"Indeed," said Charlie, a little surprised that the man should know such a thing. "So what?"

"So am I!" shouted the man. Having regained his voice, he now seemed unable to control it. Fear does funny things to people.

"*Salaam alecum,*" said Charlie. "Now how do we get to the bridge?"

"Left out of here, up the staircase, and it's on the left," the man said, staring and clutching his blanket to him. "The gate is open."

"Thank you," said Charlie in Arabic. "*Alif Shukr.* A thousand thanks."

"One is enough," said the man, wild-eyed, as the lions trooped past him, out onto the deserted, silent, midnight riverbank.

Charlie had hoped that if anybody saw them, they'd think they were a trick of the light, a cat, an urban fox. "That cat looked *huge*," they might say. "Did you see it?" But the cat would be gone, and the night would be still again. Yet from the shadows at the top of the staircase, they could see that it was still too busy for them to cross the bridge on the pavement.

On the outside of the bridge's wall, there was a ledge. It was much the same width as the ledge alongside the river, and it was several hundred feet up in the air.

"We can use that," said the oldest lion.

Charlie looked at it. If he fell, he would tumble into the cold river, or bash his head on the white stone bridge, or drown, or have a heart attack.

The lions made themselves as flat as flatfish and slithered over the wall. Charlie just held his tongue between his teeth and repeated the words "I have no choice, I have no choice."

Just in time he realized that of course he did have a choice. The lions, it was true, couldn't be seen wandering the place without being picked up and taken back, but nobody would question a boy crossing a bridge. Why should they?

"See you on the other side!" he hissed, and ran and jumped across the bridge, doing cartwheels and backflips, just because he could, and because he was so scared, he would do anything to pretend that he was not.

Chapter 18

The Chief Executive smiled at them. He was short. He had springy hair and pinkish gray skin and a very clean white shirt. He looked extremely ordinary.

He'd had all their bindings removed. "No need for that kind of thing," he'd said in a voice that suggested he was surprised they had been used at all.

"Now," he said. His desk was very big. "You know why you're here."

"No, we don't," said Magdalen. She wasn't feeling too well.

"To work with us!" cried the Chief Executive.

"We don't want to," said Aneba.

"You don't want to complete research on your asthma cure in a calm and happy environment, with all the money and help you need, and the promise of plenty of investment in the future?"

"Oh!" said Aneba. "Is that what you're offering? And there we were thinking you'd kidnapped us and brought us here bound, gagged, and threatened because you know full well we wouldn't cooperate with a bunch of crooks like you."

The Chief Executive looked hurt. "Doctor," he said, "the Corporacy works for the advancement of mankind! What could be more marvelous than a cure for this dreadful scourge of asthma, which torments our children and blights their futures? We have for years been making the drugs that treat asthma and give the little ones some relief—but how much better to cancel out asthma forever!"

Magdalen gave a low, nasty laugh.

"Tell me," she said, looking up suddenly. "How much money do you make each year from asthma drugs?"

The Chief Executive made his hurt look again, but she kept talking. "And how much do you expect to make from a cure? Which would be better for your profits—a one-off cure, or continuing to sell medicine for the rest of time? Do you want to use our cure? Or do you just want to make sure nobody else does?"

She started coughing.

The Chief Executive veiled his eyes. "Well, if you're going to be like that about it," he murmured.

Magdalen threw up.

The Chief Executive raised one eyebrow and lifted the telephone.

"Miss Barakat?" he said. "The professor and the doctor seem to be ill. May I suggest a visit to the Wellness Unit? They don't seem to be very well at all. But nothing we can't sort out, I'm sure. Nothing a couple of weeks of treatment won't solve."

He put the phone down and smiled.

"I'll see you in a couple of weeks then," he said. "I'm really looking forward to working with you!"

The lionesses easily, swiftly followed the scent the others had left. They negotiated the ledge and terrified the Moroccan, and they were just about to set out on the ledge across the river when something extremely peculiar happened.

At that moment, Charlie and the lions were at the other end of the bridge. They only needed to cross a small square, Place Valhubert, and the station would be just there to the left. But as they hesitated at the far side of the bridge, waiting for a quiet moment to cross, they heard it too.

It was a howl. It was a howl of such intensity, loneliness, and longing that Charlie's hair stood on end. It sounded like the end of the world, like losing your mother, like looking in the mirror and not knowing your own face. It sounded like the loss of all you held dear. Tears came to Charlie's eyes, and terror to his heart, at the sound of it. What could make so sad a noise? Who could be that sorrowful?

But if Charlie was shocked by the sound, the lions were more so.

The lionesses stopped stark still and listened. The three lions with Charlie stopped dead, dropped low to the ground, and turned their heads in the direction it was coming from—across the square to the right. They were baring their teeth and wrinkling their noses; their whiskers were quivering, alert to every vibration. The young lion started to growl, a low, mean, motionless sound that Charlie had never heard before. They were all terrifying.

Charlie desperately wanted to say something, to calm them, to change the situation. He'd calmed them in the Moroccan's chamber, perhaps he could now too . . . He started to speak, but the oldest lion flashed his eyes and gave a tiny, authoritative twitch of his ear that left Charlie in no doubt that he was to do nothing, say nothing, and probably even think nothing.

Up by the bridge, the lionesses began to run.

The howl came again—lower than the first one, but longer, and if anything, sadder and more piercing. The lions' ears twitched. Charlie knew that lions can judge distances from noise, and if two noises come from the same direction, they can tell which comes from nearer and which from farther away. Were they doing that now?

Their faces showed total concentration. As they were now, free, desperate and united, he could imagine them in the wild, hunting in a pack, alert to every movement on the African plain, hearing things he couldn't hear, running faster than he could ever run, leaping and slaughtering.

The young lion was looking to the oldest lion. The oldest lion held his concentration, thinking, considering. Finally he blinked.

He turned to the young lion and said, "You stay and guard our friend and your sister—"

At this the young lion's eyes flashed green and furious, and he tried to contradict his father, but the oldest lion raised his head the tiniest amount and gave his son a look of such haughty scorn that the young lion immediately fell back and turned his head a little to one side . . . but you could see he didn't like it.

Charlie said: "Sir—what is it?"

The oldest lion didn't reply. He merely twitched his ear again, and then he was gone, his tail hanging on the air behind him as he picked up speed, bounding like an uncoiling spring into the darkness toward the direction of the noise. For a moment he waited for a gap in the traffic, then he flashed across the road and across the bridge, a quick shadow in the night, a streak of darkness.

Charlie went to the edge of the bridge. The young lion and Elsina had hidden themselves—only a low growl called him to where they were lurking in a tiny patch of park on the corner. He sat down against the wall, suddenly exhausted. What was this thing? Why were the lions so upset about it? And how long was it going to take? They didn't have that long to find the train, and find a way on.

The night was cool, and the ground was cold beneath him. Maybe there was a change in the weather coming. He shivered.

Elsina prowled over and arranged herself beside him. She felt warm and comforting, and he was pleased to be able to be near her without having to hide their friendship from Maccomo or anyone else. The young lion still stood, his face in the direction of the howl—alert, mysterious, both scared and scary.

"What's down there?" asked Elsina quietly.

"Well, I don't know," said Charlie. "I thought you knew—the way you all reacted."

"I don't mean what's making the noise," she explained. "I mean what thing, or place, is there. You've been looking at maps—you know where things are."

Charlie ran his mind back. "The Jardin des Plantes is down there," he said. "It's a park. And the museums of natural history and so on, and—and the zoo."

"The zoo," she said softly.

"But that wasn't—that wasn't just an animal, was it?"

"I don't know what it was," she said.

Charlie wanted to call the young lion. He wanted to know what *he* thought. But the young lion was a million miles away from him—not in space, but in spirit. He was pure animal at that moment, pure watching animal. Charlie felt that he wouldn't even hear him if he called.

"Do you have an idea?" Charlie asked. "You must have an idea. Why did it upset you all so much?"

"It upset you too," said Elsina.

"Yes," said Charlie, and he shivered again as he thought of the belly-curdling, tear-making cry. "But not as much."

"Because it's not your—" She broke off.

"My what?"

"I don't know," she said. "I don't know."

She laid her chin on her folded paws and lay still, eyes open, no longer available for conversation. Charlie felt very alone.

Several minutes passed.

We're going to miss the train, Charlie thought, and a great fear and worry came over him. But anyway, how could they take it without the mothers? Why had the oldest lion gone rushing off without explanation? Had Charlie been wrong to trust them? He could hardly believe so . . . they were all in this together. But why hadn't the lion explained before he left? Charlie didn't like it when the grown-ups who were meant to be with him just went off without saying where or why. Even if they didn't mean to.

Charlie turned over sadly, and found himself snuggled up with Elsina. She didn't mind; she patted him absentmindedly with her tail. But she, like her brother, was fully occupied, silently watching and waiting.

After another few minutes, Charlie lost his patience.

He jumped to his feet.

"Everybody else seems to have forgotten," he said, "but we have a train to catch, and if we don't catch it, then who knows what's going to become of us, and I for one don't want to risk it, so would you please, one of you, go and get the grown-ups so we can get a move on?"

The two lions turned and stared at him—but whatever they were going to say in response will never be known, because at that moment the howl came again, much, much nearer, and an immense form came bounding out of the darkness toward them, from the direction of the Jardin des Plantes. Behind it, looking small in comparison, low and slinking against the river wall, came four lions.

The young lion and Elsina leaped out to block the form's way. The oldest lion and the lionesses moved up behind it to make a circle. Charlie stood back in horrified fascination. Were they hunting it? Were they going to kill it?

And quite apart from that, what was it?

The creature at the center of the circle of lions was—well, it was a lion. Charlie had no doubt about that. But it was like no lion that Charlie had ever seen. For a start it was enormous—nearly twice as big as the oldest lion. Its forequarters were taller than its hindquarters, hugely powerful and muscular. It had short, strong legs and a long head sloping into a long neck; its back sloped down rather like a hyena's, and its tail was short and stumpy-looking. Its eyes were flat and defensive, but its face gave an impression of fear, anguish, and deep exhaustion. However, Charlie hardly noticed that, because this face also bore something else, something rather more immediately impressive.

This lion had a set of saber teeth. The phrase came straight into Charlie's mind as he looked at them. That's what they were. Two big, long, strong, sharp teeth, gleaming white and hard in the darkness, curving down and back from the creature's upper jaw, like tusks, so big, they could never fit inside his mouth. Saber teeth. The creature looked across at Charlie, and bared them at him.

Charlie took one look and screamed. He screamed and screamed. The sound broke the standoff between the lions.

The creature turned as if to leap on Charlie—provoked no doubt by this sound of weakness, he forgot for a moment that he was the victim of the rest of the lions.

The oldest lion roared, and leaped over to Charlie to protect him. The young lion roared, and pounced, and tried to bite the creature's leg. The lionesses all jumped on top of the creature. The creature howled again.

"No no no!" yelled Charlie. "Stop it! People will come! Shut up and stop! Stop stop stop stop!"

He was yelling, of course, in Lion.

His lions, amazed that he should be so bossy to them, stopped for just long enough to stare. The creature, no doubt having never heard a human speak Lion, was so astounded that he suddenly cringed, and in that moment all the fight and the running away and the attacking and defending went out of him. He slumped down on the pavement and just lay there, his great teeth reflecting the lamplight, his great mouth uncloseable. And though, as Charlie knew, lions don't cry, it seemed as if there were tears in his eyes.

Surrounded by this troupe of wild beasts, Charlie for a moment understood what Maccomo must feel in the ring. He had controlled them—he felt strong and powerful. But how could he communicate with them? Could they really understand him? Now that they were free, and out of the artificial environment of the circus, could he and they really be a team? And who was this new thing? Was he an enemy?

Charlie pulled all his courage and intelligence together, and spoke. "Into the park!" he said. "Get invisible. Now!"

The animals slunk swiftly into the shadows.

Charlie spoke quickly and urgently to the oldest lion. "Sir," he said, "we have a train to catch. Has our plan changed?"

The oldest lion eyed him. Then: "No," he said.

"You've brought someone. Is he joining us?"

The great creature raised his head and looked at Charlie, and at the oldest lion. The oldest lion twitched his whiskers.

"Quickly!" ordered Charlie. "Someone could appear at any moment."

The creature bowed his head again, and spoke in a low, harsh, difficult voice.

"Yes," he said.

Charlie breathed out a long sigh of relief.

"Lionesses," he said. "What happened?"

"There's no time now—" said the oldest lion, glancing around, but Charlie interrupted.

"Where is my enemy?" he asked. He desperately needed to know that Rafi was—what? Alive? Dead? Off their trail?

"He's coming after us," said the yellow lioness. "We only delayed him. He's got our scent and he'll be along as soon as the lock opens again."

The fear returned. Rafi could cause a commotion; Rafi could ruin their escape. Charlie wasn't afraid of him, but he was afraid of what he could do.

"Then let's get a move on," said Charlie. "We've no time to lose."

The front of the station was bright and busy, so they skirted around to the back. The tracks, Charlie knew from the map, led out behind the facade they were approaching, so they took a dark, quiet street down the side. The strange new creature fell in behind them, keeping to the dark corners and the walls as the others did.

The houses were dark. The lions sloped from garbage heap to closed-up snack cart, from dim doorway to darkened stairwell, landing in shadows, being shadows. The street led into the freight yard, where the lions found some mail carts and lay quietly beneath them, out of sight, panting a little as they rested. The creature found a separate one. No one was talking. Charlie was reasonably sure that the fight wouldn't break out again while he went ahead to check out the best way to get to the Orient Express.

He strolled back around and into the station. He wanted to run, but he didn't want to draw attention.

He knew it was supposed to be at platform one.

There it was.

He strolled up the platform. His legs were tense and his feet heavy.

The train was fine and high and long—so long that the front of it extended beyond the end of the platform. Beyond that, the tracks faded into darkness, to be lit only by the headlights of the trains passing beside them. And just beyond that darkness was the freight yard, dark and closed now, where the would-be stow-aways were waiting. All they had to do was come around through the darkness to the front of the train, and get on board on the far side, hidden from the light and crowds of the platform side. There was no train on that far side. No one on the platform. With just a little luck, nobody would notice them at all. There was no time to spare.

Charlie hurried back to the lions, who hooded their eyes again. The timing was good: twelve-twenty. "Quick!" Charlie called, low and hurried. "Before another train comes. Good luck! Quick!"

Yellow eyes flashed. Charlie flipped himself onto the youngest lion's back with all the skill of a trick rider, and they were off, hurtling out and across—speed gave them invisibility. All the time Charlie's mind was flicking over the things that threatened them:

Who is this new creature? Does he put our plan in danger? Where would Rafi and Troy be by now?

The freight yard led directly to the tracks, gleaming beneath the lions' paws. They lifted their feet high to avoid the cold metal, stepping over onto the wooden slats.

Huge and dim in the darkness with the station lights behind it, the train looked tremendously tall. Charlie hoped and hoped that he had not underestimated the height, and that the lions had not overestimated their strength and prowess. And anyway—they were all tired by now.

First, the engine and fuel car. Then the luggage car: their destination. No one would be there to hear them as they jumped aboard.

Go go go! Charlie urged, silently, in his head as he hopped down from the young lion's back.

The lionesses went first. One, two, three, they slunk along in the darkness by the wheels, seemed almost to halt as they swayed back on their haunches, and then took off in the great curving leap that brought them silently and magnificently onto the roof of the train. How could he have doubted them—these fabulous animals whom he had seen bounce all over the ring cage? Of course they could do it.

Next, Elsina. She wasn't as strong or practiced, but she had the energy of youth, and her aunts and mother were there to catch her.

Then the new creature. The jump was no problem to him. He was so big, he almost could have stepped on, but he gave a short, powerful leap with his strong back legs.

Next, the oldest lion. Charlie was worried about him too—he was old, could he make it?

The oldest lion looked superciliously at the train, calculating the height in his mind, and he took a few delicate paces back. Then he shook his head and seemed to change his mind. Rather than take a running leap, as the lionesses had done, he paced directly to the front of the car and swiftly, elegantly, scrambled up on the maintenance ladder. All six lions were now lying flat, spread-eagled on the roof. Charlie couldn't see them at all. Just as it should be.

He glanced around him. Nothing. Nobody. His heart was hammering. A few platforms away an engine was starting to chug and rattle.

The young lion was now preparing to leap, and Charlie was thinking that he too might take the maintenance ladder. And just at that moment, he heard voices.

The young lion flashed his yellow eyes at Charlie, blinked, and flew. He was right to, of course, because though there is only very little excuse for a young boy to be wandering alone in the dark on a railway track, there is even less excuse for a lion.

It was the extra engineer and the extra conductor, coming on duty a little late, frankly. The engineer was complaining about having to come out into the dark, on the tracks, to the cab.

Although the bulk of the train was between him and them, Charlie dropped to the ground. He was right by the gap between the cars. Did he dare scurry farther out of view? He really did not want to have to explain himself. Not now. Not after all they'd been through.

It was cold and wet and grubby down on the track. He could smell metal and dead leaves and damp wood. The wheels towered huge above him. He tried to think himself invisible. "I am a pile of rags. I am an old plastic bag," he said quietly under his breath. "I don't exist, you can't see me, you'd never notice me, I'm just some glop left over after the storm . . ." He peered under the heavy, dirty car links, hoping and hoping to see legs walking along on the other side of the train, legs that would belong to people who would walk on by, and get on the train, and never see him, and never know that he existed.

But they did see him.

"What's that?" said one in French.

"*Je ne sais pas,*" said the other. *I don't know.* They came over and peered. "It's a person—a child."

Charlie's heart sank. He had to think quickly.

What was his priority? To get on the train.

What must not be allowed to happen? Not getting on the train.

When was the train leaving? Any minute.

What would make these men put him on the train?

Think, think, think.

Bingo!

"Mummy! Mummy!" cried Charlie pathetically. "I want my mummy!"

He started crying—just a bit. It was quite easy to fake, because his feelings *were* running high, and actually—now that he was crying it out—it was true, he did want his mum, badly, although that would not be quite how he would have chosen to express himself on the subject.

"He's lost," said one of the men. "What are you doing down there? Are you all right? Here, get up."

Charlie stood, trying to look as small, young, innocent, and pathetic as possible. They had to see him as lost and sad, because otherwise they'd see him as trouble and bad, in which case they'd cart him off to the stationmaster . . . Charlie rubbed his eyes. His face was filthy.

"Where was the platform?" cried Charlie. "I was looking for Mummy and there was no platform . . ." All of which was true, of course. He *was* looking for his mum and there *was* no platform. But the drivers took it to mean—as Charlie had hoped they would—that he had fallen off the train. So now they began to worry about getting into trouble for not having a platform beside the train, and putting small boys in danger. And the nearest car was the first-class car. They didn't want any fuss from worried mothers and irate fathers with expensive tickets and high standards of travel safety.

The engineer and the conductor looked at each other, perplexed.

Hurry up, hurry up, hurry up, thought Charlie. It was 12:28 according to the station clock.

They were in a hurry—in fact, they should have been in the cab ten minutes ago. It was due to leave. They didn't want trouble.

"Oh no," said the guard. "There's Monsieur Blezard."

A small group of people led by a man in a very sharp uniform was marching determinedly down the platform.

The engineer rolled his eyes.

So they did what Charlie hoped they would do: They picked him up, opened the door of the train, and popped him inside.

"You're all right now," said one, looking firmly at him. "You don't need to mention it."

Charlie smiled bravely. "I won't," he said. "I'll just find my mum."

The trainguys rushed on up to the cab, and the head engineer swore at them for being late.

Charlie, knowing that the lions had seen and understood what had happened, looked up and down the elegant wood-paneled corridor in which he found himself, and heaved a massive sigh of something like relief.

He couldn't quite believe it.

12:29.

The first door on the corridor was open. He slipped in and swiftly locked it after him.

He was in a bathroom. It was fancier than anywhere he'd ever seen before. The sink was porcelain, with a pattern of pink rosebuds scattered across it. The toilet seat was polished dark wood. The little table was glass. The little curtain was crisp lace. The towels were fluffy and white. The walls were wood-paneled, and there was a small painting of a lady in a pink dress, on a swing, surrounded by garlands of pink roses and two fat little cupids. It reminded him of Madame Barbue on her horse, and Pirouette flying through the heavens of the big top on her trapezes. Nothing could be less like slimy canal sides, dangerous ledges, filthy railroad tracks, trash-filled dens. He had to blink.

Gosh, he was tired. This had been a long, long day. He sat down on the polished toilet seat and finally, finally, let himself take a breath. He was here on the train. The lions were too. All had gone more or less according to plan in the end—except for the new creature, of course, with his teeth and his howl. He wasn't part of the plan. He was—well, what on earth *was* he?

In thirty seconds the train would leave.

Please God, please everybody, keep Rafi away for thirty seconds.

It smelled wonderful in here—like Christmas and honey and oranges. For the moment, the lions would just have to look after themselves. The new creature would just have to look after himself. Charlie was in a warm, dry place, about to leave for Venice, and he was exhausted. He pulled a fluffy white towel toward him: The moment the train started to move he would *sleeeeeeep* . . .

The distant sound of a dog barking was almost part of his dream . . .

But it wasn't. It was here. Right outside the crisp white curtain. Loud, insistent, and accompanied by shouting, in English and French. Charlie jerked his head up.

"You must stop the train! You must stop the train! *Il faut arreter le train! Il y a des—des animaux à bord! Il faut arreter le train! Il y a des—*"

Charlie stared at the curtain. Very, very slowly, he lifted the corner.

"Listen, man, you must stop it! They're criminals, they're runaways . . ."

It was Rafi. He looked appalling. Wet, furious, shouting, with green scum smearing his leather coat, and blood down his face, his lips gray, his arm hanging limp, and his big ugly dog slobbering at his feet, jumping and barking, as if desperate to get at the car and tear it up piece by piece.

A guard was shouting at Rafi—telling him to control his dog.

Someone shouted *"Fou!"*—madman!

The train was beginning to creak and crunch. Doors were slamming, guards shouting to one another.

Charlie couldn't see whom Rafi was yelling at. He couldn't see what was happening.

"Stop the train, man!" Rafi yelled. He looked like a lunatic.

Charlie pressed his face to the cool glass of the window.

Rafi turned. His little beard was matted with blood. His eyes were livid.

He saw Charlie.

Charlie saw him.

The whistle blew. The train lurched. In slow jerks, Rafi's furious face disappeared from view.

CHAPTER 19

❧

Charlie was asleep, his head on a fluffy white towel folded up on the edge of the sink.

He was not disturbed by the footsteps of the seven lions on the roof of the train as they cautiously prowled around, looking for a place to lie safely through the night, snug in a pile, as far out of the wind as possible. He slept through the rattle and hum of the train speeding up as it left Paris, heading south. He slept through the polite, gentle French voice of the conductor inquiring whether everything was just so, and was anything else required, and through a smooth English voice replying "Yes, yes, thank you so much," in a way that clearly meant "Now just go away and don't bother us."

Even the shock of Rafi's wild, riverswept face at the car window, caked with blood and fury and demanding that the train be stopped—even that could not keep Charlie awake. He had been working, and planning, and running, and fearing, and in this moment, in this clean warm place, with the train rushing him away from everything he feared, not a thing in the world could keep him awake. Sheer relief had knocked him out.

Charlie was dreaming that he and his mother and father were all at home around the kitchen table eating fish sticks and playing a game of Scrabble. Charlie was extremely happy in this dream, and had no plans to leave it. Mum was being particularly clever, making words Charlie didn't know, like "spasmodiacal" and "leavensome." Actually, perhaps they weren't real words. Dad was laughing. Their hands were squabbling over the board: hers pale and strong, his big and black and silky-skinned. Charlie was putting his hand out, in the dream as he had so often in life, to see his brownness next to them, when he was awakened by a sharp rat-a-tat-tat on the door.

Charlie bolted awake in a state of shock. Where was he? What was happening?

"What?" he cried.

A gruff foreign voice was saying, "All right, you can come out now."

Charlie shook his head, trying to clear it. He had been very deeply asleep, very deep in his dream of home.

"Open the door," said the voice. "You must be very tired, it's late for a youngster. Come on out and Edward will make up a bed for you."

Charlie was so amazed that like a sleepwalker he stood up, opened the door, and stared out at the person who had called him. It was a fat, dark man in a gorgeous purple dressing gown.

"Dear oh dear," said the fat man. "Edward—pajamas for my young friend. Washing can wait till morning. Are you hungry?"

Groggily, Charlie admitted that yes, he was.

Ten minutes later he was sitting up under tartan blankets in a small, tight, incredibly clean train bed, with a chicken sandwich on a heavy white plate with a gold crown on it, and a large glass of milk—or rather, a goblet of milk. Really, he thought, this glass could only be called a goblet, with its leg, and the weight of it. It's so—gobletty.

Gobletty. That's not a word.

Should be, though. Nice word.

Two minutes after that, he was fast asleep again.

Eight hours later he was awakened by the smell of bacon. He'd become used to his ropelocker bedroom on board the *Circe*. He had sort of considered it home. But this tiny bunk was really very comfortable, and so deliciously clean. He yawned, and tried to roll over, but it was difficult. He was tucked in very tight—rolled in like a caterpillar in a chrysalis, because it was so small.

Had he perhaps died, and gone to heaven?

He was in a tiny compartment, with a little window outside of which a cold, bright, clear morning was racing past. Inside, all was as snug and luxurious as could be imagined.

How very warm it was. And dry. And comfortable.

And then there was the smell of toast. The smell of golden butter melting on toast. The smell, he almost persuaded himself, of beautiful, ruby-red strawberry jam melting into the golden puddles of melted butter . . . It gave him a sharp memory of home.

He pushed back the tartan blankets and got out of bed. He was starving. But then—on the other side of the door, a strange man with a grand dressing gown, who had extracted him from the bathroom the night before, would almost certainly be waiting, wanting an explanation. Charlie hesitated—but not for long. There was nothing else he could do, so he pushed the door open.

The man was not immediately there. The little corridor with compartments leading off of it was empty. Apart from his own, the doors were closed. First Charlie turned left. The corridor seemed quiet, but then, at its end, Charlie came up against an extremely large man in a very grand uniform, holding a rather long gun, and standing legs apart across the door to the next car, with his back to Charlie. He was as black as Dad, and nearly as big. Given the choice of either tapping this huge, armed man on the small of his back (which was about the highest Charlie would be able to reach) to ask for information, or going the other way, Charlie decided pretty easily that going the other way was a very good idea.

At the other end of the car there was another large man, in the same sort of uniform, but apparently gunless. He stood astride the doorway, like his companion, but he was facing Charlie, so there was no avoiding him. Charlie put a polite smile on his face, and wondered what on earth he was going to say. But he didn't have to wonder, because as he approached, the guard saluted smartly, turned on his heel, and gestured for Charlie to pass.

Charlie had never seen a railway car like the one he now entered. For a start, it was one big room: no rows of gray plastic seats, no little rooms off a corridor, no luggage racks and aisles. It was just one grand, old-fashioned sitting room, with embossed leather sofas and armchairs, a grandfather clock, a fireplace, a *piano,* oriental carpets, beautifully polished wooden paneling (teak and mahogany, though Charlie didn't know that, as both these woods came from trees that had long since died out, and their wood was very rarely seen nowadays) and a painted ceiling, and three chandeliers. The bookshelves had little balustrades at the bottoms, to prevent the books from falling off when the train went around curves. Sitting in one of the armchairs, taking his toast and bacon from a tray on a side table and reading a newspaper, was the gentleman, looking very fine in a yellowish tweed suit with big checks, for all the world as if he were at home.

Charlie blinked.

The gentleman looked up. His hair was very black and shiny, and so were his eyes.

"Good morning, my little friend," he cried, putting down the paper. "How did you sleep? Edward!"

Edward came in. He was pale and extremely polite. The gentleman told him to bring more bacon, toast and milk, and strawberries and cream, and cake. Edward bowed and set off.

He must be a servant, thought Charlie. He had read about servants in books, but he had never seen one, or met anybody who might have one. How terribly old-fashioned! He was fascinated.

"Sit down, my dear boy, and tell me why you locked yourself in my bathroom. I wouldn't have minded," said the gentleman kindly, "except that I usually lock myself in there until the train has left, so I was a little discommoded . . . ha ha . . ."

He started to laugh.

"Discommoded," he said wheezily. "Do you get it? Discommoded. The commode is the WC, discommoded means put out or made uncomfortable, and I was discommoded—banned from the WC, and put out." He laughed a lot.

"Sorry," said Charlie. He could see that it was a good joke, but a bit complicated, and he preferred jokes that didn't have to be explained. No doubt he'd like that one if he were older, and knew about commodes.

"Never mind," said the gentleman. "So who are you?"

"Charlie," said Charlie. That was an easy question.

"Last name?" said the gentleman. "Ah, no, perhaps not . . . And going to . . . ?"

"Venice," he said.

"No ticket?"

"No," said Charlie, shamefaced. Well, it would be pointless to pretend he did have one. If the man was going to hand him over to the guards, a lie now would make no difference to anything, so he might as well tell the truth.

"Why not?" asked the gentleman. "No money, no time to buy one, on an adventure . . . ?"

"Yes," said Charlie.

"Wonderful," said the gentleman. "Well, if it's not too luxurious for you, please join me in my car until we reach Venice. I'm sure you will have plenty of other discomforts as you go about your business, so perhaps a little comfort now would be acceptable."

At just that moment Edward brought in a tray of comfort that was so acceptable to Charlie, particularly the toast, the melting butter, and the ruby-red strawberry jam, that it needed no discussion. Though he was most interested in the food, Charlie did notice that the tray was gold, the cutlery was silver, the plates were of porcelain, and the mango juice was in a heavy crystal glass—i.e., the best of everything, in the old-fashioned way. Normally, these things would be in museums.

Something was bothering Charlie. Ah, yes!

"Why do *you* lock yourself in the bathroom?" he asked.

"Ah," said the gentleman. "Danger of assassins."

This perked Charlie up. "Are you in danger from assassins?" he asked.

"Oh, yes."

"Why?"

"Oh, you know. They love blowing things up and shooting people and so on. And I'd rather not."

Charlie wondered if this man thought assassins always wanted to blow everybody up, or just him. He couldn't quite work it out, but then Edward came in and said, "Excuse me, Your Majesty," and suddenly everything looked much clearer, in a fairly complicated sort of way.

"Are you a Majesty?" cried Charlie.

"I am King Boris of Bulgaria," said the gentleman.

"Crike," said Charlie. There weren't many kings left, and he felt rather pleased to meet one.

"Your Majesty," said Edward again, in a very deferential yet rather stern manner.

"Yes, Edward, what is it?"

"Members of the staff of the railway are expressing an interest in a small boy found last night on the rails, and put aboard the train, but now no longer apparent, Your Majesty," said Edward suavely.

"Are they?" said the king. "What will they do with him when they find him?"

"Hand him over to the police, Your Majesty, for having mis-represented himself as a bona fide passenger who had lost his family when in fact he is a mere stowaway and a jackanapes, Your Majesty."

(Charlie smiled. Jackanapes reminded him of Julius.)

"Dear oh dear. Well, he's probably no longer on the train, I'd have thought," mused the king. "Would've disembarked, wouldn't he? Anyway, where could he hide?"

"Exactly, Your Majesty."

"Of course if I see him, I'll inform the authorities. Tell them so, Edward, won't you?"

"Of course, Your Majesty. Good day, Your Majesty."

The moment Edward had withdrawn, King Boris started to giggle.

"When I was a little boy," he said, "about your age, I was traveling on this lovely train and my father, King Ferdinand, went to dinner and told me to keep the blinds of the compartment down, but I didn't. I peeked out. And one of the conductors spanked me. I like cheeking the conductors!" the king said with an air of conspiracy.

Charlie giggled.

"Shall we play backgammon?" said the king, but Charlie didn't know how, so the king taught him, and then they played for mile after mile after mile, running down to the Alps, through Dole and Lausanne toward Lake Geneva and Simplon, where they would take the long tunnel through the mountains.

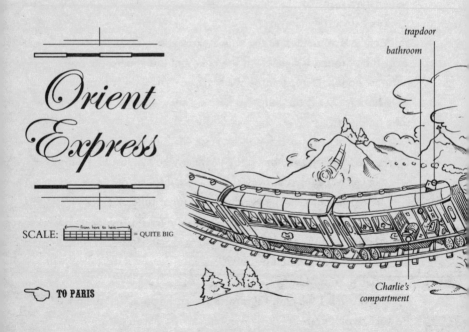

Orient Express

SCALE: ⊢from here to here⊣ = QUITE BIG

TO PARIS

trapdoor

bathroom

Charlie's compartment

Between games King Boris told Charlie about the glory days of the Orient Express, when it was the height of luxury (Charlie thought it seemed the height of luxury now) and all the world's spies and adventurers and mysterious, beautiful ladies traveled on it, before the Great Wars of the twentieth century.

And King Boris recited the names of places the great train passed through: "From Paris to Dole, Lausanne and Lake Geneva, Brig, Simplon, Milan and Verona, Mestre and Venice, Trieste, Ljubljana, Zagreb, Vinkovki, Belgrade, Nish, Sofia, Plovdiv, Adrianople, Corlu and Istanbul . . ."

The names sounded like poetry. Charlie especially liked Plovdiv.

"I drive it sometimes, you know," the king said suddenly.

"Really?" said Charlie.

fuel car

ladder

luggage car

King Boris's car

TO VENICE, LJUBLJANA, NISH, PLOVDIV AND THE EAST

"Yes. They tried to ban me, and in fact I cannot drive now in most places because after I crashed it, they said they would fire anyone who let me. But in Bulgaria, of course, they can't stop me—they couldn't have built the Nish to Plovdiv section if we hadn't allowed them to. Whenever we get to the border now, if they know I'm aboard, they just stop until I come up to the cab. I have my special boiler suit." He sent Edward to fetch it. It was white, and very well tailored. Charlie admired it. "I wish I could drive you now, but if you're getting out at Venice we won't have the chance. What a pity." Charlie agreed it was a great pity.

There was a pause.

"So tell me about your parents," said King Boris.

For a moment Charlie couldn't speak. He had been thinking about them a lot, but he hadn't really talked about them for a long time.

They were just his parents. He didn't know what to say.

"They're scientists," he said at last. "Dad's from Ghana and Mum's English. I went home one day and they weren't there. They've been kidnapped. I'm looking for them."

In the Wellness Unit of the Corporacy Gated Village Community, Aneba and Magdalen were sitting on fake wood chairs, being talked to by the Motivation Management Officer, a smiling woman in a gray suit.

"And after your individual sessions, you'll be entering the group therapy, where Corporacy colleagues will be sharing with you their experience of the Motivational Adjustment Program, showing how it has helped them to truly achieve and become what they have aspired to achieve and become in their professional and personal lives . . ." the Motivation Management Officer was saying, smilingly.

Magdalen didn't like her smile. She smiled too much—all the time. It was sick and weird.

"Are you feeling all right, dear?" said a lady in a white coat. This was the Medications Officer. "Have a pill."

"No, thank you," said Magdalen politely. "I don't want your pills and I don't want to listen to any more of this garbage. Could you just go away, please?"

The Motivation Management Officer smiled some more.

"It takes time," she said soothingly. "Resistance is part of the process! Soon enough you will find yourself able to embrace your aspirations and be immersed in the loving, unifying aspirations of the Corporacy."

"Oh, bog off," said Magdalen.

Aneba stifled a giggle.

The Motivation Management Officer stood up, smiling still. "Embrace your aspirations!" she said, and moved gently, smilingly out of the room. The Medications Officer, shooting Magdalen a dirty look, followed her. As she closed the door behind her, Aneba and Magdalen heard the lock clunk shut.

Aneba started to laugh. Magdalen, after a moment, joined in.

"But it's not going to help, is it?" she said. "How long are we going to be able to hold out?"

A voice came over the loudspeaker. It was backed by gentle but insistent music, and it was saying, "Come on, friends and colleagues, potential friends and potential colleagues! Unite! Come and be with us, be among us! The rewards and pleasures of united, corporate life are so many. You can't be expected to get by on your own—who can, in this difficult world? It's too much to ask. Do yourself a favor! Go with the people who know what's best. Listen to them, learn from them, and contribute! Become one of us, and build a better world the Corporacy Way!" And on. And on. And on.

Magdalen and Aneba smiled at each other. "Come on then," he murmured. "What'll it be today? Verdi? Robbie Williams? Bob Marley?"

"'When the Saints Go Marching In,'" said Magdalen. Sticking their fingers in their ears, they started to sing out loud—very loud.

"So do you know where they are?" said King Boris. But Charlie suddenly did not want to talk about them. He didn't know what he should reveal, and what to keep secret. He didn't want to lie to King Boris, who seemed like a sympathetic man. But he had to be careful. Charlie just frowned.

King Boris seemed to understand. "Let's have a look at the menu for lunch," he said, and called Edward.

The menu was on thick white card, printed in gold lettering: oysters and turtle soup, capons and saddle of venison, lobsters in aspic, ice cream served in miniature railway cars made of marzipan and nougat. Charlie stared. He didn't want to eat a saddle, didn't know what a capon or aspic was, wasn't at all sure about turtle soup . . .

"I'll order all of it, and you can try what you like," said King Boris kindly. "And saddle doesn't mean the saddle, it means the bit that the saddle would go on."

Charlie didn't know what a venison was either.

"Deer," said King Boris.

Oh dear. "What's a capon then?"

"A kind of chicken," said the king.

Then, as Charlie was thinking that a kind of chicken was better than saddles and deer, he noticed that, though it was snug and warm within—with the fireplace and the backgammon and the promise of an exotic lunch—outside it had begun to snow.

The lions! He had forgotten all about the lions! In a moment, his sluggish mood of comfort slid off him. How could he have been so selfish?

CHAPTER 20

"Aaahhhh," Charlie said. "I should stretch my legs a bit."

"Good idea," said the king. "Stretch mine while you're at it! Lunch won't be for a while anyway. Don't go beyond my cars, will you? See you later."

The king took up his newspaper again, and Charlie scurried back to the second car, with its little corridor off of which were the bathroom, his little compartment, and the others. (The king had a grand bedroom at the other end of the main car.)

How could he get out onto the roof? Those poor creatures. But he wasn't going to waste time feeling bad. He must take them water, food, and blankets. Swiftly he stripped his bed and grabbed the towels, and put them in a pile so they would be handy when he had found a way up. Then he put on all of the clothes he had with him, including his gloves, and tied his scarf around his face.

He thought hard.

Maintenance ladders! The luggage car had one, so maybe the other cars would too. He went to the far end, to the door connecting the king's car to the rest of the train. The guard wasn't there at the moment, but the door was locked. It was very thoroughly locked, actually. Against assassins, Charlie supposed.

How about the other end then? The luggage car was the next along, toward the head of the train. But that was through King Boris's bedroom . . .

So how else might one get onto a roof?

Trapdoors? He surveyed the ceilings of the corridor and his own compartment looking for one. He dared not look in any of the other compartments—the huge man must be somewhere, and Charlie didn't like the idea of disturbing him. Or Edward.

At first Charlie thought he was having no luck, but then, in the bathroom, he realized that the ornamental panel above the tiny bathtub was, in fact, on hinges, and that—yes!—those were bolts along the side. He clambered into the bath, and by standing carefully on the edges, he was able to reach. He pulled the bolts back— they slid easily—and pushed hard to lift the trapdoor, which was extremely heavy.

Trapdoors in train roofs are not designed to be opened while the train is racing along through a snowstorm. Charlie had to push hard, banging and straining. But he was a strong boy, made stronger by his time with the circus. Finally he managed to get the door to lift—then the wind rushed in through the gap, and violently, suddenly, lifted the trapdoor and slammed it open.

First, a pile of cold, wet snow fell in on Charlie's head. The wind hurtled around the bathroom like a tornado, flapping the curtains and throwing the towels on the floor. Charlie hissed through his teeth, put one hand on each side of the trapdoor's frame, and pulled himself up. In a moment he was lying half in and half out, his legs dangling and his face burning from the bite of the wind.

Outside was like a different world. The cold nearly took his head off. He had to lie as flat as he could because of the speed of the train. Holding on tight and sheltering his eyes, he could see that there was a sort of channel down the middle of the train's roof that was slightly sheltered. That's where the lions would be. But he couldn't see them.

Oh well, of course he couldn't see them! They weren't on this roof, they were on the next but one, the luggage car. He was going to have to go and fetch them—traveling against the wind rushing over the train. Narrowing his eyes, Charlie looked up ahead, and he didn't like the look of this challenge at all.

Pulling his jacket around him, trying to tuck his pants farther into his boots, he lay along the top of the train and wriggled himself into the channel. It was better in there—quieter for one thing, and with less wind against him for another—but it was still extremely uncomfortable. He'd heard tales of how flesh can stick to freezing metal. He hoped it wasn't that cold.

Flat on his stomach against the cold metal, Charlie shimmied himself along the train. As he went, he began to get scared. Physical discomfort can do that sometimes—the worse your body feels, the worse your mind feels. It's hard to be brave when you're cold or hungry or tired. But Charlie, though cold, had slept the previous night in a cozy bed, and he was full of toast and strawberry jam. So as he pushed through the wildly eddying snowflakes, working his way along, he was thinking only about his friends, and how to help them.

When he found them, he was horribly afraid it might be too late. They were lying in a pile, bedraggled and shivering. They were wet, and if a lion could look pale, they looked pale. Their ears were down flat, their whiskers limp. The snowflakes falling onto their golden sides weren't even melting. They looked terrible. Charlie was furious with himself, and his fury gave him energy.

How could he have left them out there all night? They relied on him and he had let them down. How stupid. How stupid of him.

One of them seemed to be better off than the others. It was the new creature who had joined them last night in Paris. He was talking to the lions in a low voice, and though Charlie couldn't work out what he was saying, it sounded comforting and strong. He was in the middle of them all, so that the smaller creatures were sharing the warmth of his bigger body.

Charlie crawled over to them, cursing himself, and gently called out to them, but they couldn't hear him over the sound of the train. He stretched out his arm and stroked the nearest flank—one of the lionesses, he thought.

"Lions, lions!" he called. "Come on! I'm here! Come with me, we'll warm you up, come on, we can go inside the train! Come on! Come on! Young lion! Elsina! Come on!"

He patted desperately at the flank, and even thought about taking hold of the beautiful paw, and pulling it, but he couldn't quite bring himself to. Instead he clambered farther along, and sort of lay among them, wriggling and stroking and patting and talking. "Come on, come on!" he said.

The new creature joined in, and gradually the lions came to themselves and realized that Charlie was with them. They began to move.

Getting the poor creatures back along the train's rooftop to safety and warmth was one of the worst experiences of Charlie's life. He was so scared that they had become too weak, that they might lose their footing and roll off the train to the speeding land below. He was scared they might stick to the metal or slip on the snow. He was terrified when they had to pass over the gap between one rattling car and another, scarier than the gap between the circus ship and the shore when they had fled the *Circe*. He was scared as well that even if he got them back to the bathroom, they would be so ill that he might not be able to make them better. And even if he did make them better, how could he possibly keep them from the King of Bulgaria?

"One thing at a time," he said sensibly, and he repeated it over and over. "Just let's get them inside. Let's get you inside." He sounded like a mother. That idea cheered him up just a little bit, because it was so absurd: him being mother to all these lions. He laughed, and the laughter made him feel a tiny bit warmer. Jokes at the worst moment are good. Even feeble jokes like that.

The snow swirled and danced furiously around them, whooshing over their heads as the train snaked through the storm and the wind whistled past.

"One thing at a time," he murmured. At least they were going with the wind now.

There was the trapdoor ahead of him.

He almost pushed the lions through, and they landed in a big pile, filling up first the bathtub and then the whole room. Charlie clambered through last, pulling the trapdoor behind him—and that wasn't easy either. While he'd been out on the roof the bathroom had been filling up with cold, crunchy snow that had whistled in, and was now starting to melt in drips and lumps. Outside, the snow was beginning to cover the low slopes of the Alpine foothills.

Charlie was more relieved than he had ever been in his life to have everybody in out of the storm.

But there was work to be done. As quietly as he could, he swept the melting snow into the sink, and ran warm water on top of it so the steam would warm up the room even more. He rubbed the lions down with the towels, and checked their paws and ears for signs of frostbite.

"Don't go to sleep!" he said, and set them to examining each other to keep them busy. He'd read somewhere that if you go to sleep when you're that cold, you can die. "Keep moving around! Don't go to sleep till you're warm!" he hissed. "And keep quiet!"

He gave them some meat. That perked them up a bit. What else could he do for them?

Mum's Improve Everything Lotion! He still had it in his bag, from the day he had left home. During his time with the circus he hadn't ever had to use it. He knew it was just for emergencies—but this, for sure, was an emergency.

He gave them each a couple of drops: more than a person would have, because lions are much bigger than people. More for the huge new creature and the oldest lion, less for the young lion, the lionesses, and Elsina.

"That'll help," he murmured to himself. "They'll feel better soon." The strange new creature looked at Charlie with his large, sad eyes, as if taking him in.

They were all more or less all right—cold and tired, stiff and hungry, but they would be all right.

Oh lord, thought Charlie. What on earth am I going to do now?

What happened next was not up to Charlie.

The Orient Express suddenly stopped rattling. It drew to a halt.

Charlie and the lions looked at one another, looked around, shrugged, and the lions continued to rasp at the meat with their hungry, sharp-surfaced tongues.

Charlie went to the window, clambering over the lions, and peered out. Snow everywhere—soft and white and beautiful, swirling and circling and filling up all the space beyond the glass. How calm it looked in its silent dance. How different watching it through glass was to being out in it! After a while the lions began to snooze and Charlie, sitting in the steamy bathroom with their breath adding a musky scent to the steaminess, realized that the snow level was beginning to creep up the sides of the train. Ice half-covered the windows the way the water had half-covered the portholes on the middle deck of the *Circe*. With the engine no longer chuntering and the wheels no longer rattling and singing beneath them, it was extraordinarily quiet. Snow muffles sound, Charlie knew. And things always sound quieter when a loud noise has stopped. But even so—it was extraordinarily quiet.

He supposed they were stuck. Too much snow on the tracks or something.

How long could he keep the lions concealed? How much more of a problem was this going to be?

One of the lionesses snuffled. The young lion, piled in the tub with Elsina, opened an eye, and looked at Charlie.

"Thank you, friend," he said in a very low voice roughened by his hard cold night on the roof.

Charlie wondered for a moment if he was being sarcastic. He must have realized that Charlie had neglected them for hours and hours. But he wasn't—he was genuinely grateful.

"It turned cold very quickly," said the lion. "It is good that you came when you did. If it hadn't been for"—here he gestured at the creature—"I don't know what would have happened. Thank you for not forgetting us."

Charlie felt awful because he had forgotten them. Blinking, he flung his arms around the lion's neck. "I am so glad you're safe," he said. "Safe for now."

"Why only for now?" asked the young lion, fear coming into his eyes. "Is there more danger here? Should we—"

Charlie calmed him. "No immediate danger," he said. "But this bathroom belongs to somebody who may want to use it . . . We must be very quiet."

He had locked the door, but who knows how long it would be before Edward or one of the guards would want to use the room. Should he try to move the lions to the cabin where he had slept? No—he couldn't risk their being seen.

The snow and ice made the light in the bathroom curiously pale and greenish, like underwater light. Cold light. He could still make out the tops of icy trees on either side, painted in frost. What had looked swirling and beautiful was now starting to look crisp and evil. He put his face up to the window: Hailstones rattled against it and gave him a shock. He shivered. We must be quite high up in the mountains, he thought.

The next thing that happened was that the Chef du Train—who was not a chef but the train's boss—came to the door of King Boris's cars. Charlie could hear him clearly, talking first to the first guard, then to someone else, then walking past the bathroom door and addressing the second guard. Very politely, but very firmly, he was insisting on speaking to the king.

In the end the king was informed, after much use of phrases such as "impossible" and "I'm afraid, monsieur" and "I think you will find"; and "with every respect" and "as a matter of security" and "for any lesser reason we would not dream of discommoding . . ." (Discommoding again! Charlie very much hoped that he and the lions were not about to be discommoded, i.e., turned out of the bathroom, in front of the Chef du Train.)

The Chef du Train was ushered into the king's sitting room, and

Charlie, having instructed the young lion to lie behind the door in his absence to prevent it opening, quietly slunk to a position behind the door of the king's car, where he could eavesdrop. The bodyguard guy had gone in with the Chef du Train, so the coast was clear. Charlie wasn't being sneaky—he was desperate. He needed to know why the train had stopped so he could plan accordingly.

"Majesty," the Chef du Train was saying, "please forgive this unseemly bursting in on your esteemed privacy. I come bearing the apologies of the company, directors, and staff of the Societe Nationale des Chemins de Fer for disturbing you in the seclusion of your own august car, the very purpose of which is to prevent the likelihood of such disruptions . . ."

"If the matter is so important, just tell me what it is," said the king kindly.

"Your Majesty will have noticed that the train has stopped," said the Chef du Train.

"Indeed I have," said the king. "Why?"

"The reason we have offered the majority of the passengers is indeed the truth, though not the whole truth, Your Majesty: The unseasonable bad weather has produced an avalanche on the tracks ahead, and short of drive into it we have no choice but to stop for the duration. We had not expected such a thing so late in the year, and the snowplows we use in winter have already been removed. No other snowplow is conveniently near, though we are trying to locate one. We have positioned braziers along the tracks to stop the switchgears from freezing, but in the meantime unfortunately our valves have frozen up, so the brakes are frozen into position, and even if we could move, we cannot."

"Oh, dear," said the king. "And?" Charlie could imagine from his voice the friendly look in his eye as he inquired what "the whole truth" was.

There was a pause before the Chef du Train's voice came again, and when it did, he sounded like a worried man pretending not to be worried.

"There was a report from Paris, Your Majesty . . ."

"Really?" said the king, sounding interested. "What report?"

Another pause.

"Wild animals, Your Majesty."

"Wolves?"

"Not as such . . ."

"On the train?"

"On the roof, Your Majesty."

"While the train was going along?"

"Well . . ."

"Before it had stopped?"

"Yes."

"How on earth could they have got there? The train goes quite fast." The train went at least a hundred miles an hour.

"Well, in Paris, Your Majesty . . . A young man said . . ."

"Well, where are they now?"

Silence again. Charlie tried not to breathe.

"We don't know, Your Majesty. They disappeared from a circus, apparently, and—"

"Wolves in a circus? Unusual."

"Well—lions, Your Majesty."

"Lions!"

"Yes, sir, from the circus. They ran away, and . . ."

"And decided to take the train to Istanbul? Marvelous. So, the question remains, where are they now?"

"There have been no sightings and no footprints, Your Majesty."

"The snow would have covered them up, I suppose. Or perhaps they missed their train. It happens."

"No doubt, Your Majesty, or else—"

"Or else what?"

"They might have boarded the train, from the roof, Your Majesty."

"How would they do that? Beasts can't open doors, can they? And I imagine most people had their windows shut this morning . . ."

A flurry of icy snow hurled itself against the windowpane, rattling wildly and proving the king's point.

"There may have been a person with them, Your Majesty," said the Chef du Train in quite a small voice. Charlie felt that he was a little embarrassed to offer such an absurd story, and to a king of all people.

"What kind of person?" said the king.

"A small one," said the Chef du Train. "I believe you were informed earlier . . . A . . . small one."

Charlie was thinking fast. He could get to the bathroom and get the lions out now—they could go through the window. It would be a squeeze and a leap, which was difficult but perfectly possible, then—then what? Lost in a snowstorm somewhere in the Alps? When it's cold enough to freeze brakes? Sick and weak as they were?

Best to stay on board. Best to hide—but was the bathroom the best hiding place? Maybe go back on the roof . . . ?

Rats rats rats. Was there any alternative?

The king was speaking again. "Let me help you out, monsieur," he was saying in an amused voice. "You have received a report about some wild animals on the roof of a speeding train in a howling storm, you have put this together with some tale about a disappearing boy who is either on the train or not, and you fear they may all be hiding in my coffeepot, and you are embarrassed to ask me to have it searched. Is that it?"

"Yes," said the Chef du Train, in a tiny voice this time. "The boy was put on the train in your car."

"Tut, tut," said the king. "That wasn't very security-minded of your people, was it?"

"No, Your Majesty," said the Chef du Train.

"He could have been a tiny assassin," said the king.

"Yes, Your Majesty."

"My dear fellow," said King Boris. "You are quite absurd. Go and have a glass of brandy, and wait for the snowplow to arrive. It is hard to be the person in charge when there is nothing to be done, but really, we are just stuck in a storm and there *is* nothing to be done. Don't worry about a thing. Good-bye!"

Charlie, fascinated and terrified, only just remembered to leap away from the door and conceal himself before the Chef du Train came out, looking bemused and confused, on his way back to the rest of the train. Charlie ducked behind a coatrack, holding his breath as the man passed, his boots squeaking a little on the polished floor. In a second, Charlie was back in the bathroom, shoving the young lion out of the way to let himself in, and thinking furiously.

"Edward!" he heard the king call. "Where is our young friend?"

He couldn't make out the reply.

Go out the window, or stay here?

Aaaargh! Decide!

The young lion looked quizzically at him. Charlie gave him a grin, which he hoped was convincing. The others, thank goodness, were all still asleep.

There was no time to decide.

A knock came at the door.

"His Majesty would like to see you," came Edward's voice from outside, as calm and polite as always.

Charlie wiped the steam off the little mirror and took a look at his sooty, pale, and frightened face. White people go even whiter when they are scared, or perhaps scarlet. Charlie went a sort of greenish yellow.

"One moment!" he called, as if he were just finishing on the toilet and washing his hands, rather than trying to gather himself together having been up on a train roof in a storm with a gang of half-frozen lions only to find himself—and them—in danger of either arrest or a snowbound attempt at flight. He washed his face and his hands, dried himself off, rubbed at his growing-in hair, and tried his best to look respectable.

Here goes, he thought, and stepped out of the door, closing it swiftly and tightly behind him.

He smiled brightly at Edward.

"Your friends can stay in the bathroom," Edward said politely.

Charlie gulped. What did he mean?

Edward bowed and gestured him along the corridor. It was a chastened and nervous Charlie who went in to explain himself to the King of Bulgaria.

CHAPTER 21

In the great freeze of 1929," said King Boris, sitting on a velvet cushion in his high-backed, elegant chair, "the Danube froze solid from Budapest to Belgrade, Yugoslavia was thirty degrees below freezing day and night, and there were thousands of cases of frostbite throughout the East. Frost and snow closed roads as far south as Beirut and Damascus—the palm trees had snow on them, in the desert. Can you imagine? The Orient Express was snowed in for seven days. No news could get through from the Balkans to Western Europe, so nobody knew where it was . . ."

Charlie stood silently in front of him, his head cast down, like a naughty boy in the principal's office.

"They didn't know how long they would be stuck there, so food was rationed, three-course meals instead of five. The wolves howled all around them in the night, and nobody knew for sure that they wouldn't get into the train and eat the passengers. Nobody knew where they were, or how close. Then late at night would come sounds like pistol shots, as the ice cracked . . ."

Charlie shivered. It was impossible now to see out the windows: The layer of ice made them opaque and greenish like a frozen river, and let only dim light come in.

"The train ran on coal then, and the coal soon froze . . . it made a tremendous hissing sound. Soon enough it ran out and the train grew gradually colder, the floors and the walls . . . the heating pipes froze. The train was in an enormous snowdrift, with nothing but brandy and crackers to eat. The lines were down; they could only wait. In the end they soaked rags in kerosene, wrapped them around the brakes, and set fire to them to thaw the brakes out. The walls of snow towered higher than the train itself on either side."

"Were you there?" asked Charlie. He couldn't not.

"Of course not, it was years ago," said the king. "But you know it wouldn't have been made any easier by having a pride of lions asleep in one's bathroom."

Charlie gasped.

"Small boys do not deceive the Bulgarian security police," he said. "Edward is the most efficient security officer in Eastern Europe. Now what on earth are you up to, and what do you intend to do?"

"They're good lions!" cried Charlie. "Please don't turn them over to the Chef du Train, please don't be scared of them!"

The king looked at him in some amazement.

"Do I look like the kind of king who would hand stowaway lions over to a railway functionary?" he said. "You insult me."

"No no, Your Majesty," cried Charlie in horror. "I don't mean to, it's just I am very scared for them, and I am responsible for them, and if anything were to happen to them, I don't know what

262

I would do. They're my friends . . . They're my friends," he finished up. That said it all, really.

"Just tell me your story," said the king. "Edward! Hot chocolate! With cream and curly chocolate shavings on top!"

So while the hailstones rattled the window, in the green icy light, the king drank coffee laced with brandy, and Charlie drank hot chocolate and told him the whole story. Well—almost all.

When he had finished, the king's eyes were shining and his mouth was curved in a smile, but there was a wariness in his face as well, as if he could foresee some danger.

"You are a very brave and foolish child," he said.

Charlie could not disagree.

"And why do they obey you? Why don't they try to eat you, and run off?"

One detail Charlie had kept from the king: the talking to cats bit. He was always reluctant to speak of it—fearful, to be honest, that people would want to exploit it, to use him in some way, and perhaps make him do things that he didn't want to do.

But he could trust this kind king, surely? Couldn't he?

"They are circus lions," said Charlie after a moment. "They're used to me, and they're used to doing what they're told." In his head he apologized to the lions for this bit of misrepresentation. Used to doing what they're told, indeed! He was glad they weren't there to hear him say it.

"I'd like to meet them," said King Boris. "Can I?"

"Um," said Charlie.

"Later," said the king. "First—what do you intend to do with the lions in Venice?"

"We're going to hide, Your Majesty, and we're going to find my parents and rescue them, and then the lions are going to stow away on a boat to Africa."

The king just looked at him.

"They want to go home," Charlie explained.

The king kept on looking.

"To Africa," said Charlie.

The king sighed.

"It's not your motives or intentions that I'm worried about," he said. "It's your methods. How on earth are seven lions going to hide in Venice? Or stow away on a boat? They haven't a chance of success. And you and your parents . . . I'm very worried, Charlie. I don't see how you can succeed in any of this. You will sneak from my car and go off into the night, no idea where you're going, with hope in your heart and danger on your heels . . . I don't like it, Charlie."

Put that way, Charlie didn't like it very much either. They would be hiding in a city they didn't know, and they had already been very lucky in escaping from potentially dangerous situations.

"Charlie," said the king, "they're lions, not little mice you can put in your pocket. People notice lions. Especially Venetians! They're crazy about them."

The king rubbed his nose. "Charlie," he said. "You leave me with no choice." He stood up.

Charlie's heart sank. He knew what was going to happen. King Boris was going to take charge, and send him home, and send the lions back to the circus, where Maccomo would drug them again. Everything would be safe and sensible with grown-ups in charge, and Charlie would have betrayed Major Tib and Julius and all his circus friends for nothing, and they would all hate him, and he would have to just keep going to his lessons and staying who knows where until maybe, one day, his parents might come back, and the lions would never get back to Africa, and as for the strange new creature, who knows what would happen to him . . .

"*No!*" shouted Charlie, jumping to his feet. "I won't! I'd rather we all just ran away *now!* We'll take our chances in the snow rather than go back, we're never going back, never never never!!"

"Be quiet," said the king. "And sit down. Of course I'm not going to send you back. You wouldn't go even if I did. I'd like to know how you intend to find your parents when you don't even know who has them, or why."

Charlie sat down. He couldn't make heads or tails of this kind, bossy, pessimistic king. Could he trust him? Tell him how the lions and the cats were going to help him?

Charlie was chewing his lower lip as he looked over at King Boris.

"I have some friends who are very good at finding things out," he said at last.

"So do I!" cried the king. "Edward!"

The pale quiet Englishman came back into the car and stood by his master.

King Boris said to him: "Why have two British scientists, a married couple, been kidnapped in London and brought to Venice?"

Edward raised an eyebrow and looked at Charlie. "Ah," he said. "This would be *that* boy then. I wondered."

Charlie didn't appreciate it. *That* boy, again. It was what the French canal cat had said.

"*What* boy?" he said, a little rudely, imitating Edward's intonation.

"The boy whose parents are missing, who is missing too," said Edward.

"Am I missing?" said Charlie, in some surprise.

"You were last seen stowing away in a policeboat on the Thames. You are feared drowned."

"Oh!" said Charlie. "So where are my parents then?"

"En route," said Edward. "They have been traveling south, and when they arrive, we will know their whereabouts."

"And who has them, Edward?" asked the king. "And why?"

Edward looked a little blank. "It isn't clear whether in the full process of—" he began. The king stopped him.

"Edward," he said. "Charlie deserves to know everything that we know."

Edward tightened his mouth a little. It seemed he didn't agree.

"The likelihood demonstrated by current investigations—" he started again.

"Edward," said the king warningly.

Edward blinked, and gave in.

"Your parents were working on a cure for asthma, weren't they?" he said.

"They were always working on cures for everything," said Charlie. He spoke cautiously, but inside him a light went on. This was the first human information he had had yet. Was he about to be proved right? Was it for their knowledge that they had been taken?

"It seems that they were working on asthma prevention, and furthermore they have found something quite important," said Edward. He looked at the king. It was clear he didn't want to tell Charlie.

King Boris sighed. He thought for a moment and then he took over. "There are people in this world, Charlie, who make a great deal of money from selling medicine," he said.

Charlie didn't understand.

"Asthma in particular has been a problem. Though automobiles now hardly exist, there remain many allergies, to cats and so on. People—especially children—need a lot of asthma medicine. If, however, everybody were to be inoculated against asthma, or if the asthma gene could be identified—do you know about genes, Charlie?"

"Yes," said Charlie. "They're the building blocks of human beings. We all have a different pattern of genes, which make us who we are. We get a mix from our parents."

"Exactly," said King Boris. "So if the gene that makes a person susceptible to the allergies that cause asthma could be identified—are you following me, Charlie?"

"Yes," said Charlie. But for a moment he heard another word in his head. Allergies, genes. Allergenies. Were they something to do with this? Were they drugs? Or people? Or genes? Or what?

King Boris was still speaking. "If the gene were identified, it could be modified or changed or removed, and people would no longer need asthma medicine, and the people who made money from asthma medicine would stop making money."

Charlie shook the Allergenies from his mind, and concentrated on what the king was saying.

"But everybody would be happy if asthma were prevented!" he said.

"Not people who put money above the ability to breathe clearly," said King Boris.

Charlie frowned. "Couldn't they make money out of modifying the genes or something?" he asked.

"If they had the imagination, perhaps," said the king.

Charlie was staring very hard at the floor.

"So somebody took my mum and dad because they have invented something that would help everybody?" His voice sounded thick and tight, even to himself.

"We believe so," said the king gently.

Charlie stared and stared at the floor, holding his face straight with determination.

"But it can't be!" he burst out. "Rafi doesn't have anything to do with—" He was confused.

"Rafi?" said Edward.

"Rafi Sadler is the name of the boy who kidnapped them initially," said King Boris.

"Ah," said Edward, pocketing the name for future reference. "Charlie—big groups would employ lesser characters to, as it were, perform those functions not considered appropriate to an institution interested in maintaining a facade of respectability."

"What?" said Charlie.

"A group big enough to use your parents' information would pay villains to do their dirty work," said King Boris. "Edward, do try and talk clearly. I am Bulgarian and my English is clearer than yours."

Charlie was running through the scene in his head—Rafi saying to some faceless, powerful, greedy person: "Yeah, Ashanti and Start, I can get them. I know 'em. Make it worth my while and I'll get 'em for you." He felt a surge of hatred and incomprehension. He would no sooner kidnap Rafi's mother than he would run over his own head with a steamroller.

"Does everyone know about all this?" he asked. "All grown-ups? Why do you know about it?"

"I know because I like to know everything," said King Boris. "But no, very few people know about it, Charlie. It's complicated."

Charlie felt very young. Even if he asked about what made it so complicated, he probably wouldn't understand the answer.

"Is anyone going to get them back?" he asked tightly.

"It did appear that there were intentions to set in motion the requisite preparations," said Edward, "but budgetary obligations combined with some outstanding diplomatic issues—"

The king gave Edward a withering look, and interrupted. "Edward seems to be saying that the government of Britain thinks that it can't afford a search," he said. "And they don't want to offend the medicine companies."

Charlie was silent. He knew that the big companies were bigger than some governments: bigger, richer, stronger, more powerful. Some big companies had even bought small countries, so they could make up their own laws and do what they wanted. They ran them like the New Communities: Only certain types of people were allowed; you had to be rich, or working for the company, that kind of thing.

"So nobody cares about them," he said. "Just me. You just said they were 'traveling south.' How come you don't even know as much as I do? People can be stolen and nobody cares and only a kid does anything about it . . ." Charlie couldn't tell if he was sad or angry. Or both. "It doesn't—it doesn't . . ." A phrase of his mum's came into his mind. "It doesn't fill me with confidence!" he burst out.

Edward and the king were staring at him.

Charlie felt sick.

"Excuse me," he said politely. "I'd like to talk to you later if that's okay." Very quietly he stood up.

As Charlie reached the door, the king said, "Charlie—people do care. Your parents have been stolen precisely because they are valuable. That may seem small comfort, but if the people who stole them care about them, it means they won't hurt them. They are safe, Charlie."

Charlie paused for a moment, his head hanging down.

"Charlie," said the king. "Much against my better judgment, I am going to help you."

He sighed. "I know you're upset. But listen—I have a little place in Venice. You and your lions can go there. Brave and foolish boy."

King Boris's black-olive eyes were filled with sadness as Charlie left.

"Find out all you can," he said to Edward.

Edward bowed slightly, and retreated. The king sat a while in thought. Outside, the snow kept falling.

Charlie went back not to the bathroom but to his little cabin, where he sat on the bed with his head in his hands. He felt a million miles away from anything and anyone, far away and very small. He felt as if he might as well not exist. How stupid to be a small boy, powerless against these grown-up things! How stupid that stupid grown-ups should have all the power, when they do stupid things like take somebody just because they've thought up something really clever! A child wouldn't do that. Any child would say, oh, great, they've done something really good, let's give them a prize. They wouldn't steal them away from their home and their son . . .

Charlie cried a bit. Though he was too big for toys, he got out his tiger and lay down for a while with it over his face. He thought about Rafi, stealing his parents to sell them for their knowledge and ability. He pictured Rafi in the canal, bitten by the lioness, and how worried and scared he had been, and now he thought, Good riddance, I hope you get blood poisoning. He thought about Maccomo, plotting with Rafi, planning to sell Charlie to him. He knew they were out there somewhere. He knew he was going to have to face them again sooner or later. The thought made him feel sick with anger.

He wished he knew where they were.

He wondered what was going on in Paris. What would Major Tib be saying about the lions having gone? He was sorry to have had to cheat him. One day perhaps he could find a way to make it up to him.

Then, as is so often the way after crying, he had a headache. He took his little bottle of Improve Everything Lotion from his bag and looked at it. Dear Mum. He didn't need to take any, though. He'd be all right.

The piece of parchment lay there, tucked in the side of his bag.

Ah.

Charlie took it out, unfolded it. There it was—and Charlie was in no doubt this time about what it was. His mother's blood, his parents' knowledge: These numbers and letters were the cure for asthma.

And he had it.

Was the bag a safe enough place for it? He resolved to find something to wrap it in so he could keep it in the long pocket down the leg of his pants, and have it with him at all times. For now, he tucked it back where it was and took out his mum's ball of lapis lazuli.

He lay down on the bed, holding it, listening to the silence of the snow, watching the curious reflections of light from the ball's shiny surface on the ceiling of his little room. Powerless in so many ways, but actually not powerless at all. He fell asleep.

Charlie was awakened by a dark purring sound in his ear, and a whiskery tickle and a warm breath on his cheek. It was the young lion.

Charlie rolled over, and found himself face-to-face with the lion. "Hello," he said.

"Oh, I'm sorry," said the young lion, "I didn't mean to disturb your rest. But we must speak. Nobody has been into our strange chamber, so when all was silent I came to find you. Come to us? Are you all right? We heard you sobbing and we feared for you. The lionesses said that though you are brave and strong, we should remember you are just a cub . . ."

"I suppose I am a cub," said Charlie. "Yes. I'm a cub."

It made him smile.

"Pretty tough cub!" said the young lion, looking—yes, impressed. Charlie smiled again. He'd impressed a lion!

"Well, you must come and tell us what's happening anyway," said the young lion. He turned to the door of the compartment and for a moment held his head absolutely still, whiskers perked, ears twitching. He could have been on an African plain, listening out for the hoofbeats of a distant animal, alert for the chase . . . But he was in a snug little railway car in a snowdrift, listening out for guards and waiters.

"All clear," he said quietly, and together he and Charlie slunk out into the corridor, and into the bathroom.

The lions were lolling about, for all the world as if they were at a Turkish bath. They looked much, much better. The lionesses had regained their shine, and the oldest lion was deep in conversation with the strange creature. When Charlie came in, they all turned to him, and the lionesses moved to accommodate him. The yellow lioness rubbed Charlie with her head, and he had the strangest feeling—pride, and tears in his eyes, and a sense of comfort. They really were his friends.

Charlie said: "Why don't you come into my compartment?

There would be a bit more room in there."

The lions all stared at him.

"Um, Charlie," said the young lion. "We're hiding. Remember? In fear for our lives?"

"Oh!" said Charlie. "Yes—I mean, actually—well, no. You're not. You see . . ."

"What?" asked the lions, all together.

"The king knows about you," said Charlie. "He wants to meet you."

The lions went suddenly still again, and the atmosphere froze.

"Do you trust this king?" asked the oldest lion.

Charlie thought for only a second.

"He's kept the railway people away from us," he said. "Twice. He's lied to them to protect us. He's fed me. He's found out things about my parents, and made Edward tell me. He's found out about you and isn't scared. He says we can use his place in Venice—"

"Good," said the yellow lioness.

"And he said . . . he said my parents aren't really in danger, because the people who stole them value them."

"And do you believe what he said about your parents? Because you know, of course, it is true."

For a moment Charlie hesitated. It seemed so wrong that his parents were away from him that he could hardly accept that they might not be in actual, direct danger.

But it did make sense. These people had taken a lot of trouble to steal them, for their skills and knowledge. Yes, he could believe that his parents would not be hurt.

"Yes," he said slowly.

"So you trust him."

"Yes," said Charlie.

"Then we are safe," said the oldest lion, as if it were obvious and he was surprised that Charlie saw it any other way.

Charlie was puzzled.

"We are in a very good position," said the oldest lion. "We are safer than we were on the streets of Paris; safer than when Rafi Sadler and his foul dog were chasing us; safer than we were when Maccomo was drugging us in the circus, or when we were out in the freezing storm on the roof, or when we were shocked by our friend . . ." He stopped and looked with a gentle expression over to the new creature, who was lying hugely in the bathtub. I wonder what they've been talking about, Charlie thought.

"We are warm and dry, and we have eaten, and we are together," continued the oldest lion. "We are free, and healthy, and we have a friend with power and knowledge—and accommodation. Someone else is going to mend the train that will roar us through this mysterious, dangerous weather to the place where your parents are, closer to our home. Tomorrow perhaps the sky will fall on our head. Tomorrow may never come. If it does, then for sure it brings our new adventure—going home, winning your father and mother back. But now—now we are safe."

He blinked cheerfully at Charlie.

Charlie hadn't looked at it that way. He ran through it in his mind.

The silver lioness rolled over, knocking Elsina, who had been lying on her back, to the floor. Elsina purred, and batted Charlie in a friendly fashion with her paw. The other lionesses smiled their mysterious lioness smiles. The young lion was perched on the toilet seat, his tail hanging down, his expression encouraging.

"Don't worry, little cub!" he said.

Charlie, squatting with his back to the door, this sea of lions around his feet, smiled again. Look at me, he thought, stuck in a frilly pink bathroom, on the Orient Express, with a friendly king next door and a wild snowstorm eddying outside, and a pride of lions comforting me and cheering me up.

"Little cub!" Charlie said. "Little cub! You smart-alecky little pussycat!"

"Pussycat!" cried the young lion. "Who are you calling Pussycat?"

So Charlie jumped up and pulled his tail, and he knocked Charlie across the room, and the lionesses told them to calm down, and Elsina joined in the rolling around, and the snow rattled the windowpanes, and when Edward stuck his head around the door to say His Majesty would see them now, for a moment he couldn't tell whether he was witnessing a terrible fight, or fun and frolic.

But Charlie knew. Charlie felt wonderful: fine, and strong, and ready for anything.

To Be Continued . . .

Acknowledgments

To Yaw Adomakoh (aka Daddy).
To Rebecca Bowen for helping with the diagrams of the *Circe*.
To Francesca Brill for introducing us to Mabel.
To Jacob Yeboa and Mrs. Elizabeth Adomakoh for help with the Twi and "Tuwe tuwe, mamuna tuwe tuwe"—the traditional Ghanaian children's song that Aneba sings.

To Fred Van Deelen for the maps and diagrams—use a magnifying glass! To Paul Hodgson for copying out the music so elegantly.

And special thanks to Robert Lockhart for the beautiful tunes. If you like the *Lionboy* tunes, and want to play them on the piano, you might like to know he's written more, including "Pirouette's Flying Habañera," "El Diablo Aero's Highwire Violin Melody," and a rather scary number called "Hello Charlieboy, Rafi Calling" . . . They're published by Faber Music Ltd: Visit www.fabermusic.com for details.

And thanks to all the ladies at Dial: especially Lauri Hornik for her patience with our different ways of pronouncing *tomato*, Katrina Weidknecht, Nancy Paulsen, and Kimi Weart for the golden cover (and the pink skull ring).

And to the agents: Derek Johns, Linda Shaughnessy, Sylvie Rabineau, Rob Kraitt, Teresa Nicholls, Anjali Pratap—so tough on our behalf! So nice to deal with! So many of them!